The Girl With 35 Names

by

D. J. Colbert

CONTENTS

PART ONE

PART TWO

PART THREE

Author's note

Dear Reader,

Molly is the girl with 35 names, each one of them special and not one the same ... but this book is not only about Molly, it is about you too. Before you begin reading Molly's story, take a moment to think about your name. Why was it chosen for you and what does it mean? Take a moment to think about where your family came from, and take another moment to consider your roots as far back as they might go. Think about how an ancestor's decision to immigrate has made a difference in the life you now lead. Think about the talents, values, and desires you have; might these have come from someone before your time? How have you been touched by someone you may never meet? When you do, you will discover how very special and unique each one of us is. We each have a story to tell. I have made this journey of discovery and that is how I came to write *The Girl With 35 Names*.

The character of Molly is based on the life of my Grandmother Malkah who grew up in a small village in Russia. She was married to a man she first met on her wedding day and because of the war that came to her country, she was forced to emigrate and build a new life in America. Her strength and courage, her adaptability and endless optimism, her joy of giving to others as well as her deep and tender love of family, inspired me to write this narrative of her life.

It is my hope that readers today will discover through Molly's experiences the joy of giving to others, and the importance of learning who we really are and where we come from. Together, let's make connections to our past and understand the impact these connections may have on our future.

Molly's journey of self-discovery and sometimes magical experiences is one that readers of all ages can relate to today. Her story celebrates women and the individuality of spirit that binds us all together.

Los Angeles, 2018

PART ONE

CHAPTER 1

Molly

In the coldest of cold Russian winters in the year 1892, when the snow piled higher than anyone in the small village of Zhitomir could ever before remember, a tiny baby girl was born in a small stone house on the edge of a wide and ancient wood. Eagerly awaited and somewhat of a miracle, she was a very special baby because her parents had long ago given up hope of ever having a child. And so this baby had been dearly loved from the first. Outside the little house that night the snowflakes that fell were as big as dinner plates, and the stars sparkled and their light bathed the trees with silver. The snow covered the ground with a beautiful glow. Inside, all was warm and light. A fire blazed in the hearth and the smell of cinnamon and cloves and fresh bread baking filled the little house with fabulous aromas.

Nestled comfortably in her mother's arms in a bed near the fire, the new baby cooed softly. The baby's mother Moriah smiled at the sound and cuddled closer to her newborn. Whispering softly in her ear, she said,

"Precious daughter, I promise to be the best that I can be for you. I will teach you and you will teach me and I will see the world anew once more, through your eyes." Moriah kissed the downy soft head of her baby daughter. She felt a sudden rush of love and protectiveness and, looking up at her husband Ari, she stretched out her hand. "Isn't she beautiful?" she asked, her eyes brimming with happy tears.

Ari kissed his wife and smiled. "Indeed she is," he responded and sat down gently beside her on the bed.

"We shall call her Malkah," said Moriah, "I have always liked that name."

"Ah," replied Ari, "you have decided and chosen well. It will be as you wish my love, it is your decision after all, and I like the name too. It means 'Queen,' and if this little one is anything like her sweet mother, it is well deserved." Ari looked down at his wife with a loving smile and gave her a wink.

Moriah blushed and cuddled the baby close. "We need to let the family know of our decision," she said. "I have a feeling they will be here soon."

"I almost forgot. That's right ... yes, the *family*," said Ari with dread in his voice, and he rose up from his wife's bed too agitated to sit still any longer.

Suddenly, just as Moriah had predicted, there was a loud knock at the front door followed quickly by a large gust of wind and a whirl of snowflakes as the door banged open and there on the mat stood the family. There were so many. Aunts, uncles, cousins, parents of cousins, grandparents, great-great-great-grandparents, and they all pushed into the room crowding the small space and jostling each other around Moriah's bed. The room was becoming warmer and warmer as more and more people continued to squeeze into the little house. Soon steam began to rise in the tiny room and the snow began to drip from the hats and coats of all the relatives, and their voices rose too as everyone ooohed and ahhhed at the new arrival.

"Ahem ..." said Ari, trying to remain calm amid the press of people. "Beloved family ... Moriah and I have decided to name the baby Malkah, and our decision is final!"

"Bravo Ari!" whispered Moriah softly from behind him in the bed.

At first there was total silence, then everyone began to speak at once. And as usual, no one could agree. Everyone had a special name they wanted to give the baby. Everyone wanted to bless the child by giving her a name of someone special who had come before. In the end, in order to please everyone and to keep family harmony as best as Moriah and Ari were able, the little girl was named Malkah Hannah Laurie Judith Phyllis Elaine Beth Bella Esther Chaya Dobrisha Elishah Alicia Marsha Pearl Sally Edie Sylvia Maria Raina Sophie Sarah Lily Francis Miriam Bette Rachel Evelyn Agnes Lucy Sadie Mary Ethel Goldah Ann. But everyone just called her Molly.

Molly grew strong and sweet and extremely curious about the world around her. In the spring and summer she played happily amid the tall grasses and picked handfuls of wildflowers, her long blond braids and the tails of her apron trailing in the wind as she ran and played. In the winter, when the heavy snows would begin to fall and the drifts that formed outside her front door made venturing out difficult, Molly would sit for hours in the cabin, wrapped snugly in a blanket in a chair by the fireside, and read. Molly adored reading. In the heart of the frozen winter, she could travel to distant islands and play on sandy beaches in the warmth of the sun, and she could imagine herself in the stories she loved as a princess in a fairy tale castle, or a pirate on the deck of a ship. Moriah had saved her childhood books in hopes of sharing them someday with a child of her own, and gave them to Molly as soon as Molly was old enough to enjoy them for herself. It did not matter what Molly read or how many times she re-read the books Moriah had given her; the books were Molly's special treasures, too.

When the spring thaw would finally arrive and the heavy snows would begin to melt away in the warmth of the sun, Moriah would unlatch the shutters from the windows and push back the curtains. The front door of the little house was opened wide and the warming breezes and the rich aromas of springtime would flood in, filling the house with light and blowing away the stale air of winter. Molly would run from the house as fast as she was able, soaking up the sun and breathing in the fragrant perfume of spring. Molly knew then it was time to prepare the earth for planting once again. There was always so much to be done.

Behind the little house, Ari and Moriah worked together in their large garden. They planted many things each year, but the thing that grew the best was potato. As long as Ari could remember his family had planted potatoes to sell on market day in the village. Of course he and Moriah brought other things to sell as well, but the potatoes seemed to be everyone's favorite. Molly loved to be with her parents in the garden, too. And as she grew, she spent more and more time there.

On a beautiful spring day when the sun rose high in the sky and the earth began to warm and the rich soil behind the little house beckoned with promise, Molly followed her father from his tool shed down the path towards the garden. Over his shoulder he carried a variety of rakes and hoes and shovels. Ari pushed open the wooden gate and put down the tools he had been carrying, and took a deep breath.

"Ah ..." he said, "the world smells like new beginnings. I just love this time of year ... but not so much all the hoeing and weeding that needs to be done." He turned to the piles of tools he had brought along and found among them a small rake and hoe just big enough for a child.

"Are these for me?" Molly asked excitedly. "They're the perfect size!"

Ari was pleased with his daughter's reaction when she saw the rake and hoe. "Well," he said, smiling down at her, "our family has farmed this plot of land for a very long time, and they had to make their own tools themselves through the years in order to work the earth in this garden.

These tools were made for my father by his father, your Great-Grandpa Joseph, and when I was a boy of eight, just about as old as you are now, my father gave them to me. I remember that day very well. When he passed them on to me, I was so happy that I had my own tools to use so I could help my family work our land and grow the food we needed. Each spring when I had an opportunity to use them again, I always felt important and connected to my family and all those who came before. These tools certainly have seen a lot of use in this garden. They have all lasted a very long time. Using them, I learned how very important it is to care for the things you have, and if you can do that, they will be there for you to use as long as you need them." For a moment Ari stopped speaking as the memory of a long-ago day ran through his mind. He looked down again at his daughter and, placing his hand upon her shoulder, he said, "It is also important to fill your life with good memories and take care of them, too. If you do, I promise you that they will both last a very, very long time."

With that, Ari wiped the back of his neck with his checkered hand-kerchief and stuffed it into his back pocket. "Shall we get started?" he asked with a grin, and he patted Molly on top of her head. Molly picked up the shovel and hoe and followed her father excitedly through the old metal gate and into the garden. She stroked the wooden handles of the hoe and shovel and they were both smooth and warm in her hands. As she did, her thoughts became filled with images of her father as a little boy using these same tools, and she smiled to herself.

Molly did not quite understand everything her father had just told her, but she surely knew who her Great-Grandpa Joseph was as there was a picture of him in the hallway of her parents' house. She had always thought the photograph a bit scary, and she hurried down the hallway in order to pass it quickly. The photograph was old and the image was black and brown and there was what seemed to Molly a mean and unhappy scowl on his face. Molly had never really heard any stories about Great-Grandpa Joseph from her father before, but she could sense from the way her father had handled the tools, and the memory he had shared, that he remembered his grandfather with love. Molly's eyes grew wide with that revelation as she looked again at the little hoe and shovel. It seemed as though they had traveled a long way through time to come to her. She felt proud and happy to receive them, and excited to have them for her own. *Maybe Great-Grandpa Joseph is not as mean as I thought,* she said to herself. Then, taking the small hoe, she began to follow her father as he walked along the rows and furrows.

Ari stopped for a moment and watched Molly begin to scrape the earth, removing small weeds at the corner of the garden. The edges of her dress dipped in and out of the damp earth as she moved her new hoe back and forth, covering her boots to her ankles. She smiled happily as she went about her work, and Ari smiled too just to look at her. How wonderful to see his lovely child so carefree and so happy. He prayed while he watched that her life would always be like this. That she would never be touched by the evils that he had experienced as a boy and then again as a young man, when crop failures, war, prejudice, and misunderstanding had harmed many of his relatives and neighbors, turning their lives upside down. The Imperial Russia that Ari had been born into was a place of great beauty, with fish-filled seas lapping along its vast coastline, great plains and ancient forests filling its interior, the treeless and grassy steppes in the south, and the rugged snowy caps of the Ural Mountains in the west. But the constant skirmishes, high taxes, and struggles between the wealthy and those who had very little made the daily living of her citizenry feel as though one lived on the razor edge of a sword.

Ari looked up to the vivid blue sky that stretched like a soft blanket above him and watched as brilliant white clouds scuttled in front of the sun, creating cool shade and shadows that ran along the loamy soil at his feet. His great boots were already heavy with dirt. As he began to move forward he gave each foot a great shake, sending clots of earth flying. *I will never let harm come to my child or my wife or our family. I will never allow anyone to destroy what we have built here,* he thought to himself. *Each day will be a blessing, each and every day I will believe that all will be well.* Ari sighed deeply and looked again at Molly. Her rosy cheeks glowed while her lips formed a wide and delighted smile as the clouds above moved swiftly away and a warm sun shone down on her golden curls.

CHAPTER 2

The Spectacles

This year Molly was ten, and it seemed to everyone who knew and loved her that she grew almost as fast as the plants did. It made her feel important to no longer be thought of as a little girl, and she worked eagerly and happily alongside her parents in the garden. Since receiving the tools from her father, Molly looked forward with excitement to every spring when she could feel the grass beneath her bare feet and smell the warmth of new beginnings in the earth. Each year she would take her rake and hoe and join her mother and father to begin the long process of turning over the soil to make it ready for planting. Working in the garden came naturally to Molly, and she took great pride in her work. In her eagerness to get started, she was always first down the path to the garden gate. Just as her father had told her, the work was long and hard and required everyone to participate, but Molly never minded.

She always waited a bit impatiently for the end of winter, when the sun's rays would slowly grow stronger and gently warm the earth, melting away the heavy snows that surrounded the little house. The icicles that clung to the roof and eaves would drip endlessly, creating little rivers in the topsoil of the yard. Then, Ari would don his high boots and hitch his team of oxen to his plow. He would drive them forward, pulling on the reins as he led them back and forth across the field creating neat furrows, preparing the soil for Moriah to plant her seeds. From early morning to late afternoon, Molly delighted being in the garden. It was her job to hoe, weed, and water. Using her watering can, Molly would walk between the rows, dreaming of the day when she would pick sweet red berries and pull bright orange carrots out of the earth. It was indeed true that Molly had grown taller in the last few years, but she was still quite a bit shorter than her parents and therefore much closer to the ground. So it had become her job to take away any small rocks and stones that happened to be in the way.

One day as she was bending down to struggle with a particularly troublesome rock, she noticed a bright sparkle at the edge of the row where she was working. *What is that?* she asked herself, and since Molly was always naturally curious, she had to look closer. Just then a cloud scuttled in front of the sun and the sky grew darker and at first she could not tell the source of the sparkle. Then, just as quickly, the cloud blew softly away and the sun blazed down and then ... she saw the sparkle again, this time brighter than before. A silver sliver of bright metal poked through the earth. *What could that be? Is it a wand?* Molly wondered to herself, stopping just a moment before she touched the shining metal. *It can't be, those are parts of fairy stories and I'm too old to believe in those anymore.* Curiosity got the better of her though and she reached down, grasped hold of the thin metal piece, and pulled up slowly. Out of the muddy soil came a pair of spectacles. They looked so very old, as though they had been in the ground for a thousand years.

"Look!" Molly called to her parents as she wiped the damp earth from the spectacles. "Look what I found!" She slipped the spectacles on her nose and her eyes grew wide. Even though the spectacles Molly found had been in the earth a very long time, the lenses still shone like new and the thin silver frame felt as though it fit Molly perfectly. She put them on and pulled them off several times in succession and then she looked through the lenses. As she did, the light of the garden began to change. Molly was thoroughly surprised and she was not sure exactly what she had seen at first, but there seemed to be a subtle shift in her vision and the beginnings of soft colors that slowly formed and seemed to wrap themselves around her when she looked down at her hands and feet. It was an exciting feeling unlike any other feeling she had known before and Molly's heart beat a little faster. From what seemed like somewhere far away, Molly could hear the sound of her parents' voices. Moriah and Ari had been keeping an eye on Molly as she worked and they too had seen the bright silver sparkle that Molly had pulled out of the damp earth. They were curious to see what Molly had uncovered.

"What did you find, Molly love?" they called.

Molly was a bit startled by the faraway sound of her parents' voices when they called out to her and she quickly slipped the spectacles off her nose and held them in her hand. Molly did not know what to think about what she had just experienced. She was amazed by all the colors that seemed to surround her, and she almost doubted that what she had seen was true. Looking up, she could clearly see that her parents were coming toward her from where they had been working. "It's just a pair of old glasses," she called back to them, holding the spectacles out for her parents to see.

"Well look at that," said Ari, coming to stand beside his daughter. He examined the spectacles carefully. "I think you just found Great-Grandma Ethel's spectacles! They have been lost for as long as I can remember. Isn't that so, Moriah?"

"Yes, I think they are," Moriah said in awe. Taking the spectacles in her hands, she looked at them closely for a moment as she remembered the grandmother she had known and loved. "How wonderful that you found them, Molly. We always wondered what had happened to them."

"Can I keep them Mommy?" Molly asked. "Can I keep them Daddy, please?"

"I don't see why not," said Ari.

"I don't see why not," said Moriah happily. "I don't see why not!"

And so she did. Carrying them with her in her apron pocket, Molly tried the spectacles on many times throughout the day. When she looked down through the lenses, she could see a rainbow of colors twirling and twisting around her feet in the dirt, so beautiful and clear that Molly was filled with happiness and joy. Nothing had ever made her feel this way before and she wondered what it all could mean and if the spectacles were some sort of magic meant for her to find. Molly was not frightened by what she saw and felt. *They are Great-Grandmother Ethel's glasses, after all*, she reasoned to herself. She was only very curious.

Later that evening, Molly placed the spectacles on her bedside table as she prepared for bed. She had not stopped wondering about them all day since she found them buried in the garden. What were the interesting feelings that came to her when she had put them on? The shift of light and color and the intensity of emotions that filled her each time she had put the spectacles on were too vivid to ignore. It was a puzzle, and as Molly drew back the quilt and got into bed, her head was full of questions to which she had no answers. From her bed, Molly could hear soft footsteps coming towards her from the hallway. She held the spectacles close in her hand and waited anxiously for her mother to come in to say goodnight. Moriah made her way slowly along the corridor that led to Molly's bedroom. She carried a small lantern before her as she approached Molly's bedroom door, and the light from the single candle within cast large and ominous shadows along the walls. Moriah knocked softly on the door and pushed it open with a squeak.

"Molly, are you ready for me to say goodnight?" Moriah asked as she stepped lightly into the room. The shadows grew smaller as Moriah placed her lantern on Molly's bedside table. The light in the room was now soft and gentle and Moriah's presence eased Molly's swirling thoughts, just as it always did when she was hurt or troubled. She breathed a little easier knowing that Moriah was near. Almost before she realized it, Molly had slipped the spectacles onto her nose as soon as her mother had entered her room. She looked intently through the lenses at her mother and as she did, she felt a warm breeze that seemed to ruffle the bed covers and blew sweetly through her hair. She saw soft sky blues and the delicate white of scuttling clouds, and her heart filled with love and serenity. Moriah sat down on Molly's bed and leaned in to look closely at her daughter. Through the lenses, Molly's eyes were so hugely magnified that Moriah laughed aloud as Molly stared back at her.

"What do you see, my love?" Moriah asked quizzically.

"I'm not sure exactly," Molly replied. "It's as if I see and feel things all at the same time. I have never, ever felt anything like this before. I am not scared by what I see and feel ... they are just a pair of old glasses after all, and I don't think they can hurt me in any way. I just wonder why I see what I see. Everything is different when I put them on, like I am seeing things in a new and different way. When you came in just now, and I looked at you through the glasses, it was as if I saw you for the first time. I saw you, but I saw you deeper ... I sensed that there were bright and moving colors that surround you, colors that I have never noticed before and I felt you deeper, differently than ever, and in my heart I felt love, happiness, and safety." Removing the spectacles, Molly handed them to her mother. Moriah held them lovingly, turning them over in her hand for a moment, and then placed them tenderly down on the quilt next to Molly.

Moriah had listened closely as her daughter spoke before saying, "The spectacles you found today were lost long ago, just as your father told you they were. They belonged to my Grandmother Ethel. She was so very old when they were lost and she was never quite the same without them."

Moriah stopped speaking for an instant as she suddenly recollected a vivid dark memory from a time long past when Grandmother Ethel had come to visit her and Ari shortly after their marriage. It had been a lovely spring day and she and Grandmother Ethel had been busy planting seedlings in the newly plowed earth of the garden. She remembered the sweet sounds of birds chirping in the sun-filled sky and then an abrupt and eerie silence as the birds stopped their song. Then came the roar of staccato blasts of rapid-fire gunshots that shattered the stillness all around them. She could hear just as loudly the terrified screams that seemed to come from everywhere at once. Moriah could almost feel again the firmness of her grandmother's hand clasped tightly in hers as they began to run forward and away towards shelter. Her heart began to beat a little more rapidly as the memory of that horrible day returned with crystal clarity, reminding her in that moment of the instant that her grandmother's spectacles were lost forever.

Moriah sighed deeply and looked at Molly cradled softly amid the quilts on her bed. Her eyes were misty as she worked to push away the memories that she would never give to her child. Then she smiled gently and taking a short calming breath, she continued on. "Before they were lost there was never a day that I can remember when she didn't have her spectacles perched on the tip of her nose. I don't know if it was the spectacles that made Grandmother Ethel special but my grandmother had an insight into people that was truly amazing. She was gifted in many other ways as well. She understood the natural world and used its bounty for the benefit of her family, friends, and neighbors. Her curatives were sought after and her wisdom was respected. My grandmother learned her craft from *her* mother Chaya and Chaya from *her* mother Dobrisha, and so forth … back and back as far as you can imagine. The women of our family have always been strong in spirit. Our traditions, our stories, our individual talents, and our connection to one another — it's like a ribbon through time. I think your Great-Grandmother Ethel would be delighted that you found her spectacles. Each time you use them I think you will feel that special connection to her and to all the women in our family, especially those women whose names you share, and that's the ribbon that holds us all together.

"And now, my sweet girl, it's time for sleep, and while you sleep, dream of all the thirty-five women who share their names with you, and know that you are especially loved." Molly was soothed by what her mother had said and so happy to be reminded once again of all the women whose names she had been given, and she smiled as she looked deeply into her mother's eyes. Moriah bent forward and kissed her daughter's warm cheek. "Goodnight," she whispered, and picking up her lantern she turned and walked to the door, closing it behind her with a soft click.

Molly lay back among her pillows but she could not sleep. Her head was too full of excitement from the events of the day and the story that her mother had told her. Sitting up in bed, she reached once again for the glasses that lay next to her on top of her blanket. The metal was cool in her hand. *I wonder what Great-Grandmother Ethel would think if she knew I had found her glasses, would she tell me how to use them and explain what I see and feel? ... I must be very like her for the glasses to work for me,* Molly reasoned to herself. *Great-Grandma Ethel loved the garden and watching things grow as much as I do, and I am named for her and so many others. Am I like them too?* she wondered.

Returning to her pillows, Molly's eyelids began to droop. Soon she was fast asleep, and as she slept, she saw Laurie playing piano and Francis teaching school and Pearl singing as she turned the pages of a book, and all the other women were singing too, a song Molly knew more than any other. In the morning, when Molly awoke, she knew that there was so much more she needed to discover and the seeds of a plan were beginning to grow.

CHAPTER 3

Market Day

From that first day, Molly was never without her great-grandmother's spectacles. She kept them safe, wrapped in a grey felt bag and tied up with a red string, tucked away in her apron pocket. Whenever Molly put the spectacles on, the people she saw through the lenses always looked so different. Not because the lenses were for someone with very different eyesight, but because it seemed each time that she looked around her, she could just *see more*. It felt to Molly as though she were able to see deeper into things, sense things differently. When she took the glasses off, the world and the people she saw seemed to retreat to a less shiny self. Molly wondered about this new sensitivity and awareness that came to her whenever she wore the spectacles. The intensity of color, the sensations and emotions that filled her whenever she put on Great-Grandma Ethel's glasses and looked at the people around her, felt more meaningful than anything she had experienced before.

For Molly, the spectacles remained a wonderful mystery that filled her mind with questions. Why did she see so many colors? What did the many colors she saw really mean? Often during the day, she would slip the spectacles from her apron pocket and, placing them gently on her nose, look carefully around. The sky, the earth, the trees, and birds would all remain the same, but when Molly looked at her father Ari, she was aware of a gentle warmth spreading through her body. She felt safe and protected and laughter bubbled up inside her. The color that surrounded him and floated just above his head was a verdant emerald green. Moriah's color was blue, as soft as the sky, roiling and gusting and changing to deep marine, swirling in waves all around her. Molly felt an intensity of love and comfort that filled her so completely that even after she had put the glasses back in her apron pocket, the glow of what she had experienced remained with her. Each day as she went about her chores in the house, barn, or garden, Molly was happy. When she visited her aunts, uncles, cousins, grandparents, and friends, the happiness and love she felt inside bubbled over and everyone loved her.

Molly always enjoyed watching the fruits and vegetables grow in the garden, but she loved going to town best. She looked forward to the end of each week with excitement, because everyone in the village attended market day. The night before market day was always very busy. The family worked together to fill their little wagon with all it could carry, and in the back of the wagon there were crates and baskets. Some of the crates were filled with potatoes, some with vegetables, and some were filled with cheese wrapped in cloth. There were also large tins of milk and eggs for sale or trade.

In the morning, the family rose early and dressed quickly. Ari hitched the horse to the wagon and helped Moriah and Molly up onto the front seat. The cart shifted and bumped over the long country road. Molly couldn't wait to get to town. She put her hands deep inside her pocket and felt the spectacles that she always kept with her. Her father began to whistle. Her mother began to sing:

Molly's the girl with thirty-five names,
Given with love, not one the same
Each name is a special message, each name a brand new page
A journey of discovery, a new beginning, a new age.
Thirty-five names made you special. There is no one else like you.
Follow your heart and let your strengths shine through.
Molly is the girl with thirty-five names. There is no one else like you.

Molly always loved to hear that song, and she laughed along with her parents as they finished.

"Can you even remember all of my names?" asked Molly.

"I have them all written down and safely kept," replied Moriah giving Molly a hug, "I just have to remember where!"

Molly looked from her mother to her father and her blue eyes grew large. "Oh you don't really mean ...?" Molly began. Then she saw a grin growing from the corner of her father's mouth.

"Moriah!" laughed Ari, giving his wife a soft push on her shoulder. Then they all began to laugh and sing.

"Molly's the girl with thirty-five names ..."

CHAPTER 4

Mrs. Eos

Molly knew everyone in the village, and they all knew her. They also knew about the spectacles she had found and carried with her in her apron pocket. But Molly was the only one who knew about the strange power the glasses held for her alone. Both her parents had tried them on once or twice, but they had never commented on anything strange or different when they wore them. All that Molly could see when she watched first her mother and then her father try on the glasses was that their eyes looked as if they grew wide and enormous. *But that always happens when you look at people who wear thick glasses*, Molly had thought, *It's quite the mystery*. Molly had talked to her parents about the colors that she saw. Moriah had suggested once that maybe the spectacles helped Molly understand people better, just like Great-Grandma Ethel had been able to do. That explained some things, Molly had agreed, but it did not explain why she reacted so strongly to the colors she saw. That was something Molly thought she had to discover for herself, so she decided not to share her true feelings just yet. And so even though she had never kept a secret from her parents before, Molly hugged her feelings and her spectacles closer.

The morning sun was rising and the earth was still damp with dew when Molly and her parents pulled up to the market square. There were so many people pushing carts and setting up awnings that, for a moment, the crush of people was precarious. Molly could smell the wonderful aromas of frying foods and see her friends in the crowd. She couldn't wait to get down from the wagon. Molly's friends waved and called to her as she rode past. Molly waved back happily, stood up on the front seat of the wagon, and taking the spectacles from her pocket, slipped them on her nose. She looked eagerly around. All the hustle-bustle of the crowded street seemed to slow, the colors intensified, and a soft aura rimmed the crowd and swirled in rainbow arcs above them, filling the sky. In that moment, she felt a sudden and intense sense of belonging and community that touched her deep inside. Sliding the glasses a little further down her nose so that she could peer over their tops, Molly watched as the world around her shifted back just as she had expected. Returning the spectacles to her apron pocket for safekeeping, she jumped down from the parked wagon and began to help her mother and father set up for the day's selling.

The village children laughed and played among the carts and stalls and ran happily through the crowd that filled the small street. Molly ached to join them. This year she was twelve years old and it was time for her to be allowed to be on her own a bit. "May I go now, mother?" asked Molly excitedly. She could not wait to run and play with her friends.

Moriah stood up. She had been busy packing a woven wicker basket. "Your father and I will be very busy today," she said. "If you can deliver these few packages for me this morning, you can have the rest of the day to do as you please. You have been such a tremendous help already to your father and me. Maybe we can even have some time later to buy you some new ribbons for your hair." Moriah reached down and stroked Molly's golden braid. "You're growing up so fast," she said with a wistful smile.

Moriah knew that her daughter wished to join the many friends who called to her. She could see it in her eyes and so she said, "I am trusting you to do this for me today. I think you will find out for yourself how very important the task really is." Moriah bent down and kissed her daughter's pink cheek. Molly breathed in lavender and vanilla, her mother's favorite scent. It was warm and comforting.

"I love you," Molly whispered and gave her mother a hug and slowly released her. She felt proud that her mother was trusting her to be on her own and she was also very curious about what she would discover as she did her errands. Moriah reached down and handed Molly the basket she had packed.

"Off with you then," she said. "Everything in the basket is labeled, you should have no problem getting everything right. Just stay on the main road, it will lead you to where you need to go."

Molly took the basket from her mother. Considering the basket's size, it was lighter than she had expected and she carried it easily in her hand as she began to walk away. At first Molly was excited. She was on her own for the very first time. But soon disappointment nagged at Molly's heart. She longed to be free and run with her friends. They still called to her as she passed, "Meet us at the corner! C'mon Molly!" they yelled, and she called back to them, "I'll be there soon!" *But first I have to do these errands for my mother*, she thought to herself a little sadly as she kicked a loose rock angrily with the toe of her shoe. How she wished she could just run off and enjoy the day, and for a short moment, she almost did. But Molly could not disappoint her mother and she was still very curious about what she would find on her errands. Carrying the basket easily on her arm, Molly walked slowly away from her parents' tiny stall and followed the main road that led out of town and into the big world. The sun was shining brightly in the sky and the day was blue and beautiful. Molly thought about her friends as she walked. Most of the kids in town were her friends, but not everyone.

Some of the children didn't like her for one reason or another. Sometimes the older boys teased her about all the names she had. They called her weird and stupid and they teased her mercilessly about her glasses and her names. Usually she did not mind too much, but today was different; she was alone. The road she followed led past an old run-down shack that stood on the last corner out of town. From a short distance away Molly could see a group of boys standing together and laughing. She recognized Billy Lenda and Ivan Bilco among them. When the two boys noticed Molly, they elbowed each other and pointed at her.

"Hey! Molly!"

"What a strange one you are."

"Crazy Molly with all those stupid names."

"Where are your dumb glasses, Molly?" they yelled and roared with laughter.

When Molly heard them call at her from across the road and tease her about her names, her first instinct was to turn and run away as far and as fast as she could go. After a moment she thought better of it, and remembering her idea, she quickly put the basket down next to her and reached for the spectacles in her apron pocket. She slipped them on and looked defiantly, directly at Billy and Ivan. Instantly, her view of the boys shifted. Instead of seeing the boys who bullied her, she saw an impenetrable darkness as deep as the ocean surrounding both Billy and Ivan. She felt a cold, hard heaviness in her heart, and she wondered for a moment about the source of the evil darkness that rose up around the boys. *Was it the color that made the boys so mean or did their mean spirit make the colors that surrounded them?* Molly did not know. She slipped the spectacles down so once again she could peer over the tops of the rims and, as she did, the boys on the other side of the street came back in focus. The wildly spinning blackness that had flown about their shoulders disappeared in an instant. Still they called angrily to her.

"You're so strange, Molly," they yelled. "You're so strange with your glasses and names, strange, strange, strange."

Molly's eyes filled with tears that fogged up the lenses she still wore. She was feeling terribly sorry for herself. *Maybe they are right*, she thought, as she turned and walked quickly past the boys without looking in their direction again and trying hard to ignore the names they called her. As she passed, she took the spectacles off and held them tightly in her hand. *Maybe I am a little strange,* she thought sadly, and for a moment she was filled with self-doubt. But then she began to think better of herself and her courage returned. *I don't know why the spectacles work the way they do. But whatever they say, I know what I see. I know these glasses are special for me in some way. I just have to learn what it is.*

Molly's thoughts still ran fast and furious as she continued to walk away and she was a bit breathless when she reached the far corner that led out of town. Looking back over her shoulder, she could no longer see or hear the boys. Relief flooded through her and she stopped for a moment and put the basket down. She removed the checkered cloth that covered the contents and wiped her eyes. As she did, she noticed several labels in her mother's neat handwriting: *Mrs. Eos, Mrs. Teresky, Mrs. Lieben.* Just the sight of her mother's writing gave her comfort, and she wiped her eyes once more and placed the cloth back in the basket. As she did, she suddenly remembered the dream of the women she had not so long ago and the seeds of the idea that had come to her when she awoke. A huge smile lit Molly's face.

"It's time!" she said aloud. "I can begin right now!" She picked up the basket once again and started on her way, more excited than ever to continue with her errands and her plan of discovery.

Molly had met Mrs. Eos, Mrs. Teresky, and Mrs. Lieben many times before, but she had always been accompanied by her mother whenever they had stopped by for a visit. The women were each a distant relative in one way or another, Molly knew, but she could never remember exactly how, so she always called them *Mrs.* when she spoke with them, just as she had been instructed to do. *It will be very different this time though*, thought Molly, remembering back to when she had been much younger. She had often come along with her mother on her errands when she visited her friends and family, but she had not really paid much attention to any of her mother's conversations with the women she visited. Molly had never been invited to participate in any way. It had never bothered her, and truly she had never really cared before. It had always been much more fun to tease the cat with a feather at Mrs. Eos's house or roll around on the rug with her best friend Miranda's new puppies whenever they would visit the house of her mother, Mrs. Lieben. This time would definitely be different. Molly was not so little anymore. She had a plan and she knew exactly what she wanted to ask Mrs. Eos.

At the end of the village in a secluded grove lived Mrs. Eos. Moriah and Mrs. Eos had known each other for a very long time, since Moriah was a young girl herself. Mrs. Eos had always lived alone, with just her fat black cat for company. In her large garden she grew an array of strange and wonderful flowers and herbs that Moriah would sometimes use in the medicines and curatives for which she was known. Many other people from the village visited Mrs. Eos's garden to buy the fruits and vegetables she had for sale, but Mrs. Eos always saved the best of what she grew for Moriah.

In the middle of this seemingly secret grove, surrounded by sunlight and flowers, sat Mrs. Eos's shiny white painted house gleaming brightly in the sun. It was a very old and traditional dacha house, the kind of small and well-crafted home that most people would travel to from the cities to spend a quiet weekend here and there in the country. It had been built many years ago when Mrs. Eos had been just a child. She had many wonderful memories of her own youthful summertime adventures and she had enjoyed the time she spent there so much that when it came time for Mrs. Eos to make her own way in the world, she had decided to move permanently to this idyllic home and its surrounding gardens. The house itself was not very large, but the land on which it sat was wide and sprawling and lushly planted. It was warm and comfortable and the perfect space for Mrs. Eos and her ancient cat, whom she affectionately called Kiska.

Mrs. Eos's dacha was made of planked wooden siding that had greyed in the weather, but each window, column, and door frame was contoured by lacy gingerbread trim that shone brightly in brilliant white. There was a large covered porch surrounding the little house and its roof sprinkled with a flowering vine of pink geranium. A neat pebble path led to the front door, and Mrs. Eos, who loved all things light, had painted it a shiny warm yellow that seemed to bathe the shady porch with a sunshine glow. She took great pride in her home. It was spotlessly neat and tidy inside and out and, even though it was well hidden from the road amid a stand of exceedingly old and very tall pine trees, the sun always seemed to shine brighter and stay higher and longer in this magical grove. Mrs. Eos's gardens were always well tended and overflowing with wonderful flowers, shrubs, and herbs, which grew in profusion and perfumed the air with marvelous aromas that smelled dreamily of lilies, lilacs, and tuberoses. At the windows, the white linen and lace curtains rustled in the breeze, and from the path Molly could see Mrs. Eos at the door, a broom and dustpan in her plump little hands and a crisp white apron tied firmly about her round middle. It was almost as if she had been waiting for Molly to arrive. From her doorstep, Mrs. Eos raised her hand in greeting. Molly waved back and began to walk a little faster. As she went, Molly thought back to all the other times she had visited Mrs. Eos in this beautiful garden. She had always loved coming here.

"Good morning, Mrs. Eos!" she said quickly.

"Child, child," said Mrs. Eos happily. "Come in. Come in. How very lovely to see you my dear, truly it is! Come in. Come in!" Molly bent down to rub the fur of the fat cat that lolled in the sunshine near the front door, then she carefully wiped her feet on the mat and stepped inside Mrs. Eos's shiny house. Inside, the windows were open to capture the sweet-smelling breeze, and everything felt cozy and serene.

"Sit down, sit down," said Mrs. Eos in her sing-song voice, indicating a large floral chair in the corner. "You've had a bit of a walk, haven't you?" she said, not waiting for an answer. "Let me get you a glass of lemon water, my dear," and she toddled off towards the kitchen. Molly sat down on the edge of the overstuffed chair and pulled her spectacles from her pocket. From the kitchen she could hear the sounds of tinkling glass and water being poured. She placed the spectacles on her nose and waited. Quite soon, Mrs. Eos returned to the room balancing two large glasses and a yellow pitcher of lemon water on a shiny round tray. Molly watched her as she entered the room. Through the spectacles she saw a brilliant yellow halo of light appear around Mrs. Eos's silver head, a light that looked as vivid and golden as the sun. Molly's heart filled with beauty and compassion. She slipped the glasses down her nose once again, and as the golden light faded, she looked at Mrs. Eos as if for the first time. Molly clasped her hands together in her lap and leaned in a little closer to the old woman.

"How are you, Mrs. Eos?" Molly began politely.

"Oh, I am well child, very well," replied Mrs. Eos as she slumped heavily into her chair. "Well, as well as can be expected and truly child, I don't wish to complain."

"Is anything wrong, Mrs. Eos?" Molly asked.

"Well since you mentioned it, my dear, I love the sunny days, but the nights are so dark. I am not at my best in the dark, you know. My bees give me lots of wax and plenty of honey, but it all means nothing without a wick."

"I'm so sorry," said Molly, "I do wish that I could help you." Reaching into the basket she pulled out the package labeled *Mrs. Eos* and handed it to the old woman. "My mother sent this to you," Molly continued, "I'm not sure what it is, but I surely hope it can help."

Mrs. Eos took the package in her small plump hands and untied the wrapping. A large spool of candle wicking fell into her lap. A bright and glorious smile lit Mrs. Eos's round face and a tiny tear fell from the corner of her eye. "Oh! Thank you, Molly dear. You have made me so happy. Now I can spread my light whenever and wherever I wish!" she said with glee.

Molly felt her heart fill with the most amazing lightness. How did her mother know exactly what Mrs. Eos would need today of all days? "Mrs. Eos?" asked Molly, adjusting the spectacles on her nose so that she could see through the lenses. Once again a bright yellow mist glowed softly about the old woman's head. "Mrs. Eos, my mother told me you were in the room when everyone named me."

"Oh yes! Oh yes! Of course I was there. We all were. Everyone so excited, so excited!"

"And do you remember, Mrs. Eos, which name you gave me?" asked Molly a bit nervously. She had waited with excitement to hear what Mrs. Eos would say and she trembled a little as she waited for her answer. "Do you remember whom you named me for, what she was like and why you wished to bless me with her name?"

"Do I remember?…of course I remember. I'm not quite as old as I look," Mrs. Eos replied, her stout little body shaking with laughter.

"Well—" asked Molly, "which one was it?"

"Lucy, I think," said Mrs. Eos, scratching her head. "No…no, yes. Yes, definitely Lucy, definitely Lucy. It was my mother's name. How could I not remember, and since I had no children I thought I would pass it on to you. My mother was such a funny, happy soul. Everyone should be happy as she. I was lucky to receive such a gift from her. Every day when I rise, I start a new day. New possibilities to seek and new beginnings with which to embark. Even when it rains I wait for the clouds to clear until once again I can bask in the warmth of the sun. I think each one of us has a responsibility to be happy. My mother surely did. I gave you her name so that her spirit of happiness could be part of you too, and because of the joy you feel, it will be easy for you to pass it along to others." As Mrs. Eos told her story, Molly had slipped the spectacles back onto the bridge of her nose. She thought to herself, *Our name is Lucy,* and listening to Mrs. Eos's words, Molly began to see a rich dark red plume emerge from the bright golden mist that had first surrounded Mrs. Eos's head. The colors separated into tendrils and the tendrils curled into themselves and then floated away as if they danced on the wind. Happiness bubbled up inside her and she felt like giggling and laughing; she felt warm and light and graceful. Molly was so very delighted and grateful for the name Mrs. Eos had chosen for her.

She stood up from the chair in which she sat and went over to Mrs. Eos. Taking the old woman's plump hand in hers, she gave it a tender squeeze. "Thank you so much for telling me about Lucy," she said, and then she bent down and kissed Mrs. Eos's soft cheek and gave her an enormous hug. "Thank you for your gift, Mrs. Eos," Molly whispered in her ear. "I have to go now, but I promise I will be back."

"You have made me very happy, child," said Mrs. Eos, getting up to walk Molly to the door. "Please tell your sweet mother how grateful I am for her timely gift."

"You have made me very happy too, Mrs. Eos. I promise to remember all you have told me." Molly left Mrs. Eos at the front door of her tidy white house, a delighted smile shining on her face, and a large spool of candle wicking in her plump little hands. "Goodbye," Molly called as she stepped out into the sun-filled yard and began to skip down the path. "Lucy," she sang to herself, "Lucy."

CHAPTER 5

Mrs. Teresky

The trees began to grow closer, blocking out the sun and created long shadows on this part of the path. It was always a little darker here and a little cooler too, Molly remembered, from her previous walks through this part of the road with her mother. But the trail was familiar, and as she walked, she listened for the sounds of the birds far above the trees and she knew that at any moment she would see the blue of the sky around the next bend. At least she thought so, but as she continued on, the sky turned suddenly dark and cloudy, and a heavy mist began to conceal the path. Molly felt as though she walked through thick grey clouds when a chill wind began to pick up and fat raindrops began to fall. Molly had walked quite a long way already and she began to feel angry and sorry for herself again. *It can't be much further*, she thought. Whenever she had walked this way with her mother before, it had never seemed to be quite this far or to take so very long.

Molly shivered in the brisk breeze that now blew coldly at her back, and she put her hands in her apron pockets for warmth. As she did, she felt for the spectacles. They were cold and hard in her already chilled hands. She fumbled with them as she tried to place them on her nose. She had hoped that they might help her find a way through the gloomy mist somehow, but her now wet hands made them difficult to hold. When she tried to remove them from their bag, they fell at her feet, splashing into the middle of a large and muddy puddle.

Oh! No! thought Molly anxiously. "Please!" she breathed aloud, her anxiety rising. "I hope I haven't ruined them … oh I hope not … !" She quickly plucked them up from the muddy puddle and rubbed them on her sodden apron. Molly's hands shook a little as she handled the spectacles. She was so cold, and a sudden and unreasonable fear clutched at her heart. *What if the magic had been washed away? How silly,* she reasoned. *I did find them buried in the mud in the garden. Even so …* she thought to herself once again, *anything is possible.* Molly placed the spectacles back on her nose, and the contact of her skin with the icy metal of the frame made her shiver and cringe.

Although the lenses were no longer as muddy as they had been, they were now so badly steamed up that when Molly put them on and peered through the streaked wet lenses and looked slowly around, she could see only darkness and feel only growing despair. Her mind felt empty and black too, just as she had when she had looked at Billy and Ivan. The fear and emptiness that filled her deep inside scared her with its intensity and made her heart beat faster and pound loudly in her ears. She looked carefully around her, struggling to see the path through the heavy mist. The foggy darkness was so complete that she wondered if the rain along this part of the path would ever cease and she longed to see the sun and bright colors again.

Suddenly, from somewhere closeby, Molly heard the loud, throaty yelp of a large animal. Listening carefully, she tried to turn towards the sound, but the fog and wind made it impossible to know for sure where the noises she heard were coming from. Molly remembered that Mrs. Teresky had a dog named Jasper and she only hoped that the wild noises were from him. *Jasper*, she thought nervously, *I hope that's Jasper.*

The loud yelping seemed to be coming closer and a small, frightened sob rose in her throat as she called out. "Jasper! Is that you boy?" Molly heard the sound of heavy paws slapping through puddles and approaching her rapidly, and she looked quickly around herself again, trying to place the direction of the loud and persistent noise.

"Please," she whispered aloud, "please let it be Jasper." The large animal's paws hit her shoulders hard from behind. Before she could tell their direction, they smacked her squarely with such force that she fell face forward in the mud. Fear and anger filled her body and she struggled mightily to fight off the heavy weight that held her down. Thoroughly sodden and covered in grime, she tried again and again to roll over and push away her attacker, but the large paws of the animal and her twisted skirts made moving nearly impossible. She was more frightened and more miserable than ever as she struggled to free herself. Fighting to stand, she felt the heat of the great animal's breath heave against her neck and along the side of her face. She lay pinned beneath it, barely able to move as her heart began to race crazily. Then suddenly, the great weight upon her shifted and she felt the gentle lapping of a slobbery, wet tongue wash against her cheeks. A wetness that was warmer and scratchier than the rain.

"Jasper, it *is* you!" Molly cried out with relief and happiness, giving a mighty push to rid herself of the enormous dog and to scramble up from the muddy puddle where she lay. Her long skirt and apron were dripping and clung tightly to her legs, but the spectacles were still there. Molly quickly retrieved the wicker basket from the ground where she had dropped it, and began to run as best as she could in her mud-caked skirts to keep up with Jasper as he trotted away through the heavy mist. Coming around a bend in the path, Molly smelled the smoky fire before she saw it.

She heard Jasper's deep woof just ahead of her on the path and knew she had arrived at Mrs. Teresky's.

"Mrs. Teresky!" called Molly, "are you here?"

"Yes, girly," replied Mrs. Teresky gruffly. The old woman stood under the overhang of her tiny cabin gathering wood from the pile by her front door. "Where else would I be?" she replied in a sarcastic tone. "It's much too wet to be out and about on a day such as this. The cold and wet make my bones ache so. And where would I be a goin' even if I could?"

"You could always move to town," said Molly with a shiver, shaking out her thoroughly wet and dirty clothes.

"Town!" exclaimed Mrs. Teresky, "oh, no, never that. Not *town*! No, No, No."

"I'm so sorry," began Molly, "I didn't mean to upset you."

"Well, girly," said Mrs. Teresky, "some folks was meant for town and some folks just aren't. My family has lived in this spot for generations you know, and if it was good enough for them it is good enough for me!" With that, Mrs. Teresky spun abruptly around and began to walk hastily back inside her tiny cabin. "Well, are you comin' or not?" she yelled over her shoulder at Molly, without once turning around.

The wooden door to the cabin creaked on its rusted hinges when Mrs. Teresky went inside. She barely left the door ajar, but there was just enough space for Jasper to wriggle through. Molly followed the large wet dog and stepped into the smoky interior. She could hear the constant dripping of the rain as it fell down from inside the chimney and landed hissing and popping on the struggling fire below. Molly had to rub her eyes in order to clear them of the hazy smoke. When she opened them again, she could see that the cabin was bare except for a small table and two chairs placed close to the fire. Above the hearth in a little alcove just large enough for a mattress was Mrs. Teresky's bed.

"You are Moriah's girl, aren't you?" Mrs. Teresky asked in her rumbly voice.

"Yes ma'am I am," Molly answered shyly.

"Then what are you waiting for, girly? Come in, come in. Sit by the fire and try to warm yourself. Believe me, I know what it is to be cold. Even in the summer, I shiver. Let me give you some hot tea from the kettle. It is all I have, but it will help spread the warmth inside you." Mrs. Teresky turned her back on Molly and began to assemble her cups and saucers. "And maybe a washcloth to wipe you off a bit." She rustled around in front of the fire and as she did, Molly slipped the spectacles on her nose. As she had hoped, the small room began to darken and change. Around Mrs. Teresky's thin, stooped body, a grey blue light dimly shone. Molly felt a chill that seemed to permeate deep into her bones. She shivered and her body screamed to be warm, but as Molly watched, a green vine began to grow slowly through the grey blue and a slow warmth began to creep back inside her. The vine twisted, turned, and began to bud. She felt hope fill her heart like the promise of spring and of new growth and soft green shoots beginning to bud in the garden.

"Here we are, girly," said Mrs. Teresky turning slowly around. "'Tis all I have, but praise be it should help." The green vine continued to swirl and blossom. Molly slipped the glasses off and laid them in her lap. She reached for the cracked clay cup and saucer that Mrs. Teresky held out to her, and wrapped her still chilled fingers gratefully around them.

"So," said Mrs. Teresky, "you're Moriah's girl. She is special, that one. Let's see that dirty face of yours and maybe I can see your mother in your eyes," she said, reaching for the washcloth. "Ah … there you are! There you are!"

"Mrs. Teresky," said Molly, trying not to squirm as Mrs. Teresky rubbed at her face with the scratchy wet cloth, "my mother sent along something for you. I don't know what it is but I hope it will help." Mrs. Teresky stepped back as Molly bent down from her chair and reached inside the basket. Several labels with her mother's neat handwriting popped out at her. One after the other Molly began to hand them to Mrs. Teresky.

"Oh my!" exclaimed Mrs. Teresky, as she took a large square package from Molly.

"Let's do this slowly. All good things come to those who wait, and anticipation is almost more fun than the gift itself," she said with a chuckle. The first package was large and floppy. Inside was a knitted shawl of a soft grey blue. The fringes on the end were green and viny, and at the very tips of the fringe almost hidden from sight the beginnings of tiny buds could be seen.

"How lovely!" exclaimed Mrs. Teresky, wrapping herself delightedly in the shawl. The next package was quite a bit smaller. Molly leaned forward to see better in the dim light of the room. Mrs. Teresky pulled the string on the package and peeled back the paper. "Oh," said Mrs. Teresky again. "Thank you, Moriah," she breathed in a heartfelt whisper. Inside the package that lay in Mrs. Teresky's lap was a pair of soft warm gloves that matched the shawl exactly. The palms of the gloves were a soft grey blue, the five fingers were a rich new green, and if you looked closely at the very tips, there were the beginnings of tiny buds all set to grow.

"Perfect," sighed Mrs. Teresky, snuggling deeper into her shawl and admiring the gloves in her lap. "But I can't very well open the last package with gloves on, can I? Here, girly," she said wiping a small tear from her eye and handing the gloves to Molly. "Put these on. You look like you might need them more than I at the moment. Mind you though, I want them back!" she sniffed. Taking a handkerchief from her apron pocket, she blew her nose loudly. "What's next?"

"I don't know," said Molly reaching back into the basket. "Let's see. I am finding that my mother is even more surprising and remarkable than I ever knew before."

"Her name means 'the wind,' you know," explained Mrs. Teresky. "Seeds travel on the wind. The universe makes its desires known through the wind and rain, the changing tides and seasons and the movements of the planets in the sky. My people have always been listeners to the earth and growers of necessary and beautiful things. I can never leave this place … but, sometimes my old bones find it cruel. I always wait for spring." She gave a small shiver more from past memories than from cold.

While Mrs. Teresky spoke, Molly lifted a rather large and heavy jar from deep in her basket. She was surprised once again at the weight of the jar, since while she had carried it in her basket on her errands it had not seemed as heavy as it was now. As Molly raised the jar, she saw yet another oval package wrapped in a green checkered cloth. Molly lifted that out too. By now, she had guessed that the contents of the jar held one of her mother's delicious soups, and her stomach rumbled in hunger.

"Look, Mrs. Teresky, soup!" cried Molly with excitement. She knew if her stomach was rumbling after just a short while that Mrs. Teresky's had to be very empty indeed. "It's my mother's special soup!" Molly felt a sudden and wonderful sense of gratefulness and relief, but it was not just because of the food she would soon receive.

"Yes, girly," replied Mrs. Teresky. "Moriah's soup is very special indeed. On a day such as this I will enjoy it immensely," she said. Taking a pot from the back of the stove, Mrs. Teresky poured the smallest amount of soup you can imagine into the bottom. She took two bowls down from her cupboard and placed them on the table. "Open the bread," said Mrs. Teresky in her crackly voice.

Molly opened the green checkered cloth and its folds relaxed and covered the small table. A rich, yeasty smell filled the room and combined with the delicious aroma of bubbling soup. Suddenly, the gloom inside the small room began to dissipate. Molly's stomach rumbled again but she was firmly resolved not to eat a bite of the soup her mother had provided for Mrs. Teresky. She could eat later, thankfully, but she just hoped it would be soon.

"Here we are, girly," said Mrs. Teresky turning around from the pot on the stove, "nice and hot." She placed two bowls down on the table, one in front of Molly and one in front of herself.

"I'm not very hungry. I don't—" Molly stopped mid sentence. Looking across at Mrs. Teresky's bowl she saw that it was filled to the brim and steaming. She looked to the jar of soup on the stove — it was full. She looked down to her own bowl of soup, and so was hers. *How could this be?* Molly asked herself in amazement, her eyes growing wide with wonder. She looked at Mrs. Teresky, who was eating her soup in large hearty gulps, as though nothing strange was happening.

After a long moment Mrs. Teresky looked over at Molly and said between spoonfuls, "What a lovely treat for such a rainy day. Moriah's soups are always delicious. Eat up, girly, eat up," as she passed Molly the spoon that lay on the table next to her bowl. "Your mother is special indeed. I for one never question any of her gifts," she added with an air of finality, and she went back to spooning up the last bits in her bowl.

Molly did not know what to say, and for a long moment she just sat there marveling at what she had seen. Since Mrs. Teresky had told her not to ask questions, she picked up her spoon and began to eat, but Molly hardly tasted her food; her mind was whirling with questions. *How did that happen?* she wondered. *Was it really my mother like Mrs. Teresky said?* Molly didn't know what to think, and it was certain that Mrs. Teresky would not answer any questions about the soup. Molly had other important questions to ask her; she held her breath a moment and gathered her courage.

"Mrs. Teresky," Molly said with a small quiver in her voice, "my mother sent me on this errand today, and I am very happy that I came. But before I leave, can I ask you a question, please?" She was more than a little nervous asking anything after what Mrs. Teresky had said, *but this is important,* she thought, *I need to know.* So she waited anxiously for a reply.

"A question?" huffed Mrs. Teresky in her gruff and rumbly voice.

"Yes, a question," answered Molly shyly. "You know that my name is Molly. You remember the girl with thirty-five names. My mother told me you were one of the people who named me. Can you tell me, Mrs. Teresky, do you remember whom you named me for, what she was like, and why you chose to bless me with her name?" The questions tumbled out, and once again trembling slightly with anticipation, she slipped the spectacles back on her nose.

Mrs. Teresky sat in quiet reflection, and then after a long moment she answered, "Sarah. Sarah, the mother of millions as she was called in the Bible. Just what is needed in a garden. Be fruitful, multiply, and all that. But you are named for my sister Sarah. She was an amazing woman herself, and in her hands our gardens and our family blossomed more fully than ever before. She had twelve children and they all went on to create and build and nurture their own beautiful families and gardens. My sister Sarah passed on her love of nature to everyone around her, and I who loved her dearly could think of no greater gift to give you at your birth than that." Molly sat quietly while Mrs. Teresky spoke and through the lenses of the spectacles, she could see the soft blues that swirled around Mrs. Teresky's head growing deeper and warmer, chill skies melting away, and the green of spring and new seedlings starting to form in the earth.

"Sarah," Molly whispered, "Sarah." She felt her heart swell with possibilities and gratefulness. *I am Sarah*, she thought to herself, *I am Sarah who loved the beauty of the garden and I am Lucy of laughter and happiness.* Molly was delighted to learn about the women whose names she carried and the stories both Mrs. Teresky and Mrs. Eos had told her. Her smile was once again as warm and bright as the sun, but curiosity still prickled at the edges of her happiness. She leaned back into the wooden chair where she sat at the table and thought about what she had just seen and heard.

Mrs. Teresky watched her for a brief moment, and though she could see that Molly's curious mind flew with questions, she said nothing more. So before Molly could ask any more of the many questions she ached to ask, Mrs. Teresky pulled her new shawl a bit tighter around her, stood up on her spindly legs and went to her front door, opening it slightly. Molly watched her and knew that the time for questions was over and she would just have to wait patiently for the answers she needed. She resigned herself to that fact and sighed deeply. It had to be enough for now.

Mrs. Teresky was waiting for her to leave. Molly took the spectacles from her nose, and placing them gently in the pocket of her apron, she rose from the table, leaned down next to her chair and picked up her wicker basket. She was so very glad that she had come on this errand today and was overjoyed with what Mrs. Teresky had told her about Sarah, but of the soup and the many colors and feelings she felt so deeply she would just have to find out in her own way. That was all she could do for now. It was all part of the wonderful idea that she had had and in good time she was sure she would discover all that she needed to know. Going to the door, Molly kissed Mrs. Teresky on her wrinkled cheek and thanked her once again. Then she walked out of the house and down the path with Jasper yelping heartily at her heels. At the top of the lane Molly turned to wave goodbye, but Mrs. Teresky was nowhere to be seen.

CHAPTER 6

Mrs. Lieben

The rain had stopped as fast as it had come and a warm sun bathed the path as Molly headed back towards town carrying her basket. She was dry and happy and full and contented as she made her way along, and the basket as always swung lightly in her hand. She hummed her special song as she walked, "Molly's the girl with thirty-five names, given with love, not one the same ... "

Molly's last errand was to visit Mrs. Lieben. Mrs. Lieben had a bakery. Her mother had had a bakery as had her mother before her. Mrs. Lieben was famous for her baking as was her mother and her mother before. The women kept their family recipes secret but the wonderful aromas that wafted through the open door were for everyone to enjoy. But as Molly entered the bakery and heard the gentle tinkle of a bell as she stepped on the mat, she noticed a little something different in the air. She put on the spectacles and looked around. The usual warm, sweet smell that always made her mouth water was definitely missing. She could smell yeast and cinnamon, and bitter chocolate, lemon, vanilla, and ginger. But the cara-mel sweetness her senses longed for was mysteriously absent as she looked along the bakery shelves. The cookies and donuts, cakes, pies, and torts that usually accompanied all the breads and buns and biscuits that the Lieben family women were famous for were gone. Even so, the whole bakery seemed to be bathed in a sweet lilac glow.

Through a swinging door Mrs. Lieben bustled into the bakery from her kitchen in the back. She was an overly large woman with large rosy cheeks, large strawberry blond curls, large blue eyes, and large hands and feet. Her bright flowered dress blew softly around her. When Molly looked closely at her through the spectacles, she saw pinks and purples and laven-der plumes swirling together like batter in a bowl, spilling and filling over and over again, and her heart felt full and as light as meringue. Before Mrs. Lieben could notice, Molly slipped the spectacles off her nose. Molly blinked and the bakery shifted back into focus. When she next looked at Mrs. Lieben, she realized anew what a very large person she was. In fact, everything was large about Mrs. Lieben including her heart. She was so very large that Molly could barely see her daughter Miranda walking behind her as she followed her into the shop. Mrs. Lieben carried a large baking sheet in her hands.

"Hot, hot, hot! " she exclaimed, and dropped the baking sheet on top of the display counter with a clatter. That's when she saw Molly.

"Molly, dear," she said happily, a sweet smile lighting her flushed face. Mrs. Lieben always remembered the names of all the children in the village. "I didn't see you there, what can I do for you today? As you can see we are not up to snuff in the sweets department these days, but we do have some very tasty poppy seed buns. I just made them this morning. Can I get you one or two?"

"Thank you, Mrs. Lieben," replied Molly. From the corner of her eye, she saw a swish of fabric and the tip of a brown leather shoe move behind Mrs. Lieben. Leaning to the right so she could see around the woman,

Molly waved. "Hi Miranda," she laughed and smiled happily. Miranda peeped out from around her mother's skirts and giggled, her eyes sparkling. Molly was delighted to see her friend standing there hidden behind her mother, because Miranda was one of her very good friends from school. Molly had hoped to meet her here when she saw that one of her errands was to stop at the bakery.

Mrs. Lieben looked quickly around her. "Oh there you are, Miranda," she said. "I wondered where you had gotten off to."

Miranda stepped out from where she had hidden. "Hey, Molly," she said with a wide smile. "Do you want to come with me to meet the other kids?"

"Sure do," said Molly eagerly. "But first my mother asked me to deliver this." Molly reached into the basket and began to bring out the package labeled *For Mrs. Lieben*. It was a very large package wrapped in brown paper and tied up with string, but it swung up easily onto the counter when Molly lifted it. She placed the package in front of Mrs. Lieben.

"Open it, open it," cried Miranda excitedly.

Molly just waited silently. If anything, that was one thing her experiences so far today had taught her. Watch and wait and listen.

Mrs. Lieben couldn't wait and so she pulled quickly on the string that tied the package and tore away the paper. Inside were four very large jars of golden honey. "Oh," she said, "Oh, have you ever seen anything more beautiful?" She held a jar up to the light and a sweet amber glow spread out along the counter top. "Your mother is truly a wonder," said Mrs. Lieben excitedly. "Now I can begin baking my sweets again. How wonderful! And if I hurry," she continued, casting a quick glance at the clock on the wall, "I can just make snack time at the little school across the street! Children need a yummy snack in the afternoon," she said and patted Miranda's chocolate brown curls. "Full tummies, full minds, I always say. It's hard to learn on an empty stomach and there is nothing more important than education, right?"

"Yes Mother," said Miranda, smiling back at Molly. "You're right, can we go now, please?" She pulled gently on Molly's arm. Molly did not move. She was determined to finish her plan and ask Mrs. Lieben the questions that were so very important to her. She smiled at Miranda and motioned for her to wait a moment.

"Mrs. Lieben," said Molly leaning in a little closer to the glass counter, "you are right. Education is very important, and I would like to learn something if you don't mind?"

Mrs. Lieben's eyes grew even larger in her round face and her smile was warm and soft. She leaned closer to Molly over the counter top. "Of course my dear, what can I do for you?" asked Mrs. Lieben in her sweet, caramel voice.

"My mother told me that when I was born, you were one of the people who named me. Do you remember which name it was? Do you remember whom you named me for, what was she like, and why you chose to bless me with the name you did?" The questions spilled out quickly as Molly placed the spectacles back on the tip of her nose and looked at Mrs. Lieben anxiously across the glass counter. Her eyes were large and magnified by the lenses as she looked intently at the woman and waited.

"Let's see," said Mrs. Lieben with a far-away expression on her face. "I remember that night. The snowflakes were big as dinner plates and the sky sparkled like diamonds. Everyone in the village was there, all the relatives and more. It was such a crush of people, I felt like an olive in a press! And I was much larger, even more than I am today, as I was expecting my own little one very soon." Mrs. Lieben chuckled and smiled lovingly down at her daughter Miranda. "I remember when I stepped into your parents' house and looked at you in your mother's arms. You looked so innocent and peaceful and smelled so sweet that I immediately thought of my Aunt Lily. She was truly a wonderful woman, an amazing cook and baker who loved to feed everyone. She was a teacher too and everyone who knew her was sweetened by having known her. Lily was her name and I loved her dearly." Mrs. Lieben sniffed loudly into her large purple handkerchief, then from the baking sheet she had just been carrying, she handed each girl a still warm poppy seed bun. With that, Mrs. Lieben spread her very large arms and gathered up all the jars of honey and turned back towards her kitchen.

Molly watched as she turned away. *A teacher, a cook, and baker who loved to take care of others*, she thought to herself. *How wonderful! I love that I am named for someone who gave to so many, and made so many people happy.* In her mind's eye she could see a fleeting vision of her mother, and it too filled her with joy and comfort. Then she slipped the spectacles off her nose once again. The colors that she had seen while Mrs. Lieben spoke of her Aunt Lily were vivid yellows, coral, and orange twirling and twisting-and they danced happily in wide circles before her eyes. Molly felt as though she could fly away the happiness that filled her was so great. "I am Lily, I am Lucy, I am Sarah," she breathed, "and they are me!" It wasn't just the story of her birth that made her so happy, since she had heard it many times before from her parents. It was just so amazing and wonderful that so many people had cared about giving her the name of someone they had dearly loved. She felt incredibly special, incredibly lucky, and even more curious than ever about all the others whose names she shared.

"C'mon Molly," Miranda said, pulling on Molly's arm once again. Molly still held the spectacles in her hand. Their crystal lenses and silver frame sparkled brightly even in the dim lavender light of the bakery. It was almost as if the spectacles were winking at her. As if Great-Grandma Ethel herself was winking at her and glad for all that she had learned today. Molly's eyes grew wide with excitement and possibility and she pressed the spectacles close to her heart.

"Thank you, Great-Grandma," she whispered.

"Let's go play, Molly," Miranda repeated anxiously. "Come on!"

Molly placed the spectacles in their grey felt bag, tied the red string, and put them safely in her apron pocket, giving them a soft pat as she did.

She reached for the wicker basket that still sat on top of the glass counter, and placing it in the crook of her arm, she and Miranda stepped out of the shop and onto the welcome mat. The sun was high in the sky and the street was bathed in golden light. The tiny bells above the shop's front door began to tinkle in the spring breeze. They seemed to sing *Lily, Lily*. Miranda must have heard it too because she started to sing *Lily, Lily*. Then she stopped and looked at Molly.

"You're so lucky," said Miranda, "I wish that I had thirty-five names." And she reached over and gave Molly a hug. Then together each holding a handle, Molly and Miranda swung the basket between them as they walked back to the Market Square.

CHAPTER 7

The Lightness of Giving

The basket felt as light as air, the way it had all day, even with the weight of all the gifts Molly had carried earlier for her mother. It was another puzzle and one Molly and Miranda wondered about as they walked along the streets that led to the town square where Molly's parents' fruit and vegetable stall stood. Both Moriah and Ari were busy with customers when Molly and Miranda arrived. The little stall was so crowded that the girls stood aside for a moment and waited. Ari noticed the girls through the crush of people; he finished bagging potatoes and vegetables for his customer and called them over.

"Hello girls," Ari greeted them happily, "I hope you had fun today." He reached over the counter and kissed Molly on top of her head and gave Miranda a loving pat on her shoulder. Molly handed her father the basket and he placed it under the counter for safekeeping. Just then, another customer approached the stall. "Well girls, back to work," Ari laughed.

"Molly," he said, "we will be leaving by four o'clock, so be back by then." And he turned away to welcome the next shopper.

At a quarter to four, Molly rounded the corner that led to her parents' stall. She was eager to talk to her mother about her day and ask the many questions that had been twirling around in her head. When Molly arrived at the stall once again, her parents had already begun the task of packing up and she helped them place the last of the empty crates in the back of the wagon. Then it was time to leave. As before, Molly climbed into the middle of the seat and nestled herself comfortably between her parents. She was so excited she could barely keep still. Moriah held the basket that Molly had carried on her lap. Ari held the reins and the little wagon moved slowly down the dirt road. Molly was just about to speak when Moriah reached into her skirt pocket and held out a small package for Molly. Molly took the package and quickly peeled back the white paper and pulled out a length of sky-blue ribbon. "Oh thank you!" she smiled happily. "It's beautiful!"

"You were such a help delivering my packages today, I wanted you to have something special." Moriah smiled back and gave her daughter a tender squeeze around her shoulders.

"Oh mother, I had the most amazing day," Molly exclaimed. "Really and truly amazing! When I saw the labels on the gifts you sent, I knew I wanted to ask Mrs. Eos, Mrs. Teresky, and Mrs. Lieben about the names they chose for me and why, and when I did, I put on the spectacles and each time I saw and felt incredible things, colors, and emotions and in the end I felt so proud and happy and very, very lucky to have such special women be a part of me. I am not just Molly or Malkah, but so much more!" Molly's eyes were large and bright with excitement as she looked closely at her mother, who returned her happiness with a warm smile and a gentle squeeze around her shoulders.

Moriah was very pleased with her daughter's discovery; it had been the real reason that she had sent her on the errands today. Still, she could sense that there were even more questions that Molly needed to ask, so

47

she sat quietly next to her on the wagon seat with a contented smile on her face and waited. Molly watched her mother, and her natural curiosity bubbled up inside her. There were so many more questions that she had wanted to ask all day. She thought for a second as she tried to decide how to begin … should she ask about the colors she saw when she looked through the lenses of the spectacles or the basket first? The wagon gave a sharp lurch as it bounced along the rutted dirt road and the wicker basket slid off Moriah's lap and onto Molly's. *The basket first*, she thought with a smile. Then, handing the basket back to Moriah, Molly asked her mother one of the questions she had been aching to ask all day: "… How did you know the one thing each woman needed?"

"Did I?" Moriah asked, smiling broadly. "Well ..." she continued, "I have been saving candle wicking for Mrs. Eos lately because I know how fast she uses it up, keeping her home as bright as the sun. Mrs. Teresky is always cold living as she does in that drafty house of hers. The winds blow through the walls of her house as if they aren't even there and I worry about her and if she has enough to eat. I try to send her things as often as I can, and I only hoped that there would be enough soup to last her for a while. I could do no more than that. You remember that your Aunt Lena keeps bees. She has so much honey that she sent me much more than I could possibly use. So I thought to share it with Mrs. Lieben. She makes the most delicious honey buns."

"What about the basket?" Molly asked.

"The basket?" Moriah repeated.

"Yes," replied Molly, "the basket, why was it always so light even when it contained so many wonderful and heavy things?" Molly could barely sit still as she waited for the answer and her fingers fidgeting with the fabric of her skirt in anticipation of what she would learn.

"Ah," sighed Moriah as she remembered a long ago day. "I have had that basket ever since I was a young girl just a little older than you are now. It was given to me as a gift for a birthday by my favorite Aunt Charlotte, who had received it from her mother, my Great-Aunt Annabella. They were kind enough to pass it along to me and when I received it, it was filled to the top and more with the loveliest sweets and pastries you can imagine, and a note on top read: *To Moriah for your special day: giving makes the load lighter.* I thought that was a very unusual thing to write for a birthday, and since the basket held far more than I could possibly eat alone, I picked it up with the intent of sharing my gift with my family and friends. I expected that basket to be very heavy since it held so much, and so I was quite amazed that when I began to lift it, it almost floated into my hands. Through the years, whenever I have used that basket to help others it has always been … *weightless.* I can't explain it more than that. My great-aunt explained to me, when I asked her, that it is in the believing that things come true."

Molly looked at her mother as a smile of understanding lit her face, and her eyes were large and bright. "I believe that what I saw and felt was meant for me to discover today, and you knew what I would find, and that is why you sent me on those errands."

"You are growing up, you are twelve now," Moriah continued. "You have always been a very curious person from the time you were very small, and since you found the spectacles, I have seen you begin to look even closer at things and to question the world around you. I thought that today would help you discover something new about yourself and your connection to the people around you and the women whose names are part of you. I hoped that learning more about all the women you met today would fill you with strength and happiness. It is so very important to understand who we are and where we come from and to share with others whatever we can, openly and with a happy heart."

"Oh," laughed Molly, "yes it's true, and it did! I did!" she exclaimed, throwing her arms out wide in delight. She was so excited and happier than she could say and her smile was bright as the sun. "I am Lucy and Sarah and Lily and so many others! Mrs. Eos, Mrs. Teresky, and Mrs. Lieben told me the most wonderful stories of how they came to give me the names they chose, and Great-Grandma Ethel's spectacles helped me to see deeper into everyone I met today and discover the special talents that make me who I really am."

Moriah looked intently at her daughter. "You are wise beyond your years," she said softly.

"*You're the girl with thirty-five names*," sang Ari, turning to look at his beloved wife and daughter. His tenor voice was strong and sweet and his eyes glowed with pride. Then, laughing softly together, Molly and Moriah joined him.

CHAPTER 8

Two Baskets

Molly always had lots of questions about that day, about the spectacles and the colors she saw through their lenses, and about everything she had experienced. In fact, each time she put on the glasses there were more and more questions, and her friends Miranda and Grace were curious as well. The two girls had tried on the spectacles, but, like everyone else who had tried them on, never felt anything or saw anything different like Molly did. Nevertheless, the girls chatted endlessly about what it all could mean.

"What was Molly supposed to learn about the many fantastic colors that she saw through the lenses?" They wondered again and again as they walked home from school together. "And why did the colors make Molly feel things the way she did?" There was certainly lots more to learn, so Miranda and Grace set about making a plan of their own.

Moriah stood at her kitchen table and put the last lid on a jar of ointment she had just made. Rich verdant aromas filled the air around her. To make the ointment, Moriah had first separated the honey from the combs her sister Lena had given her, and then melted the beeswax in a large pot which hung from an iron hook above the fire in her kitchen. When the wax was hot and bubbling thickly, she added a large handful of pink mountain rose petals that she had gathered from the bushes that grew near her front door, and several bunches of shredded wintergreen and peppermint that grew prolifically in her garden. She thinned the whole mixture with a few drops of hot pepper oil and stirred slowly with a large wooden spoon, then the mixture was left over a gentle fire to bubble and simmer down slowly. The recipe she used was one she had learned from her mother, who had prepared it for her father each year as a remedy for his arthritis. Now Moriah prepared the ointment seasonally for her husband Ari, who also suffered in the winter's cold, just as her father had. Pouring the still warm liquid into the jars she had set out reminded Moriah of her father Eli and how grateful he had been each time he rubbed the ointment into his stiff fingers and achy knees. She smiled to herself as she remembered his grateful expression as the medicine began to work. The joy this simple act brought to Moriah was enormous, and as she went about her work, she sang and was happy.

On a shelf in the tiny pantry, Moriah placed the jars of ointment she had made and as she did, she thought of the many people with whom she would share them. "Tomorrow is Sunday," Moriah thought to herself. "It should be a lovely day for a long walk and I think I may be able to make it to Pearl and Abe's as well."

The next morning, Moriah rose early and went about her chores. As she prepared breakfast, there was a knock at the door. There on the mat stood Miranda and Grace.

"Is Molly here?" they asked in unison.

Moriah could see behind the girls that Ari and Molly were coming up the path from the barn and she smiled widely. "Here she comes now!" she said with a laugh.

"Hi!" called Molly and she ran the rest of the way to the front door.

"Have you girls eaten breakfast?" Moriah asked. "There is porridge and honey, if you like."

"Oh, thank you!" exclaimed Grace, stepping delightedly into the kitchen. Grace never said no to anything that included honey. Maybe that was one of the reasons that she and Miranda were good friends, because Grace always loved going to her mother's bakery, too.

"Good morning, ladies," said Ari coming through the door. He placed the pail of milk he had carried in from the barn next to the stove and gave his wife a kiss on her cheek.

"Thank you," she said and smiled up at him. "Everyone sit down now, Molly and I will bring the porridge." And she turned towards the stove dishing up the porridge into bowls and topping them off with a golden dollop of honey and warm milk.

After breakfast, the girls sat at the kitchen table talking and laughing, deciding how to spend their day. From a cabinet in the kitchen, Moriah took down a wicker basket and began placing inside of it some of the jars of ointment she had made. Molly looked up from her conversation.

"Are you going visiting, Mother?" she asked curiously.

"I thought I would share some of my remedy with my mother's family who live close by," replied Moriah as she wrapped the jars carefully in white cloth. "I think my Aunt Pearl would especially appreciate having some to rub on her poor knees."

"I remember Aunt Pearl," said Molly excitedly. "She is one of the women I am named for, isn't she?"

Moriah looked up from her wrapping. "Actually," she replied, "it is her mother Pearl who shares her name with you."

Molly laughed. "It is a little confusing, but I think I do remember her a bit from when I was little."

When Miranda and Grace saw the basket and heard about Aunt Pearl, they looked at each other and grinned. Could this be the opportunity they had hoped for? Miranda leaned across the table and said to Molly,

"Maybe Grace and I can go with you to visit your aunt. It would be fun to meet another one of the women who named you," she continued, and Grace added excitedly, "You can bring the spectacles, too!"

Molly looked back at her mother expectantly. Moriah turned and reached into the cabinet again, pulled out another wicker basket and placed it on the counter next to the one she had already filled. "I do have more than one basket, you know," she said with a wink.

Grace was not shy and so she asked Moriah, "Can we take your special basket, the one Molly told us about?"

"Oh! Grace," moaned Miranda.

"It's alright," replied Grace confidently. "Isn't it? We'll be careful." And she turned to Moriah questioningly.

"I think it's a wonderful idea," said Moriah. "It's a lovely day for a walk, just as I knew it would be, and I think my Aunt Pearl would dearly enjoy a visit. It has been such a long time since Molly has seen her. I'll just add a few of these jars from my basket to this one and that should be enough." Grace leaned over the counter and watched eagerly as Moriah took six jars of ointment from her basket, placed them carefully into the larger one, and covered them both with a snowy white cloth.

Molly rose from her chair at the table. She was excited about the opportunity to do this errand for her mother, so she went quickly to her room and retrieved the spectacles from her bedside cabinet. She untied the string of the soft felt pouch and removed the spectacles from inside. They shone brightly in her hand, almost beckoning her to try them on. It made Molly very happy to be able to use them again, and she wondered what she would discover when she visited her Aunt Pearl. Molly wrapped the spectacles back in their bag for safekeeping and, placing the glasses in her apron pocket, she returned to the kitchen where Miranda and Grace were anxiously waiting. Moriah was waiting too, and as she stood by the front door, she wrapped a soft blue scarf on her head, tying it securely under her chin.

"Do you remember how to get to Aunt Pearl's?" she asked her daughter.

Molly thought for a moment. "Isn't it out beyond the river road?" she replied.

"Yes, that's right. I wasn't sure if you had forgotten. It's been a long time since you last visited that side of the family. Aunt Pearl's house is on Rubenki Street. You just—"

"I know where Rubenki Street is!" interrupted Grace. "My Uncle Pasha lives around the corner from there. I have been there many times before on visits with my family."

"How perfect," said Moriah. "Then you can lead the way." And she patted Grace lovingly on her shoulder. Taking the baskets from the counter, she handed one to Molly and placed the other in the crook of her elbow and went to the door. "Better get started," she said, "it's a bit of a walk."

The three girls went through the doorway and out into the bright sunlight of a brilliant spring day. Behind them they could hear the soft click of the key in the lock and around them the sky was filled with bird-song. "We can walk together until the fork in the road," Moriah said as she shifted the basket she carried to her other arm.

Grace looked up at Moriah expectantly and asked, "Would you like me to carry that for you? I don't mind," she said. Moriah had expected that Grace would ask to carry her basket.

"Well, are you sure? It is a little heavy."

"Please," said Grace, a sense of anticipation in her voice.

"Alright," replied Moriah, "if you're sure." And she handed the basket to Grace. Grace had thought the basket she now held would be totally weightless, like the stories that Molly had often told her, so she was completely startled when the unexpected weight of it in her hands almost pulled her over.

"Are you alright, Grace?" Moriah asked with concern. "I can carry it if you wish."

Grace thought for a moment. *What if the basket gets lighter the more you carry it?* she asked herself. And so she looked up at Moriah and said, "It's okay. I'd like to carry it for a while."

"Very well then." Moriah smiled at her and began to walk away down the path. Molly and Miranda were a little ahead swinging the large basket airily between them. They laughed and sang as they went. Moriah followed closely behind, enjoying the warmth of the sun on her back and the sweet breezes that stirred the petals in the trees and brushed lightly against her cheeks.

Grace struggled with the weight of the basket she carried, but finally found a manageable position as she walked slowly behind the others along the river road. She had expected that the basket would become lighter, but it only seemed to grow heavier the longer she walked. Grace did not complain, but she wondered over and over again why she had guessed so incorrectly. By the time she had caught up with Moriah, Molly, and Miranda, she was sticky with sweat and as curious as a cat. Grace put the basket down, and with a huge sigh dropped, into the cool grass beneath a nearby shade tree. Molly and Miranda joined her and passed a small cup of water between them. The cool water was refreshing and Grace was grateful for it. She could feel her cramped muscles relax a bit, but the question that was foremost in her mind energized her, and she stood up quickly.

She was just about to speak when Moriah said, "Here is the fork in the road I told you about." And she pointed a short distance ahead and to the left, then picked up the basket that Grace had put down in the grass and placed it in the crook of her elbow. "You're sure you know the way now, Grace, right?" she asked once again. Grace nodded, her mind too full to speak. Moriah bent over and kissed Molly on top of her head. "Give my love to Aunt Pearl," she added. "Tell her I will stop by sometime soon." And then she began to walk away down the path to the right.

Grace watched Moriah for a moment then called out to her, "Please, wait a moment. Please, I have a question that I need to ask you." Moriah turned around to look at Grace and waited expectantly. She seemed to know exactly what Grace would ask her, but she said nothing, a small smile working at the corners of her mouth.

"Well," Grace began slowly. Now that she had the opportunity she didn't quite know how to begin and she struggled with her words. "How come … I don't understand …" she tried again. Then she took a deep breath and asked in a rush and all at once, "Why was the basket I carried so very heavy? It should have been light as air the way Molly told me it was?" She glanced over at Molly, who still sat under the tree with Miranda. Then she looked back at Moriah, a little blush rising to her cheeks.

Moriah touched the basket beneath her arm and smiled happily at Grace. "The difference is how I use them," she said mysteriously, and turned once more to walk away.

"What do you mean, how you use them?" asked Grace, more bewildered than ever. "I still don't understand."

Moriah looked back over her shoulder. Grace stood in the middle of the path and waited. "It's really very simple," Moriah replied. "The basket that you carried for me contains ointments that I intend to sell along my way today. That is why it is so heavy. When my job is complete it will be weightless again. The basket Molly and Miranda carried is filled with love and a gift that will bring comfort and please the receiver, and that is why it is always weightless." Then without another word or a backward look, she turned and walked away.

Grace watched Moriah as she moved away down the path, then turned and went over to the tree where Molly and Miranda still sat. The wicker basket they had carried lay beside them in the grass. Grace lifted the white cloth cover that Moriah had placed on top of the jars and looked inside. Just as she had expected, there were six jars of creamy white ointment each neatly labeled *Aunt Pearl*, the very same number of jars in the basket that she had carried for Moriah. Grace reached inside and lifted out one of the jars. It felt warm and heavy in her hand, and the glass jar

DJ COLBERT

sparkled in the bright sunlight. She slowly put the jar back inside the basket and covered it once again with the white cloth. Grasping a firm hold of the basket's sturdy handle, she lifted it up slowly. It came up easily in her hand. Indeed, it felt as light as air, as though it were completely empty with nothing at all inside. Just as Moriah had said it would be. Grace looked at Molly, her eyes wide and her mouth open in amazement. Molly clapped her hands in delight at the look on her friend's face, and Miranda began to laugh out loud too.

"My mother always said that Molly's mother was special," Miranda giggled. "Now I guess we know that it is surely true!"

"How did your mother make that happen?" Grace asked, still astonished by what she had seen. "Can she do other things too?" Molly looked at Grace and there was a mischievous smile on her face. Then she stood up and gently took back the basket.

"You're right. I think my mother is more than special," Molly answered. "She comes from a very long line of healers, women with talents and special abilities that are amazing and wonderful. They are all connected to one another like a long ribbon that goes back and back through hundreds of years, longer than I can count. My mother explained to me that we are all like that. Each one of us has family to discover and connect to. She also told me that this basket was a birthday present she was given from a very old aunt of hers named Charlotte. She meant for my mother to use the basket each time she had something to share with others. My mother said that it has always been weightless each time she has carried it to give a gift to someone else. She also told me that if I believe enough, then it would always be true. Anything is possible. Maybe that is what the answer is: just believe, and impossible things can happen. That is what my mother said, and that is just what I try to do, just believe, and wait and see." The sun shone brightly all around Molly as she turned away and began to walk down the path, the wicker basket swinging from her arm.

"Wait!" called Grace, and she and Miranda hurried to catch up to Molly. "Can I carry this one now?" she asked anxiously. "I want to give something to someone else too!" Molly smiled at her friend and opened her hand and offered the basket to Grace, who reached out excitedly to take it. As she did, the wicker basket that held the six jars of ointment fairly flew into her hands.

CHAPTER 9

Moriah

The soft breezes that blew through the trees propelled Moriah forward, her step light and carefree. It was delightful to be outside on such a beautiful late spring day. The unpaved road she followed led through a sun-filled grassland. Along the edge of the dirt road, nettles and raspberry plants grew in profusion. Moriah stopped to pick the spiny leaves of the nettle plants, being careful not to prick her fingers on the spiky barbs along the stem and purple flowers. She placed the leaves gently in a leather pouch that lay inside her basket and moved along the road to where the raspberry plants drooped their fruit-laden stems within easier reach. She picked both the fruit and leaves and added them to her basket, popping a few sweet raspberries in her mouth as she worked. Moriah knew exactly what she wanted to use these plants for and she picked only the freshest and the most verdant green.

The taste of the fruit filled her mouth with delicious pleasure, reminding her of a day long ago when she had gone foraging with her sister Lena and her aunt Charlotte. There had been sweet raspberries to pick that day as well, and Lena had laughed and teased her before running wildly along the trail that Aunt Charlotte followed. But Moriah had stayed close by her aunt, watching her intently as she filled her baskets with a variety of wild plants, roots, and flowers. Moriah knew that the items that her aunt picked would later be used to make the many curative teas and balms that her family used throughout the year, and she watched carefully as her aunt worked. She was eager to learn all that the women of her family had to teach, and she asked her aunt over and over to explain what she was picking and why. Aunt Charlotte was always patient with Moriah and never seemed to mind answering all the questions she had.

Moriah smiled to herself as she remembered another day, long past, when as a very young child she sat in her grandmother Ethel's lap in a rocking chair by the fire in her mother's kitchen. The old woman's silver spectacles glinted softly and the lenses reflected the red and blue flames. There was a large black iron pot hanging over the fire suspended by a hook that hung from inside the chimney, and the aromas that filled the air were of honey and cherry and cloves. That day, her mother was making a syrup remedy for sore throats and colds, and the mixture of ingredients simmered long and slow, thick bubbles rising to the top and popping gaily on the surface.

"There needs to be more cherry," Grandmother Ethel had remarked in her old and raspy voice. "I can tell from the smell that there needs to be more cherry."

Moriah's mother sighed softly and flipped through the pages of a large leather-bound book that sat open on her kitchen table. "I am following the recipe exactly," she replied. "But, if you really think it needs more, well …"

"I do. I definitely do. It just smells a little off to me," her grandmother had replied as she gave a little *humph*. "It needs more cherry."

Moriah's mother shook her head and smiled. "All right, I'll add a little more." And from a large wooden bowl she took several handfuls of deep red cherries and added them to the simmering liquid in the pot. After a few moments, a richer, deeper aroma of cherries filled the air, and Moriah could tell her grandmother was satisfied even though she remained quiet. All around the open hearth Moriah's mother had placed bunches of herbs and bundles of leaves to dry. Tied up with string and hanging upside down, they were ready for the time when they would be used for whatever remedy was needed.

Moriah was fascinated by all the ingredients her mother worked with, and as she grew, she learned more and more. At first she assisted her mother and aunt in the gathering and foraging. There was so much to know. Not everything they needed could be grown in their garden and there were special places that the women knew of where a particular plant, or a sweetly full honeycomb, was waiting to be found. Moriah learned to carry a small sharp knife in the pocket of her apron and she used it often to cut plants and stalks and dig for roots in the soil. She also carried with her a small basket and several leather bags to use as she collected whatever it was that she found along the way. Moriah loved the process of making remedies for her family, and with practice, she became quite good at it. Even better than her mother or aunt had been. But it was not until she married Ari that the leather book of recipes that her mother had collected and carefully kept was given to her.

"Now," her mother had told her with great pride in her voice, "these recipes are entrusted to you. Do only good with them. They have been collected through many, many years and have served our family and friends well. I think that your deep understanding, intuition, and love of your craft have made you worthy to receive this gift and have set you apart from other women healers in our family who have come before. You can be the greatest of all of us."

Moriah cherished the leather book of recipes her mother had given her, knowing that it was a culmination of the hard work and experimentation of all the women in her family. She had always kept it proudly on a special shelf in her kitchen. She referred to it often and relied on the wisdom she found within its pages. But Moriah had a deeper sense of things than just what was written in her book and the medicines she created with her hands. She also had an innate sensitivity to the world around her that allowed her to see and feel what was to come, before most other people did. From the first she had thought of this awareness as a kind of protection and she had learned that if she became very quiet and still and listened to the breezes that blew softly against her skin, she could feel a connection to the deepest part of herself and the universe beyond. It was a comfort and a strength that came naturally to her, and she realized that if she believed very strongly in the work that she did, wonderful things were sure to happen. Through the years when friends, family, and neighbors had come to her door seeking the aid of her knowledge and medicinal treatments, she had treated them all happily and took enormous pleasure from her work.

Moriah sighed deeply and contentedly as she remembered the days of long ago, and she hummed a happy little tune to herself as she added another handful of berries into her basket and then continued on her way.

CHAPTER 10

Kamenka

The little village that lay just ahead on the dirt road was called Kamenka, and along its main street were an assortment of wood-fronted shops with grimy mud-spattered glass windows that were reached by a rickety sidewalk. Moriah had been to Kamenka many times before and knew just where she wanted to go to sell some of the ointment she had made. First she stopped in at the tailor shop where old Mrs. Ivanov sat in the dusty window trying to warm herself in the sun.

When the old woman saw Moriah, she greeted her happily. "Have you brought my ointment?" she asked in a soft and creaky voice.

"Yes, yes," replied Moriah and smiled tenderly at the old woman. Mrs. Ivanov suffered terribly with arthritis in her hands and feet. Even so, she continued to help in whichever way she could in her son's shop. Moriah lifted the linen cover of her basket and took out several jars of her ointment and placed one on the counter next to Mrs. Ivanov's chair. Then she opened the top of the other jar, and taking some of the creamy ointment on her fingertips, she took Mrs. Ivanov's hand in hers and began to massage the medicine into the old woman's swollen fingers. Mrs. Ivanov sighed deeply as she felt the heat of the ointment making its way into her sore hands.

"Oh, Moriah," she breathed, "you are a godsend, a true godsend!" And she smiled warmly at Moriah.

"I am just so happy to be able to give you some relief even for a little while," Moriah replied with concern.

"I know you are, my dear, I know you are," sighed the old woman.

At the back of the tiny shop a man stepped from behind a brown curtain. "Hello, Moriah, so good to see you again," he said. "My mother ran out of your ointment a few weeks ago and she has been praying that you would come back soon with more."

"Hello, Tomaz," replied Moriah with a smile. "You can always send me a message, you know. I would be happy to—" she began to say.

Mrs. Ivanov interrupted her, "I don't want to be a bother, my dear. I will just wait and in time I know you will return." Moriah looked over at Tomaz who shrugged his shoulders and smiled.

"I did offer to send for you," he said and turned to the little cash register that sat on the counter. He took out several copper coins and dropped them into Moriah's basket. "Thank you," he said, "we are grateful." Moriah put the cap back on the jar of ointment and closed it loosely, leaving it next to the other jar on the counter. She bent and kissed the old woman's wrinkled cheek.

"Be careful with this jar," warned Moriah gently. "The cap is loose so you won't struggle when you need to open it. I promise not to stay away too long, but if you are in need, please ask, it is my pleasure to help you in any way I can."

"I know you will come as soon as I ask," said Mrs. Ivanov. "You are a godsend." Moriah patted the old woman's shoulder and waved goodbye to Tomaz and went out into the sunshine.

Moriah walked along the uneven sidewalk carefully, the pride and happiness she felt deep inside from helping Mrs. Ivanov lightening her steps. Several shops down at the end of the block she reached the butcher shop of Mr. Treff. The interior of the shop was dark and shadowy when she entered. Moriah immediately noticed the woodsy smell of sawdust in the air that the butcher used to cover the shop floor and a deeper, darker, more acrid odor of fresh blood and flesh. Mr. Treff also suffered from arthritis in his wrists and elbows, which he attributed to all the carrying of heavy slabs of meat he had done through the years and the repeated use of the cleavers and knives he used to cut what he sold.

When Moriah entered the shop there was no one about, so she called out to the butcher and waited. It was not long before Mr. Treff came through the back door of his shop, carrying a large leg of mutton on his shoulder. He dropped the leg heavily on his large wooden cutting block and wiped his bloodied hands on his already dirty apron.

"Ah, Moriah!" he exclaimed loudly. "Just the woman I wanted to see today. I am sadly out of that wonderful cream you make. I was about ready to send a message that I needed more, and here you are."

"How wonderful!" Moriah replied happily. She smiled up at the butcher and placed two jars on the countertop. Mr. Treff went to his register and opened the drawer beneath, taking out two copper coins and handing them to Moriah.

"I am so glad that my ointment is working for you, Mr. Treff," said Moriah. "I made a little extra so I can leave you two jars this time."

"Well then, I guess I owe you a little more," replied Mr. Treff, going back in to his register and taking out two more coins.

Moriah took the coins that Mr. Treff held out to her and put them in her basket. "Thank you, Mr. Treff. I am so glad that you are finding some relief using my ointment."

"Indeed I am," exclaimed Mr. Treff. "That is why I have told my friend Mr. Saltzman about it. He has been suffering terribly since he took a bad fall last week. He injured his back and leg when he fell from a ladder at his work, so I shared some of my cream with him, and he told me that it was helpful. He lives at the end of the crossroads, if you have any more you would like to sell."

"Well yes, I do," replied Moriah gratefully. She had wondered where she should try to sell her remaining two jars. "Thank you. I can stop by along my way." Mr. Treff gave Moriah the directions to Mr. Saltzman's house, and thanking Mr. Treff again, she left the shop and headed down the street towards Mr. Saltzman's. The sun shone brightly in the late morning sky as Moriah entered the Saltzman's front yard. Her knock on the front door was quickly answered by a middle-aged woman in a red paisley dress and a starched white apron. Moriah introduced herself and explained why she had come.

The woman who answered the door was delighted to see Moriah. "Please come in. I am Olga," she said. "Follow me. My husband will be so very glad you are here. He has not been able to work since he fell from the ladder and the only thing that seems to help is the ointment that Mr. Treff gave him." Olga led Moriah into her kitchen and there, in a large padded chair near the fire, sat Mr. Saltzman.

"Andrei, this is Moriah, the woman who made the cream that you have been using, she has brought you more. Mr. Treff the butcher sent her along. Isn't that nice? I'll just get my purse," she said, and leaving Moriah with her husband, she bustled into the next room.

"I am so glad you have come, my dear woman. I can't thank you enough for the ointment; it is truly remarkable. I don't know what I would have done without it. I must get back to work as soon as I can. I work in the forest cutting back trees and hauling lumber. It has been weeks since I have been able to do anything since hurting my back. If I don't return to work soon, we will have no money for food or rent."

"I am very sorry for your injury and so glad that I can be of any help. I have two jars left and I will be happy to leave them with you, just rub it in thoroughly on your back and leg two times a day. When you begin to feel some relief try to walk around a bit, you must regain your strength before you are able to continue with the heavy work you do," replied Moriah, gently patting his broad shoulder. Then she took the last two jars from her basket and placed them on a nearby table and turned to go. Olga returned to the kitchen and saw Moriah as she headed for the door.

"Wait, please," she exclaimed. "Let me pay you."

"There is no need for payment," Moriah answered. "Later when your husband returns to work we can talk about payment, for now he must heal and regain his strength."

"Thank you so much, my dear woman. You don't know what a blessing you are," Mr. Saltzman replied gratefully.

"Yes," agreed Olga, "we are so very grateful, you will never know how much." She hugged Moriah close and kissed her cheek. "Thank you again," she whispered and walked Moriah to the door.

CHAPTER 11

Lena

After leaving the Saltzmans' home, Moriah continued down the road that led out into the countryside. The fields she walked through were ripe and abundant with the new growth of spring, and the air was filled with the trills and chirps of birds calling for their mates. Moriah stopped to listen for a moment. The birdsong filled her heart and she was at peace with the world that surrounded her. A quick glance at the sun told her that it was just after noon and she increased her pace a bit as she went along her way.

She was headed for the home of her sister Lena, who lived not far from the village of Gorky. Lena's wooden farmhouse stood in a cluster of similar homes and fields, and soon, from where she walked, she could see the pitched roofs and plowed fields that signaled the end of her journey. Moriah pushed open the wooden gate of her sister's house, walked up to the front door, and knocked. It was soon opened by a chubby-faced little girl with long golden curls and large blue eyes. For an instant, Moriah felt a sharp pang of memory. The little girl looked so much like Molly had when she was small.

"Babooshka! Babooshka!" called the little girl as she turned and ran back into the house, leaving the front door open wide.

"What is it, Tassy?" answered a woman's voice. "What do you need?" Coming around the corner to check on her granddaughter was Moriah's sister, Lena. Lena had dark brown hair like her sister that she wore in braids wrapped around her head in a tight crown. Her green eyes grew large and delighted smile bloomed across her round face as she recognized her sister standing in the doorway.

"Oh! Moriah! What a wonderful surprise. I am so glad to see you. The women of the village are asking when you would come back." She reached her arms wide and pulled Moriah into a warm and loving hug. "Come into the kitchen, there is chamomile tea and poppy seed cake." She took Moriah by the arm and led her to the back of the house and into her spotless kitchen. Moriah pulled out a chair and sat down at the round wooden table and placed the basket beside her on the floor. "Have you brought more leaves and berries?" asked Lena excitedly. "There is none remaining since you were last here to make the infusion that Mrs. Milesky is waiting for," she added, and placed a glass of chamomile tea, a jar of golden honey, and a slice of poppy seed cake in front of Moriah.

"Thank you," replied Moriah, stirring the honey into her cup and drinking deeply from her glass. "I was so very thirsty. Yes, I have brought more fresh leaves and thistles as well." And she opened the top of her basket so Lena could look inside. "I've brought raspberries too that I picked along the way. I thought you might enjoy them."

"Tassy loves raspberries, and so do I," remarked Lena. Taking the wicker basket from beside her sister, she removed the berries carefully and filled a large wooden bowl that she placed in the center of her table. "Shall I prepare the nettles and raspberry leaves? If we start now, the tea can steep for awhile before we send for Mrs. Milesky and we can begin brewing the infusion as well, don't you think?"

Moriah took another large sip of her tea and stood up from the table. "Yes, that will work nicely. Let me help you with the nettles and leaves I brought; this batch needs to dry out before we can use them to make the tea. We can place them in a basket to dry and you can have them on hand for use later. I have brought along some that I have dried already so we can use them today."

She reached into her wicker basket, and from under the cloth at the very bottom, she removed two leather pouches, one filled with dried nettles and the other with dried raspberry leaves. "These should brew and steep for an hour or more before they are ready to be used," she reminded her sister. "I have also brought coriander, birch flowers, and marigold, and if I can use some of your chamomile, we can make that infusion as well."

Once again Moriah reached deep into her basket and removed three small leather pouches and placed them on the counter top. Lena handed her sister a small jar of dried chamomile, and then from a cabinet near her hearth, she took out two black iron pots and hung each from a hook above the slowly burning fire. Moriah ladled water into the pots from a nearby jug and as the liquid began to bubble, she measured out the dried nettles and raspberry leaves and sprinkled them across the surface of the water in the first pot and stirred the mixture with a wooden spoon. Then she opened her bags of coriander, birch flowers, and marigold. In taking the jar of chamomile, she sprinkled three teaspoons of each into the boiling water of the second pot. Using another wooden spoon, she stirred the mixture thoroughly.

While she worked, Moriah hummed a tune, one that she always sang when she made her medicines. It was old as old could be, and one that she knew almost more than any other, and she smiled to herself as she made her preparations. When she had finished she turned to her sister, "I will need to watch over the fire. I don't want the pots to boil over; a slow simmer for a while is just what is needed. We can let the women of the village know that I am here whenever you are ready. By the time they arrive, the teas should have had enough time to steep and will be ready to cool. Then they can sit overnight and be ready for use tomorrow."

"Let me get Alexei," Lena offered. "He has been helping out in the barn today and I am sure he would not mind. He can take Tassy with him and drop her back at home. I will be right back." And leaving Moriah to watch over the pots in the kitchen, she went to the bedroom to fetch Tassy. Taking her granddaughter by the hand, she went out the door and down the dirt path to the barn.

When Lena returned a short time later and stepped through her front door, she could hear her sister humming her ancient song. As she came through the hall towards her kitchen, she could feel the steamy warmth that filled the room, and she breathed deeply of the rich and aromatic scents from the pots that bubbled slowly in the hearth. Moriah's dark brown hair curled in wisps from the steam and she wore a satisfied smile on her face as she hummed aloud.

Lena paused in the entry of the kitchen for a moment watching Moriah. "You make the world around you so special," she said with happiness as she stepped over to the hearth and pulled her sister once again into a warm embrace. "Everyone loves to know you are here and looks forward to your visits, and you do so much good with your medicines and caring. I am so amazed at all you do. I only wish I could be as capable as you are. I have tried and tried, and my curatives are never the same as yours. Maybe it is that little song you sing that makes everything you do better." Lena looked intently into Moriah's eyes. She could see that what she had thought was indeed true, and she knew deep in her heart that even if she hummed the song the very same way that Moriah did, it would still not matter. Moriah was gifted with a talent that she could never achieve. But there was no jealousy, only admiration and pride.

Moriah looked at her sister and gave a little laugh. "It is my pleasure to do this work. I am happiest when I am able to help wherever I can, and I believe so strongly that I was meant to share with others the recipes and knowledge passed down to me by all those women of our family. I only hope that that is why my medicines are sought after."

Lena squeezed her sister's hand. "I know that you were chosen for a reason. You were always the one who asked questions and wanted to learn. From the very beginning it was you who had the talent and the ability. It is indeed a most marvelous gift. Without that knowledge, I think your life would be very, very different." Still holding her sister's hand, Lena led Moriah to the table. Moriah knew that what her sister had said was true. Without that knowledge, she might never have had her own daughter.

CHAPTER 12

Moriah and The Women

Moriah sat with Lena at the table talking and remembering and laughing while they waited for the women of the village to stop by. It wasn't very long before they heard the sounds of footsteps coming from the lane outside the house. Lena pushed the shutters of her kitchen window open wide. She could see a tall and very thin young woman who carried a bundle in her arms coming slowly up the path that led to her front door.

"Come in Mrs. Milesky, we have been waiting for you. The front door is open." Lena went to the door and met Mrs. Milesky as she reached the entry. The woman held a sleeping baby cradled in her arms and carried a small basket. "Hello and welcome," Lena said sweetly and stepped back to allow the young woman to pass.

"Please. Call me Ruth. We have known each other long enough after all. Your son Alexei told me Moriah is here and I came just as soon as I could. I had to bring my baby along, I hope you don't mind?"

"Of course not, babies are always welcome," laughed Lena. "Please, follow me, Moriah is waiting in the kitchen."

Moriah stood up from the table and greeted the young woman with a smile and a gentle pat on her shoulder. "What a beautiful little one," she said, looking down at the baby.

"Oh Moriah, I am so happy that you have come. I have been so afraid …"

Moriah knew exactly why Ruth was afraid, as she had shared those very same fears herself not so long ago. She said nothing however, and just pulled out a chair and motioned for Ruth to sit. When they were all seated, Moriah reached out for Ruth's hand and held it tenderly. She could feel the rapidity of her pulse and her icy cold touch. "Now tell me Ruth, whatever is the matter?" she asked in a soothing voice.

"You know my story," Ruth began in a rush of words. "I have lost several babies before they were due to be born. It is only because of the tea you make that I have been blessed with this child." And she looked down and rocked her sleeping baby gently, a sad and wistful smile appearing on her harried face. Looking up at Moriah, tears filled her tired eyes. "I am expecting again and I haven't any more of the tea. I did not know how long it would be before you returned and I was so very worried that it might be too late. I know without your special tea I will not be able to have another child at all. I am so worried that …." Ruth was unable to continue and she struggled to hold back her tears. Her child stirred in her arms sensing his mother's discomfort. Ruth shifted the baby to her shoulder and rocked gently back and forth in her chair. The baby cooed softly. "This is my son Sasha. He is the light of my life. I cannot lose another child." She sighed deeply and her tears fell like raindrops down her cheeks.

Moriah stood and went to the hearth. She took a thick towel that hung from a peg on the wall next to it and used it to remove the heavy black iron pot that bubbled slowly over the fire, setting it down on a metal trivet that she had placed on the counter. She watched the steam as it rose in coils and evaporated into the air, and as she did, she hummed her tune. Then she went and stood next to Ruth, placing her strong hand on the woman's thin boney shoulder.

"You must be strong for your child and husband, Ruth," she said in a gentle murmur. "You must eat and nourish your body, or even the tea that I will give you today will not help. You must learn to be positive and believe with every part of you that all will be well. You must learn to be happy with the child that you have been given, and raise him in love and peace. He deserves that from both of you and you must find the courage to go on come what may. The tea is ready to take with you now, but it must steep a while longer. In the morning you will need to strain the liquid through a cloth before it will be ready to drink. I have made enough to last you a little while, and I promise to come back soon and brew more as you need it. Remember you must believe and all will be as it should be. Come now," Moriah continued as she took Ruth's hand and helped her up from her chair, "have you brought along some jars for me to fill?"

Ruth nodded slowly and wiped away the tears that still flowed down her cheeks. Adjusting the baby in her arms, she opened the basket that she had brought along and handed the jars to Moriah. There were four in all. Moriah went to the pot, picked up a ladle, and began filling the jars one by one. As she worked, she could hear the high-pitched laughter of more of the village women as they came up the path that led to Lena's front door. Moriah placed the jars of cooling liquid one by one in Ruth's basket, wrapping each one in a large piece of felt and closing the lid. Then she gathered Ruth and her little boy in a warm and motherly hug.

"Thank you Moriah, thank you so much. I promise to do as you say. I know that you are right. I believe that you are right." Ruth smiled gratefully. Then, taking several silver coins from the pocket of her dress, she placed them on the kitchen table and, picking up her basket, she turned to walk out the door. In the yard, Ruth greeted the women as they came from the village and stopped to chat for a moment and show off her baby son. She felt light and happy for the first time in a long while and so very grateful that Moriah had come. Waving goodbye to the women, she fairly danced as she walked back towards her home, bouncing her son on her hip as she went.

The three women, Natalia, Katarina, and Galina, were eager to see Moriah as well, but for very different reasons. And they all wanted the same thing. In the second pot on the hearth, Moriah had brewed her special youth elixir, a kind of beauty treatment for the body that gave the drinker strength and energy. The elixir was also believed by many to add years to one's life, while making the drinker more youthful and refreshed due to its ability to rejuvenate skin, hair, and nails. The elixir was always popular among the women wherever Moriah went and today was no different.

Natalia was a middle-aged woman with beautiful hazel eyes who worked each day in the fields alongside her husband. Even with gloves and a hat her hands would become dry and chapped, as would her cheeks and the back of her neck. She bought the elixir whenever she could as a preventative and she swore that only Moriah's elixir made the most difference. Katarina was a young woman of twenty-five, tall, and relatively thin with light brown hair and large green eyes. She worked at a local dairy farm making cheese along with her new friend Galina who had just moved to Kamenka after her recent marriage. Katarina was always tired even after a full night of rest, and the elixir that Moriah made seemed to give her the energy that she very much needed. She had told Galina about the youth elixir when they first met, and Galina, who just wanted to look as best she could for her new husband, had been eager to try the drink.

So when Alexei had stopped by the dairy to let Katarina know that Moriah was in town, the two women finished their chores as quickly as they could, packed a basket with a large piece of freshly made cheese and several glass jars, and hurried over to Lena's house.

Moriah sang softly to herself as she lifted the small iron pot that contained the youth elixir from its hook over the fire and placed it on a trivet on top of the counter to cool. She could hear voices and laughter coming from the hallway, and when she turned around from her task, the women were waiting at the kitchen door.

"Come in, come in," called Moriah and she motioned for the women to enter. Katarina went directly up to Moriah and hugged her close.

"I am so delighted to see you. Your elixir has changed my life. I have more energy than I ever expected. When I get out of my bed in the mornings, I can't wait to start my day. That hasn't happened in a very long time. I am very grateful," she told Moriah excitedly. "And this is my friend," Katarina added, introducing the woman standing next to her, "her name is Galina."

"Yes, hello," said Galina. "I am here just for a small pick-me-up in the beauty department."

All the women laughed together after that, and one by one, they offered the glass jars they had each brought along for Moriah to fill. Moriah twisted the top on the last of the jars, and as she did, she noticed a cart coming towards the house through the open kitchen window. She looked a little closer and a huge smile lit her face.

"What do you see?" the women asked curiously as they joined Moriah to look out the window. Coming slowly up the lane towards the house was a little cart pulled by a workhorse of a golden red color with a black mane and tail. Seated on the bench of the open cart was a tall and muscular man who wore a straw hat on his head and waved as he drove the cart into the front yard of the house.

Turning from the window Natalia inquired, "Who can that be, I wonder?"

"I think it just might be my ride home," laughed Moriah quickly turning from the window, a wide and wonderful smile still on her face. "Thank you so much for coming today," she said and she handed Natalia her basket. "Strain the elixir through a cloth tomorrow and then you can drink it twice a day."

"Thank you," the three women replied, and they each placed the coins they had brought in payment on the table. Katarina took the cheese she and Galina had brought along and laid it next to the coins.

"We brought this as a gift to you," Galina said. "From the dairy farm where we work."

"How lovely," Moriah replied. "I am sure we will enjoy it immensely."

"And please come back soon," added Katarina and Natalia. Moriah was delighted that she could be helpful to these women and she gave them each a warm and motherly hug.

"Moriah!" called Lena from the next room. "There is someone here for you."

Moriah gathered up her basket and placed the coins and the cheese inside. "Do you want to meet the man in the cart?" she asked mysteriously to the three women.

"Yes! Yes! Of course we do," they replied curiously. Moriah led the way out of the kitchen carrying her basket in the crook of her elbow. Lena was already in the yard talking to the man with the cart who continued to sit on the bench, holding the reins in his hands. But when he saw Moriah, he jumped down quickly, handed the reins to Lena, and approaching Moriah he bent down and kissed her soundly on her mouth. The ladies watched in shock and surprise. Moriah began to laugh as she patted the man on his chest. She turned to face the women.

"Let me introduce my husband, Ari," she said gleefully.

"I thought since you had walked such a long way already, that you might enjoy a ride home," Ari told Moriah, and he turned to meet the three ladies, doffing his straw hat in greeting as he did. "A pleasure," he said.

The women smiled and began to laugh. "Oh, Moriah, what a lucky woman you are!" giggled Katrina.

"Yes I am," Moriah replied, her smile as warm as the sun. Holding Ari's hand, she went to hug her sister goodbye. Ari helped his wife up into the cart and handed her the wicker basket. Then he joined her on the front seat and, taking the reins back from Lena, he flicked them gently, and the golden red horse began to walk slowly away down the path. Moriah turned and waved over her shoulder at the women who still stood together in the yard. "I'll be back soon," she called, "see you soon."

CHAPTER 13

Aunt Pearl

The sun was still climbing towards noon when the three girls entered the lane that led to the little village of Gorky. The surrounding farms in the area they had passed were rich and green and abundant with tall stalks of oats, wheat, and barley, whose long bright green stems and soft brown tufts waved slowly back and forth, rustling sweetly in the breeze. Black and white cows grazed languidly in the nearby meadows, the earth smelled rich and deeply fragrant, and the sky was dotted with light and billowy clouds as Molly, Miranda, and Grace walked along the main street. In the center of the little village was an imposing stone building. A sign over the front door read *Post Office* in deep black letters, and leaning against the door frame was a bright blue bicycle with large brown leather bags hanging from the rear fender.

"It's this way, I think," called Grace over her shoulder to Molly and Miranda. Grace had walked a little ahead for most of the way to Gorky, happily swinging the basket by her side as she went. Then suddenly, she stopped in the middle of the street and looked around. "I know my Uncle Pasha's house is that way," she mumbled to herself and looked to the left. "Then Molly's Aunt Pearl's house must be this way." Grace was confused; she had been so sure that she knew exactly where Aunt Pearl's house was located when they had discussed it this morning, but now that she was here it all looked a little different.

"Which way?" asked Molly when she had caught up to Grace. "My mother said it was on Rubenki Street. Don't you know which way it is?" Molly looked Grace in the eye and she could tell immediately that Grace was not in the least sure which way to go. Molly looked over her shoulder at Miranda who stood behind her, and as she did, she saw a young man in a blue uniform and cap come out of the post office. His arms were heavy with packages and letters and he began to sort them into the brown leather bags of the blue bicycle that stood by the door. Molly breathed a small sigh of relief.

"Come on, let's ask the postman. He should definitely know where Rubenki Street is." And she began to walk briskly back towards the post office. "Excuse me, sir, do you know the way to Rubenki Street?" Molly asked the young man, who was still engaged in sorting his letters. "I am looking for my Aunt Pearl who lives there," she added.

The young man stood up, adjusted his cap and uniform, and looked at Molly and her friends. "I just might know who you are looking for. I wonder if it's Pearl Zabarsky and her husband Abe? They live on Rubenki Street, number 2, I believe. Is that who you mean?"

"Oh yes, that's the one," replied Molly. "Yes, my Aunt Pearl is married to a man named Abe. That's exactly who I mean. Can you tell us how to get there, please, sir?" Molly smiled up at the young man and waited.

"I can do better than that," the young man offered. "I can take you there myself. I'll just push my bicycle along so you can follow me easily. It so happens that I have a few letters to deliver to that very address today. I'll just finish up here and we can go right away."

"Thank you so much," the three girls replied in unison, introducing themselves to the postman. Standing aside, they waited patiently for the young man to finish his task. When he was done, he took hold of the bicycle's handlebars and began to push it slowly down the street.

"My name is Pavel Skolniki," he said pleasantly. "It is my pleasure to see you young ladies to your destination. Follow me." As he walked along, he began to whistle a little tune. The girls followed close behind him, happy that they would find the address they wanted. The young man had looked back after a time and noticed the large basket that Grace was holding. "Do you want me to put that on my handlebars? It sure looks as if it might be heavy. I can easily carry it," the young man had offered with concern in his voice.

"So can I," smiled Grace. "Thank you, though."

As they walked along the streets of Gorky, they passed by a large grey wooden building. The sign over the opening read *Stables, Horses For Sale*. Its front doors were thrown wide and there were stalls lining its walls. Several tethered horses pranced and jostled each other for room as they tried to drink from an old wooden trough near the front entrance. Next door was a blacksmith's shop where the iron forge burned red hot, and the intense heat it emitted radiated into the street. The blacksmith poured sweat as his heavy hammer clanged loudly over and over. The girls looked wide-eyed at each other as they passed. On the opposite side of the street, there was a small boarding house with several rocking chairs on the porch and a faded cardboard sign that read *Rooms to Let* hanging from the top floor window.

On the corner at the front door of a small cafe, a man in a long white apron stood wiping a glass with a white napkin. "Hello, Pavel!" called the man in the apron, "Any mail for me today? All I ever get are bills anyway, I don't know why I even bother to ask …"

"Not today," replied the postman with a chuckle. "You are safe for another day," he called back over his shoulder, laughing softly to himself.

He continued to push his bicycle slowly along, turning to look back every now and then to check on the girls behind him.

"Are we almost there, Pavel?" asked Molly and she walked a little faster to catch up to the young man.

"It's not too far now, only another block or so," he answered. "Have you ever visited your aunt and uncle before?"

"No," replied Molly. "But I have met my aunt a few times when she came to our house for holidays and such when I was younger. Why do you ask?"

"I have been a mailman here in town for the last few years. Most people I deliver to only receive the occasional letter or package, but your aunt receives more letters than I can count almost every day. I just wondered if you knew why?" Pavel looked at Molly over the handlebars of his bicycle. There was a look of interested confusion on his face.

Molly shook her head. "I'm sure I don't know," she answered. "But maybe I can find out during our visit. I am bringing her some ointment that my mother made for her, that is what is in the basket my friend is carrying."

"I see," said Pavel. "We turn here, this is Rubenki Street." And he turned his bike into the road that veered to the left. The houses on each side of the street where they now walked were all built of wood and the roofs were covered with shake shingles that had darkened and greyed in the weather. The columns and gingerbread trim around the windows and doors of the houses were painted in bright pastel colors of pink, blue and green. Pavel stopped in front of one of these houses and leaned his bicycle against a high wooden fence.

"It's this one," he said as he pointed to a one-story house across the street. The house he indicated looked welcoming and well-tended. The front gate stood ajar and seemed to beckon them forward. There were tall yellow sunflowers growing in the yard and pink geraniums cascading from the window boxes. The little porch that ran along the front of the house was painted a sunny sky blue, as were the ornately carved window surrounds, columns, and the front door. There were lace curtains in the diamond-paned windows and Molly could see a neatly-tended vegetable garden to the side of the house with a large red painted barn near the back. It was a lovely little house and Molly could not wait to go inside.

Pavel took a rather large packet of mail and a small box out of his leather mailbags. "Follow me," he called to Grace and Miranda, who had lagged behind. Molly followed Pavel closely as he crossed the street, went through the opened gate, and into the front yard of the house. Near the doorway in a low braided wicker basket, a fat white cat with black and brown spots lolled in the sunshine. Pavel's arms were full and even though he tried, he was unable to knock on the door so Molly stepped in front of him and gave the door three short raps.

They heard the rustle of loud footsteps from inside and soon the door swung open to reveal a rather tall and imposing man with short greying hair and heavily muscled arms. He greeted Pavel with a wide smile. "Let me help you with those," he offered. He reached out and took the mail from the postman. And he turned away and placed the letters and the box on a table inside the doorway, then turned back and looked at Molly, Miranda, and Grace with curiosity.

"Who do we have here, Pavel, are they your new helpers?" The man asked with a laugh.

"No sir," Pavel replied, "this is your niece Molly and her friends Miranda and Grace."

Molly dipped a small curtsy. "I am Moriah and Ari's daughter," she replied a bit nervously. "I have come with a gift from my mother," she explained.

"You're Moriah's daughter ... well, well," repeated the man, "you have grown quite a bit since last I saw you. I bet you have brought my wife some of your mother's special ointment. Please, come in, come in," and he began to move aside so the girls could enter the house. Molly stopped on the doorstep and turned to look at Pavel.

"I'll just be getting along and finishing my route. It was very nice to meet you," he said, and began to walk back up the front path towards the road.

"Thank you again, Pavel," called Molly. "It was nice meeting you, too. We would never have found the house without you. Thank you." Pavel waved goodbye happily as he crossed the street and mounted his bicycle and rode away.

"Come in, come in," repeated the large man. Looking at Molly, he introduced himself. "I am your Uncle Abe," he said. "Abraham Zabarsky, that's me!" he smiled. "I know your Aunt Pearl will be very happy to see you. It has been a long while since we had a visit or were able to visit our family in Zhitomir. We are just sitting down to lunch, are you girls hungry?"

"Oh yes, I am," Grace answered excitedly. "It has been such a long time since breakfast!"

Uncle Abe laughed a warm and hearty laugh. "Well, we will just have to do something about that," he said. "Follow me." He led the way down a short hallway and into a bright and sunny kitchen. The walls of the kitchen were painted pale green and in the windows the lace curtains that Molly had seen from the street were tied back with green cords. Seated at the kitchen table in the middle of the room in an oversized chair sat a rather small sized woman. Her silver grey hair was braided and coiled intricately around her head in a tight crown and her deep brown eyes sparkled. She wore an expression of surprise on her face when she saw the three girls enter her kitchen.

"Pearl," said her husband, "Look who has come to visit. It is Molly, Moriah's daughter, and she has brought along the special ointment that you like so much."

"Molly!" exclaimed Aunt Pearl. "How lovely to see you child. Come, please sit. Have something to eat. It is a long way to walk to come to Gorky.

I am so thrilled to have you here." The table at which Aunt Pearl sat was made of shiny polished wood and covered by an embroidered cloth.

"Look!" said Grace when she entered the room. "There is chicken and noodles and cabbage soup!"

"Oh Grace!" moaned Miranda with an embarrassed look on her face. "Can't you wait?" Grace shook her head slowly at Miranda, placed the wicker basket down next to a chair at the table, and then looked questioningly at Molly and Aunt Pearl.

"How lovely," exclaimed Aunt Pearl. "You have come with friends. I am so glad. Please girls join us, come and eat." And she motioned to everyone to take a chair.

"Help yourselves," said Uncle Abe. "There is more than enough to go around."

"That is very true," replied Aunt Pearl with a little laugh. "My Abe always makes more than we can possibly eat!" Uncle Abe began passing out plates and cutlery all around. Then, taking a chair beside his wife, he served her first, filling her plate with chicken and noodles and the bowl with thick cabbage soup. When he did, Molly noticed that her aunt's small hands were gnarled and bent and it was difficult for her to hold her spoon and fork. She still smiled radiantly and thanked Molly when she filled her glass with water from the pitcher placed near her at the table.

The lunch was indeed delicious and filling, and when everyone was finished, Uncle Abe rose from the table. "Pearl, wouldn't you like to show the girls your special room?" he asked with a twinkle in his eye.

"Indeed, I would. I think Molly and her friends are old enough now to understand. Can you help me please?" Molly looked at Miranda and Grace as they stood up from the table, her eyes wide with interest and excitement. Abe stepped behind his wife's chair and slowly pulled back. The chair rolled away easily from the table and he turned and began to push it out of the room.

"Follow me," he said with a spark of amusement in his voice as he looked back at the girls. Miranda and Grace were curious too and they were quick to join Molly as she picked up her mother's wicker basket and followed behind her uncle. Abe pushed Pearl out of the kitchen and down a short hallway towards the back of the house. He stopped in front of a wide white painted door and reached inside his shirt pocket to remove a shiny brass key. Reaching around his wife's wheelchair, he placed the key in the lock, turning it back and forth easily until they could hear a soft click. Then he gave the door a gentle but firm push. The door opened slowly before them, blocking out the light in the small hallway where they stood.

The total darkness before them was startling and it seemed odd too since the kitchen had been filled with warm sunlight. It was difficult to see inside the room, though the girls tried hard to peer around the edges of the doorpost. Abe went ahead into the dark interior of the room, pushing his wife in her chair before him.

"Come girls, don't be shy, your eyes will get used to the darkness. I have some things I want to show you," Aunt Pearl called over her shoulder. Molly, Miranda, and Grace entered the room cautiously and stood closely together just inside the doorway. Soon, as their eyes became accustomed to the dim light of the room, they could see that Abe had placed his wife's chair behind a very large wooden desk and that along the walls of the room were tall wooden bookcases that ran floor to ceiling. The shelves were filled to capacity with books of every size and shape imaginable, each one bound in a fine leather jacket of varying rainbow colors and with gold and silver lettering on their spines. In fact, every surface of the room's side tables and chairs seemed to be covered with books and papers, and here and there along the floor were piles of haphazardly placed notebooks and open atlases and maps.

Abe hastened to remove a stack of books from a small red velvet sofa, piling them as best as he was able in a nearby corner. Then he pushed the sofa up as close as he could just in front of the desk since the floor around it was littered with stacks and piles of papers. Taking a match from a drawer inside the desk, he struck against a flint from his pocket and proceeded to light several amber glass oil lamps that were placed on tables scattered about the room. The lamps glowed softly a golden honey yellow and illuminated the room's interior in a warm and inviting way.

"Please," he said, indicating the sofa. "This should be comfortable for all of you." Molly, Miranda, and Grace went to the sofa and sat down, each of them taking in their surroundings with wide-eyed interest and wondering what it was they were about to learn. "That should do it," Abe announced with a chuckle. "I guess I will leave you ladies now to get better acquainted." Then, kissing his wife on top of her head, he turned and left the room, closing the door softly behind him.

Aunt Pearl sat comfortably in her oversized chair and smiled happily at the girls seated before her. She ran her gnarled hands lovingly across the green leather embossed top of her enormous desk and began to speak. "I guess you are wondering what this room is and why we have chosen to keep it in darkness as we do." Molly and her friends did not reply. All three girls were intensely curious and leaned in a little closer, listening attentively. There were so very many questions each one wanted to ask but they just sat quietly, each girl a little too shy and a bit overwhelmed to speak, waiting eagerly for Aunt Pearl to explain.

"Look closely around you," Aunt Pearl continued, pointing about her to the many bookcases that lined the walls. "You will see a library of books that I have collected and some that I have written since I was a very young girl. I am a writer of journals, a poet and a letter writer as was my mother before me. For as long as I can remember I have loved to keep diaries and journals and write stories and poems. I could write about anything, but what I choose to write about, what interests me the most, is the world that surrounds me. By that I mean my family and friends, and the everyday experiences that make us who we are. There is so much to discover if only we ask the right questions and keep asking until we can understand the deeper meaning in things. Memories can change over time; they seem to dim a bit if not shared often or quickly written down. It is my wish and my life's work to write those memories down as clearly as I can to keep them safe and to cherish them as I grow older. I am not as able as I once was. My old bones do not allow me to go very far afield as they once did before and so I write letters, lots and lots of letters, and I receive mail sometimes by the bagful. I can travel in those letters that I receive even though I can no longer leave my chair, and it is as if I were there too experiencing and learning and collecting more memories than one person could ever gather just by staying home.

"I write, not just to family and friends, but to authors and historians and poets, and I am overjoyed with their responses. We share ideas, thoughts, and feelings, and even sometimes recipes too," Pearl said with a little chuckle. "When I was a young child and learned to read and write, I thought what a marvelous gift I have been given to express myself, not just by speaking, and I filled pages and pages of notebooks with the stories and history of my family and friends that are too precious to ever forget. It is our memories and our history that help make us who we are, you know. If we forget our history than we can never learn from our past and we will continue to make the same mistakes over and over. We must learn from our failures as well as our successes, and make ourselves and the world we live in better and infinitely richer for the time we have spent here. I believe that that is the purpose for all of us and I believe that if tiny seeds for a bright future are planted early and watered well, then small miracles are sure to grow.

"I guess I am what you might call a historical collector. I treasure memories that I have experienced myself or uncovered about others and I surround myself with them. When I am in this room I am connected to the people whose memories have become mine, too. My husband Abe works in a leather factory and when I am finished collecting enough for a volume he is kind enough to bind it for me and together we fill these shelves with our beautiful books. Of course, the books must be protected too and that is why we keep this room in darkness most of the time. In sunlight, the inks become faded and the leather can become brittle so Abe and I are careful to store them as best as we can."

Molly leaned forward in her seat on the sofa. "My father Ari once told me about how important it is to keep your memories safe. I think I was a little too young when he told me that, I really didn't think about it much then. But now I think I understand what you both mean."

"I think I do too," said Miranda in astonishment. "My mother writes letters all the time to her sisters who have moved far away, and every day she waits for the postman's delivery, hoping for a letter, and she is always so very happy when there is a new one to read. She says it makes her feel close to her family even for just a short while. She tells me I should write to my cousins, but I never really have. Maybe now I should start."

"I think that is a lovely idea," replied Aunt Pearl. "You never know where one letter can take you," she added with a laugh, and the girls laughed too.

"I have never seen so many books or maps before," exclaimed Grace. "Have you really traveled so far?"

"When I was much younger, but unfortunately not for a very long while," Aunt Pearl said, a bit of the laughter gone from her face.

"Aunt Pearl," said Molly, "it has been a long time since you were able to visit us. I did not know it was because you could not walk. I have brought you some of the special ointment my mother makes. I hope it can help." Molly reached into the wicker basket at her feet and drew out the jars of ointment that her mother had sent along. She placed them one by one next to each other on the edge of Aunt Pearl's desk.

"You are very sweet my dear. Yes, it does help. I am able to walk a little, but most days the pain keeps me in this chair. Your mother is a very special woman in many ways and her ointment seems to work better than most anything else I have tried."

"I am so glad the medicine can help you Aunt Pearl, and my mother will be pleased to hear it too," replied Molly. "She told me that you were there the night I was born when all the people gave me my names. Do you remember that?"

"Of course I do, child. I would never forget such a wonderful and amazing evening. Everyone wanted to be a part of gifting you with the name of someone special who had come before. Nothing like that had ever, ever happened that I can remember, and as I said, I remember a lot."

"Then do you remember whose name you gave me?" Molly asked a bit nervously as she reached into her apron pocket and took out the spectacles from their grey felt pouch.

Aunt Pearl closed her eyes as the memory of that night came into focus in her mind and as she did, Molly slipped the spectacles quickly on her nose. When Molly looked through the lenses at her aunt, she was aware of a cool breeze and a fluttering and rustle like pages of music that swirled around her. The colors she saw around her aunt's silvery grey head were pale white and creamy beige, and they flew and whirled softly like smoke on the wind, streaked with gold and black and mossy green. Molly's heart was filled with a calm stillness. She watched her aunt closely as she continued to speak. The colors that Molly had first seen shifted to mists of rose and amber, spiraling around and around.

"I named you for my own dear mother. Her name was also Pearl and I loved her deeply. She taught me to love books and poetry and music and to listen with my heart as well as my ears," Aunt Pearl said with a tearful smile. "I think those are wonderful gifts and it was my pleasure to give those to you as well. You know, I do have a volume here somewhere that is all about that night and the people who named you. Now let me think on what shelf I would have put that ..."

"Do you really have a book about me?" Molly exclaimed in amazement, never having felt this excited. She looked around the room and back and forth across the shelves wondering where her storybook could be.

"Ah … yes! There it is. If you could help me please …"

Molly quickly took the spectacles off her nose and placed them back in her apron pocket. Her legs and arms were shaking and it was hard for her to breathe, her heart was beating so fast. Taking one deep and ragged breath, she clasped the back of her aunt's chair and pushed her in the direction she indicated. In the far corner of the room, Aunt Pearl pointed to a shelf about halfway up a high bookcase, too far for Molly to reach without a stool on which to stand.

"Here, Molly!" sang out Grace and Miranda as they cleared off a nearby stool and brought it over to Molly. The girls were excited too and they both reached out a hand to help Molly up. Standing on the stool, Molly looked to her aunt once again for direction.

"A little to the right on the next shelf, it is the wide pale green one. Do you see it, my dear?" asked Aunt Pearl happily.

Molly reached out and her trembling hands grasped hold of a large leaf-green leather bound book. The book was so large that it lay on its side, too tall for the height of the shelf on which it lay. Using both hands, she slid it gently towards her and, holding it securely close to her chest, she stepped down off the stool. Molly was so excited when she first located the book that she only glimpsed a flash of bright silver lettering running down the length of its wide spine. But now, as she stood a little more calmly beside her aunt and her friends, she looked closer. There, in beautiful deep silver lettering, was her name *Malkah* followed by the thirty-five names she had been given at her birth. And inside, on creamy white paper and printed in rich black ink, was the story of each of the women whose names she bore and the reason that she had been blessed with them.

CHAPTER 14

Mrs. Bashert

Winter turned to spring and back again. Molly was now eighteen. No longer did she wear her hair in braids. Now she wore her golden hair in a neat bun at the base of her neck. She worked with her mother in the kitchen and helped both her parents in the garden and she was content. The spectacles had long ago been put aside in the bottom drawer of her cabinet. After that long ago day of errands for her mother and the visit to her Aunt Pearl, they had seemed not to work as well as they had, even when she had worn them whenever she had read her special book. Or maybe Molly just didn't need them as much as she had before. *It's a mystery*, Molly had thought. *Like so many things there may be no answers.* Even so, not knowing if she would ever be in need of using them again, she had wrapped them carefully back in their grey felt bag, tied them up with a red string and put them away in the cabinet beside her bed, safely kept along with her other childhood memories. But the book her aunt had given her Molly could not put away and so it received pride of place and rested on a polished wooden shelf of its own that Ari had made for it, next to a small picture of Great-Grandmother Ethel wearing her silver spectacles in a shiny frame above her bed.

Through the years in the early evenings after chores were done and the fire in the kitchen hearth had been banked for the night, Molly would curl up in her bed among her quilts and pillows. With the little picture of her great-grandmother glinting from its silver frame on the shelf over her shoulder, she would read from the book her Aunt Pearl had given her. Just as her aunt had told her, the book contained the magical story of the night she was born and of all the family that had come to give her a name. Inside the beautiful leather cover, the pages were a thick silky paper and printed in ebony ink. At the top of each page in lovely lettering was written the woman whose name Molly had received.

The stories that filled the book were a rich history of Molly's family and the strong and wonderful women who had lived and loved and who were an example to friends and family. Each woman had impacted the small world around her in selfless ways and had touched many hearts as she went about her life, leaving behind an emptiness when she was no longer there. That was why so many relatives had wanted Molly to have her many names, so that each woman could live on again. When family and friends saw Molly, they were reminded of their own loved one. Their own Hannah or Laurie, Judith Phyllis Elaine Beth Bella Esther Chaya Dobrisha Elishah Alicia Marsha Pearl Sally Edie Sylvia Maria Raina Sophie Sarah Lily Francis Miriam Bette Rachel Evelyn Agnes Lucy Sadie Mary Ethel, or Goldah, or Ann.

Molly learned so much from the stories that she read, about bravery and courage, acceptance and loss and love and community. She learned about the many talents and special abilities that connected her to these women, and she was pleased and happy and a bit in awe of all that she had discovered. Molly loved the stories and she cherished the book her aunt had given her. But when she tried to read it while wearing the spectacles, the pages blurred before her eyes and there were no colors to be seen at all.

On a cloudless morning in early April, Moriah rose early. All night she had tossed and turned. All the windows in the little house were open, but there was no breeze. The white curtains at the windows did not stir. But Moriah was restless and she moved about quickly doing her chores. After Ari and Molly had eaten breakfast and left in various directions, Moriah refilled the kettle, swept the floor, and reset her table with two cups and saucers and a pot of her best preserves. Then she sat down to wait for the guest she knew would be coming. She sewed and mended as she waited. The morning seemed to last forever.

At noon the little wooden bluebird began to sing, loudly chiming the hour from its perch in the old cuckoo clock that sat on the mantel above the kitchen hearth. Its timely chirp was followed quickly by a very loud and persistent knocking at the front door. The sudden sounds startled Moriah even though she had been waiting for something to happen. She got up quickly from her chair and went to answer the door. As she opened it, a great gust of wind blew in through the doorway. The little wooden bluebird ended its song with a loud and final trill. The curtains in the kitchen windows billowed out like sails, and Moriah knew that the change she had waited for all morning had come.

"Mrs. Bashert!" said Moriah. She had known that someday her visitor would bring news that would change the future, and anticipating what she would hear, her heart began to beat a little faster. "Welcome, please come in," she said, stepping away from the doorway. A gust of wind blew wildly once again through the opening, causing the many black shawls and veils that the visitor wore to swirl and flap madly in the air and snap at the edges of the door frame. The whirlwind stopped abruptly and was gone as soon as it came. The black shawls and veils ceased their flutter, settling lightly around the shoulders of the little old woman who stood on the mat.

Mrs. Bashert was old as old can be. No one in the village could remember how old she was, and it was said that Mrs. Bashert could not remember either. "Thank you, Moriah," squeaked the old woman in a high bird-like voice, "yes, I would like to come in. I have much to discuss with you."

"Please sit down," said Moriah. "Should I try to find my husband as well?"

"Not necessary, my dear. At least not yet. Let's just keep this between us girls," she said with a chuckle. Moriah smiled too. Mrs. Bashert was not anything like a girl. She was wrinkled from the tip of her nose to the ends of her fingers. At least that was all that was visible since Mrs. Bashert was swathed in solid black from head to foot. She made people a bit nervous, and Moriah was no different. Mrs. Bashert was the area matchmaker and she had a solid reputation. For many, many years her greatest delight of her highly successful career was arranging relationships and marriages for the single young women and men in the town and surrounding villages where she lived. In fact, most of the families in the area had consulted Mrs. Bashert when it came time for their own children to marry, but even so, she did have a tendency to make people think about things.

"I am here today ..." squeaked Mrs. Bashert. Moriah leaned in closer and clasped her hands tightly in front of her on the table. "Because of—" she stopped suddenly, mid sentence. *Kerchoooo! Kerchooooo! Kerchoooo!* Mrs. Bashert let out three enormous sneezes. "Oh my allergies," she sniffled. "Oh my feet. People don't appreciate ... "

"Mrs. Bashert," said Moriah, handing the old woman a handkerchief, "I am sorry your allergies are a problem and your feet hurt, but can you please continue?" Moriah poured two cups of tea. She passed one to Mrs. Bashert then she sat down and waited, her hands again clasped tightly on the table.

"There is a young man in the next village named Sam Gold," began Mrs. Bashert. "He is a lovely boy, just lovely. Tall and straight as an oak tree with green eyes to match. He is learned and kind and makes a nice living. His father is a tailor and they work together and sell fine clothes of beautiful fabrics. Your daughter will never be cold and she will always be able to eat well. I will leave you his picture," she said, and reaching deep into her very large tapestry bag, she pulled out a small picture of Sam Gold and slid it slowly across the table to Moriah.

Mrs. Bashert sat quietly for a moment watching Moriah carefully for her reaction to the photograph. Moriah looked intently at the picture of the young man that she held in her hands. She studied his eyes and the shy expression he wore tugged at her heart a little. Her immediate response to the photograph was a deep sense of comfort. She could feel a quiet strength, compassion, and honesty come through to her as she looked at the picture and she was well pleased. But still, she was a bit nervous. It was an enormous decision after all, more important and life changing than any other decision they had faced before. Now, it would be up to Molly to decide, so Moriah hid her feelings from Mrs. Bashert.

"Let me know of your decision Moriah, this one is special, I tell you. I have a feeling about these things you know." And she gave a high birdlike giggle. With a happy and satisfied smile on her wrinkled little face, Mrs. Bashert gathered up her many shawls and veils and placed her enormous tapestry bag on her arm, then shuffled towards the door. Moriah rose quickly and went to open the front door for the old woman. Her heart was pounding in her chest, and even though she had expected this to happen, she was anxious.

When Ari came in from his chores a short time later, Moriah showed him the photograph that Mrs. Bashert had left behind. Ari was not as sensitive about things as Moriah was. He was more pragmatic and somewhat less attuned to the deeper underlying messages of people and, knowing this, he had a tendency to follow along with his wife's more intuitive opinions. So after he looked at the picture for a moment, he smiled and said, "What do you think my dear?" Moriah had expected this reaction. After many wonderful years of marriage, she knew her husband very well and loved him deeply. "He looks like a very nice fellow to me," Ari added, and he took his wife's hand and led her back to sit at the kitchen table.

As Moriah took her seat once again, the breezes that blew gently outside her kitchen window began to blow more strongly and the white linen curtains puffed out in soft billows as she spoke. "It is time for Molly to marry," she replied wistfully. "Change is coming and decisions will have to be made." Moriah took the photograph of Sam from Ari and looked at it intently once again. "His name is Sam, Sam Gold. He is a tailor, as is his father. They are from the village close by and they have a little shop there. I can see from this photograph a strong sense of character and truth. I feel compassion and goodness in him, qualities that will serve our daughter well in a husband."

Moriah looked at her husband and smiled warmly. "I am glad she will not be moving so far away that it will be difficult for us to see her often. In my heart I think it will be a good match, but we must wait for our daughter to decide."

"That is true, my love. In the end it will be her choosing. We can only stand by her and support her no matter what her decision might be." Ari took his wife's hand in his and placed a warm kiss on her fingertips. "Remember how it was for us?" he asked. "When we first met on the day of our wedding and I saw you coming towards me down the aisle, I had never been so nervous. But your beautiful smile comforted me and I knew I would come to love you completely, just as my father and mother had told me I would. That is exactly what happened and I am thankful each day that you chose me to be your husband."

"When I first saw your picture," Moriah replied, "I saw there gentleness and openness, and honesty. Your eyes were brilliant and they held me close as I looked deeply into them. I knew in an instant that you were the right man for me. I felt then and still feel today, honored and blessed to be your wife. I have never had a moment since that day when I doubted my decision. We have had our struggles through the years and we never thought we would be blessed to have a child, but now that amazing little girl has become a delightful young woman. I am so very proud of who she has grown to be. I will miss her more than I can say when she leaves us, but it is time. Now all we can do is wait and see what Molly decides; only she will know if this choice is the right one for her."

"Yes," agreed Ari as he stood up from the table, "we must wait and see." Taking his wife's hands again, he helped her up from her seat at the table, and holding her in his arms, he kissed her deeply and with all the love in his heart.

That evening, as Molly sat on the end of her bed holding the picture that Mrs. Bashert had left in her mother's hands, she contemplated the face of Sam Gold. What would it be like to be married, to leave one's home, live with a man, create a family, and face the changes that inevitably come? *I'm frightened,* thought Molly. *How scary and unknowable the future is.* Almost without thinking she reached for the knob on the bottom drawer of her bedroom cabinet and pulled. The spectacles in their soft felt covering lay where she had last left them. She had not needed them in a very long time but now it seemed she was drawn to them again, and so she placed them on and looked through their lenses at the photograph of Sam Gold. The picture blurred for a moment but the color was still bright. As Molly gazed at the photograph through the lenses, she could see spirals of golden hues turning and turning, twining together and slowly disappearing into fine mist. Sam's color was the warm gold of butter melting on toast. Molly felt a warmth spread from her heart. She felt comforted and happy as laughter bubbled up inside her.

"Yes," she whispered as she drew the spectacles off, "yes." In that moment, Molly knew deep in her heart that Sam was the right man for her to marry. Mrs. Bashert had chosen well. Molly felt light as air, enormously lucky, and so very, very happy.

In the morning, Molly dressed quickly and went about her chores in the house, barn, and garden. In her apron pocket she carried the picture of Sam. Throughout the day she stopped and took it out often to look at it. As the late afternoon shadows began to fall along the garden path, Molly returned to the house to help her mother start dinner.

Moriah stood at the kitchen sink peeling potatoes, the long brown skins dropped heavily into her bowl. She looked up as Molly came in. "I'm almost done here," she said. "Would you like a cup of tea, before your father comes in?" she asked. "I know I would. I was just waiting for you to come in before I sat down for a bit." And she went to put the kettle on.

"Let me do that," said Molly, taking the kettle from her mother. "You sit." Molly set the kettle on the stove, and then she put two teacups and saucers on the small dining table. When the water was boiled and the tea was ready, she filled the two cups and sat down at the table across from Moriah. From her apron pocket, Molly took the picture of Sam and placed it on the table. Her fingers stroked the edges of the photograph.

Moriah reached over and held her daughter's hand. "Well … what do you think?" she asked. A gentle breeze stirred the white curtains in the window.

Molly looked up at her mother. "I am afraid of change," she said quietly. Moriah smiled wistfully at her daughter and held her hand a little tighter. "Last night," Molly continued slowly, "I used the spectacles to look at Sam's photograph. The colors were bright and clear, soft yellows and warm gold and I felt so happy I wanted to laugh aloud. I knew in my heart that this was the right choice. That I needed to look no further. Yet, I feel nervous about the future and so sad to leave my home." Molly looked at her mother and her eyes filled with tears.

"It is time, you know, my love. You are eighteen, some of your friends are already married," said Moriah looking close into Molly's eyes. "I was your age when a matchmaker my parents knew brought me your father's picture. I remember feeling the same as you do right now; happy, sad, nervous — all those feelings are normal and natural. My mother told me she had felt the same when her parents chose my father for her. Marriage is a commitment, and the future is unknown, but it is also something we can look forward to with hope and love. Do not fear the unknown, you carry with you wherever you go the strength of all the women whose names you hold and with Sam by your side you will never be alone. You will care for each other and fill your home with happiness. You will work together and plan together and you will be fulfilled. I am so very proud of you, Molly. Your Great-Grandmother Ethel would be proud of you too. Her glasses have worked well for you."

Molly's eyes grew wide. "Do you really think the spectacles ..." she began to ask.

"Yes, Molly I do," Moriah answered. "My grandmother Ethel wore those spectacles every day throughout her long life. They were always perched on the tip of her nose so that she could look above the tops or through the lenses whenever she needed to really look close and examine something. They were such a part of her that they became more than just glasses; they were her. When she lost them, she lost a part of herself and was never the same again. When you found the glasses in the garden, it was like you found a part of your great-grandmother. They fit you perfectly and when you look through them you can see deeper into people, just like your great-grandmother was able to do. I think it is her spirit that helped you along your path of discovery to find out more about the thirty-five names you have. I think you have also discovered that the colors that you see are unique to each person. The movement and intensity of colors is the transformation of each person's inner energy, surrounding that person with a prism of light. That is why you feel such a deep reaction to what you see. You feel someone's personality only so very much deeper. I hope this knowledge will fulfill you and that this deeper understanding will become a blessing for you."

Moriah finished speaking and sat back in her chair. She raised her hand to the collar of her dress and touched the strand of pearls she always wore around her neck. They were warm and smooth to her touch. Molly watched her mother for a moment. She was thinking about what her mother had said. Moriah was right. Molly had always felt that the spectacles held a part of her great-grandmother's essence, and it was that spirit that had led her to learn more about herself and the women who were part of her.

"Why did you never tell me this before?" she asked Moriah.

"It is more important to discover things on your own than always to be told the answers," Moriah said with a grin. "It is important to find your own truth, whatever it may be." Moriah still held the strand of pearls loosely in her hands and stroked them lightly.

"Those are your mother's pearls, aren't they?" Molly asked.

"Yes, they are," Moriah responded, a flash of memory making her smile happily once again. "My mother received them as a wedding gift from my father on the day of their marriage, and she wore them always. When I married your father, my mother gave them to me because we would be moving very far away from my parents' village. When my mother put them around my neck, she said to me, 'Wear these pearls every day and I will always be close to your heart.' I have worn them every day since she gave them to me and I know I carry her with me wherever I go."

"Just like the spectacles," Molly said a broad smile on her face.

"Just like the spectacles," Moriah repeated and she reached across the table to clasp her daughter's hands in hers. The picture of Sam lay between them. "All will be well, Molly. You will see, all will be well," she said happily.

Molly looked at Sam's picture once again. She felt a peaceful glow and a warm contentment. "Yes," she said looking up at her mother, "yes, all will be well."

CHAPTER 15

Sam

Samuel Martin Gold stood before a small mirror in his bedroom and brushed back his honey brown hair. He looked deeply into the reflection and searched his green eyes for answers. "I'm being silly," he thought to himself. "Only in going forward can I be truly sure," and he turned slowly away from his mirror image.

Several weeks before, the Gold family had been visited by a very old woman swathed in black from head to toe. Sam's mother Stella and father Harold had sat with the old woman at their kitchen table and spoken together in hushed voices. When Sam came in from finishing his chores and saw the small figure dressed in all black, he recognized her immediately and a small shiver ran down his spine. Sam knew exactly why the old woman had come, and that Mrs. Bashert had a proposal for him. Sure enough, from the dark depths of her tapestry bag, she drew out several pictures for him to see. There were three in total, each in crisp black and white. Sam only meant to glance quickly at the photographs and to tell

Mrs. Bashert thank you, and he would think about it, but that is not what happened. One photograph seemed to call his name. He stopped and looked closer, and what he saw filled his heart with happiness. He had never felt this way before. Sam knew lots of girls and had even fancied himself in love with one or two, he was twenty-one, after all, but he had never experienced such a thunderbolt before. The image that looked back at him was of a sweetly beautiful young woman with a lovely smile that seemed to shine from deep inside. He almost could not look away.

Mrs. Bashert had watched Sam closely as he looked at the photographs and she gave a delighted giggle as she watched his reaction. "Her name is Molly," she laughed in her high bird-like voice. "She lives in Zhitomir Oblast, several kilometers from here. She is a truly wonderful girl from a good and loving family. Shall I bring her parents your greetings and photograph?"

Sam looked back at Molly's picture and then at Mrs. Bashert and slowly nodded yes. There was a look of amazement on his face. He could scarcely believe it. He had never thought that he would react this way and he stood still and rigid in the center of the room, his heartbeat fairly booming inside him.

Harold and Stella rose as one from the table and went to embrace their son. "Congratulations!" they cried as they patted him on the back. "Let's have a toast to the new bridegroom to be," sang out Harold, and he went to the cabinet near the stove and took out a small bottle of fruity schnapps and several short glasses. He poured a little of the golden cherry cordial into each glass and handed them around. Stella gave her son another quick hug, being careful not to spill her drink.

"We are delighted for you, my son. May you have many years of happiness!" she said and kissed Sam soundly on each cheek.

"Oh yes!" agreed Mrs. Bashert. "May you have a long and wonderful life together!" And she gave a high-pitched giggle. "To Sam and Molly," shouted Harold, "may they have a long and happy life together!" He tilted back his head and drained his small glass.

Sam held his glass tightly. *Marriage … years … what have I done?* he thought to himself. Then he took a quick drink, emptying his glass, and reached once more for the bottle of schnapps.

Late that night Sam was still in awe at the decision he had made and, as he lay on his back on the bed in his room, his mind was a turmoil of thoughts, ideas, and plans. He glanced frequently at Molly's photograph, and each time he looked at her smiling face, he was filled with a happiness like he had never felt before; it was a heartfelt knowledge that he had chosen well. But he was still more than a bit nervous about the magnitude of the decision he had made so quickly and he was unable to sleep.

In their bed down the hallway from Sam's, the Golds sat up among their pillows and talked softly together. "Well, well," said Harold, turning towards his wife, "what a very interesting and exciting day."

"Oh, yes," replied Stella. "Very interesting. Amazing really, I have never seen Sam react so strongly before. It was truly incredible to watch his response to Molly's picture. It was as if he had found what he always wanted and it hit him like a shot. I wonder if this girl Molly will feel the same when Mrs. Bashert gives her Sam's photograph." Stella looked out her bedroom window and watched the stars in the heavens. "I hope so," she murmured. "I would hate to see him hurt in any way."

Although Sam was no longer a child and certainly old enough to make decisions on his own, he was still Stella's only child, and she worried for him and tried to protect him from harm in any way that she could. Knowing this, Stella sought to comfort her own fears and she reached for her husband's hand and held it tightly. As she did, she looked over Harold's shoulder and out of her bedroom window and watched the stars in the heavens. The sky was clear and beautiful and filled with thousands of glistening stars and the light that emanated from them was pure and strong.

Stella watched with an open heart and she felt her initial fears begin to slip away.

"Do you remember?" she asked, turning to look back at her husband. "When Sam was born, we had so many plans, so many hopes and dreams for him. He has never given us cause for worry, and always made good choices. He is a hard worker and a good friend. I know he will make a wonderful and caring husband."

"Shhhh, my dear," Harold replied, soothingly patting his wife's hand. "Our son is growing up and as hard as it is to let him go … we must. We will always be here for him when he needs us, you surely know that that will never change." Then he kissed his wife gently on her cheek and held her close.

CHAPTER 16

A Circle of Gold

It was truly amazing how fast the news of Molly's engagement spread. Mrs. Bashert told everyone she met as she went about her visits and suddenly everyone in the little town of Zhitomir knew. Everywhere Molly went throughout the village, people congratulated her on her upcoming marriage and wished her well. Molly couldn't wait for the day when she and Sam would stand together as man and wife. The day could not come fast enough, and there was so much planning to do. But what was she going to wear? It was a problem. Her friend Miranda had cut down her mother's very large gown easily, a gown she had looked beautiful in lace and pearls when she married Joseph. When her friend Grace became engaged, she had wisely sent letters to several cousins she knew in nearby towns. he had received a lovely cream satin gown from one and a beautiful long lace veil from another. Both had fit her perfectly and she had glowed with love and happiness as she walked down the aisle to marry her beloved Philip. Both friends had offered Molly their gowns to try, but they each required too many alterations in order to fit her properly and so sadly she had to decline their offers. She had considered using parts of her mother's wedding dress, but Molly had grown to be several inches taller than her mother so the gown barely touched the tops of her ankles when she had tried it on. She had considered using some of the beautiful embroidery that flowed along the bottom of the hem, but what of the rest?

Moriah tried to reassure her daughter. "Don't worry," she said soothingly, "these things have a way of working themselves out." Molly knew this was true but she was still not satisfied. Just as the news of Molly's engagement had spread quickly, so did the news of Molly's predicament.

On a breezy day in May the curtains in Moriah's kitchen flapped about and snapped against the window frames. Moriah went to close the shutters and saw ten women from the village walking up the path towards the house. Each carried a large wicker basket on her arm. Knocking lightly on the door, they called, "Molly, Moriah, company." And they all giggled together.

"You're here," said Moriah, greeting them one by one. "I knew you would be! Come in, come in!"

The ladies bustled into the house and began moving more chairs around the kitchen table. The wicker baskets they carried held spools of thread, snippets of lace and creamy white satin. When Molly walked into the room and saw what the women had brought with them, her eyes filled with happy tears. She was overwhelmed. The generosity of these women was so unexpected. She had never ever hoped that something as wonderful as this would happen. Her heart soared with happiness. For the rest of that day, and the next and the next, the ladies cut and basted, measured and sewed, told stories about how each of them had, with the help of the matchmaker, found their own husbands for better or for worse, and they laughed and sang and enjoyed their work. They spent long hours each day around Moriah's kitchen table happily absorbed in their task at hand, frequently consulting Molly on the placement of embroidered trim pieces and lace appliqué. Molly was sure that the gown they were creating for her was the most beautiful bridal gown she had ever before seen and she was overjoyed with the kindness of these talented women. When finally the gown was finished, and the last of the sewing was complete with every tiny pleat ironed into perfection, the women rose from the table and stepped back to admire their creation. There was laughter all around as Molly twirled and spun while holding the beautiful gown before her.

"Thank you all so much!" she sang out excitedly. "I cannot wait to wear it, it is so very lovely and I am truly amazed at what you have given me!" The ladies were delighted too, and as they gathered up their needles and thread and bits of silk and lace, they each kissed Molly and wished her well.

On the first of June the wind blew and the rain lashed the windows of the little house all through the morning. Molly held back the kitchen curtains and looked sadly out at the storm.

"Molly," Moriah said with concern in her voice, "You know I always say, things have a way of working out, and I just know they will for you today. Besides, rain on your wedding day is good luck." Molly looked up at her mother and her blue eyes were filled with tears that ran down her cheeks like the rain ran down the window panes.

"I'm just being silly," she said and turned back to watch the storm. Through the glass, Molly could just see her father returning up the front path. "Father's here," she said and went with her mother to open the door. Ari shook off his umbrella and leaned it against the wall by the door and stepped into the warm kitchen.

He looked up and smiled happily. "Well Molly, I have just had the pleasure of meeting your intended. He's a wonderful young man, just delightful. I sensed honesty and truth in him and I am well pleased." Ari kissed Molly on her cheek and took both her hands in his. "I think you are well suited to one another and you will be happy together," he said tenderly.

Molly felt comforted from her father's kiss and she was pleased and a bit relieved to hear that he was happy with her husband-to-be.

By afternoon the rains ceased, the winds increased and dried the dampness in the grass and trees and then stopped their blowing completely, and all was calm, still, and peaceful. As night fell, the activity in the little house grew and people came and went and went and came. When Miranda and Grace arrived, their arms were laden with dainty white roses to make Molly's wedding bouquet. They each wore long lavender silk dresses and had entwined wreaths of sweet smelling purple violets in their hair. In the middle of the front room of Moriah and Ari's home stood Molly, her golden hair piled high on her head. White rose petals and lavender sprays tucked within her golden curls held her long veil in place and the beautiful white gown she wore swept gently across the floor and flowed around her, as light and soft as fairy wings. Molly turned slowly in the mirror Moriah held up for her and she could see the delicate lace, the lovely appliqué, and the wonderful embroidery that had gone into this exquisite gift. She was overjoyed.

"How beautiful you look, Molly," Ari whispered in awe when he first saw his daughter. "You have never looked more beautiful. What a very lucky man I am to have two such lovely women in my life," he said as he brushed a soft kiss on Molly's cheek.

Molly smiled up at her father and adjusted his tie. "I am almost ready," she told him. "Just a few minutes more."

"Alright my love, I'll be right back," he replied and started for the door. Before he left the room, he looked back at Molly and smiled warmly at her. She could see in that brief moment all the love and pride that her father had for her. "So lucky," he repeated and closed the door behind him.

When he had left, Molly went to a carved wooden dresser in the corner of the room and took up a small felt bag from where it lay among an assortment of family photographs. She could feel the sleek surface of the spectacles inside the bag and she held them close for a moment. Then

Molly heard a soft knocking. Once again, the door to the room opened and Miranda and Grace came in carrying the wedding bouquet they had made for her.

"Oh! How wonderful!" she exclaimed. "Thank you both so much for doing this for me, it is such a lovely gift." Molly sighed with pleasure as she breathed in the sweet fragrance of the roses and lavender stems that her friends had used to make her wedding flowers, and she hugged Miranda and Grace tenderly and took the bouquet and held it tightly in her hands.

"Look, Molly," said Grace and she pointed out the window. "The sky is clear and the first stars are beginning to appear."

Indeed, the stars that began to fill the sky that night were glorious in their brilliance. As the girls watched through the window, one by one, more and more began to appear. Then there was a louder knock on the door again and Ari stood in the opening. "It's time, Molly dear," he said, reaching out to his daughter. Taking her arm, he led her through the door. Moriah joined them and Ari took her hand in his and proudly with a smile from ear to ear, he led Molly and Moriah out of the house and down the path, with Miranda and Grace leading the way.

As they walked, the people of the village came out to join them, lighting the path with candles and throwing flowers at the feet of the bride. Over a small bridge and into a round glade surrounded by towering trees came the wedding party. A small group of musicians began to sweetly play. The guests took their places and watched excitedly as the bride passed slowly by.

Molly first saw Sam standing under a small canopy draped with white roses, lavender sprays, and deep green rosemary. From a distance she could see his happy smile. In anticipation of this first meeting, Molly had carried the spectacles with her hidden amongst the flowers of her wedding bouquet. She slipped them on and looked around her, taking in all the guests who stood in awed and delighted silence around the edges of the glade. Then she looked ahead of her to gaze directly at Sam, where he stood patiently at the end of the aisle. She could instantly see the deep golden glow of the color that surrounded him. In a flash and before Sam could notice, she quickly took the spectacles off. In that one moment that she had worn the spectacles, the colors that she had seen spoke to her heart and she became keenly aware that the decision she had made to marry Sam was the right one. Molly squeezed her father's arm and smiled up at him. The strains of music played softly as they continued to move forward together. The sky sparkled with a million stars filling the glade with a beautiful glow.

"What a magical evening," whispered Moriah, just loud enough for her daughter to hear.

"Yes it truly is," replied Molly softly, looking down the aisle at her husband-to-be. She thought to herself that what she had seen and felt whenever she looked at Sam through the lenses was magical too.

Molly and her father took their places just in front of the flower-bedecked canopy. Ari turned to his daughter and lifted the veil from her face. He leaned in to her and placed a warm and gentle kiss on her cheek, and as he did, he whispered softly in her ear, "Be happy." Then he replaced her veil carefully and turned towards Sam who had stepped forward to greet his bride. "Take good care of my little girl," he said to Sam with a wistful smile. He offered Sam his hand to shake, then he turned slowly away to join his wife who stood close by. Molly moved forward with Sam and they both took their places for the ceremony. She held the stems of her bouquet tightly and she could feel Sam standing stiffly beside her as they waited for the officiant to begin. The officiant stood tall and straight and held a book open in his hands. He smiled warmly at the bride and groom. The guests moved in a little closer and the sweet strains of the wedding music became softer before stopping completely. Sam reached out to hold Molly's hand in his. For the first time, their hands clasped and their eyes met, and Sam smiled at her with his heart.

"Ladies and Gentlemen," said the officiant, "we are gathered here today to celebrate the wedding of two wonderful young people. Sam

Martin Gold," said the officiant in a deep and melodic voice, "do you take this woman to be your wedded wife?"

Sam had never taken his eyes off Molly. "Yes, I do," he replied and his voice was strong and sure.

"And do you, Malkah Hannah Laurie Judith Phyllis Elaine Beth Bella Esther Chaya Dobrisha Elishah Alicia Marsha Pearl Sally Edie Sylvia Maria Raina Sophie Sarah Lily Francis Miriam Bette Rachel Evelyn Agnes Lucy Sadie Mary Ethel Goldah Ann take this man for your wedded husband?" asked the officiant as he turned to face Molly, a wide and glowing smile lighting his face.

"Yes. I do," replied Molly in a breathy and excited voice. "Yes, I do." Sam reached over and lifted Molly's veil away from her face and gazed at her with wonder. As Molly looked deeply into Sam's eyes and listened to the list of thirty-five names that so many loving people had given her, she could see in her mind's eye each of their individual colors rising and swirling around her and Sam, a rainbow of colors floating in and around all the people of the village. Molly's eyes grew misty as she looked from her new husband to her parents and then out into the crowd of guests. The love she felt for all those around her and for the many women whose names she carried filled her with strength and peace.

Then, to the strains of a small violin, Molly could hear her father's rich baritone and her mother's sweet soprano as they sang together. "*Molly is the girl with thirty-five names ...*" Their voices were sweet and true blending together as they continued,

> Given with love, not one the same.
> Each name is a special message, each name a brand new page
> A journey of discovery, a new beginning, a new age.
> Thirty-five names made you special. There is no one else like you.
> Follow your heart and your strengths will shine through.
> Molly is the girl with thirty-five names. There is no one else like you.

As the song finished, the little grove filled with the soft laughter of the guests and then everyone began to sing Molly's special song. Standing under the canopy, hand in hand with her new husband, Molly felt the greatest happiness she had ever known, unlike any before, and she knew she had found her heart's true connection and the bright promise of new beginnings.

PART TWO

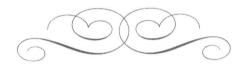

CHAPTER 17

Under the Apple Tree

The morning sun streamed in through the window of Molly's bedroom. She snuggled down deeper into the covers and stretched. As she did, her arm brushed softly against the shoulder of her new husband. Sam opened his eyes and smiled at his new bride.

"You are even more lovely now in the morning light than you were last evening," said Sam. "When I first saw you walking toward me on your father's arm, I wondered suddenly if I were worthy of such a wonderful gift. I could feel the strength and love that surrounded you, and I hoped that you could teach me to love and be loved as you are." Molly's heart filled with joy. Sam's words touched her deeply and once again she felt blessed that this man had come into her life and lucky that her husband was indeed a man of tenderness, insight, and compassion. Molly turned on her side among her pillows and took Sam's hand in hers.

"When I first saw you," she breathed, her eyes sparkling brightly in the early morning sunshine coming through the window, "the sky around you was filled with a golden light. I was drawn to that light, and to the tenderness I saw in your eyes. With each step I took towards you, I grew stronger and my nerves seemed to melt away. I don't know what the future holds for us, but wherever it takes us, I will work beside you, and I will always remember the golden light of promise that surrounded you." Sam looked deeply into Molly's eyes and saw there all that he had ever wished for. Then he leaned in and kissed Molly deeply on her lips, a kiss that spoke of all the love and joy that he felt in his heart. The morning sun flooded the room with a warm golden light and in the barnyard a rooster began to crow.

The brilliance of the rising sun had also awakened Moriah and she sat up in bed, her head filled with a long list of to-dos for the wedding breakfast. "Ari! Wake up, it's late. I need your help! Ari!" and she shook his shoulder gently but repeatedly.

"Mmmmmm," sighed Ari, rolling slowly over and pulling his pillow over his head.

Moriah dressed quickly and bustled into her kitchen, tiptoeing past Molly's bedroom. She hummed happily to herself as she lit the stove and ovens and opened the windows wide to let in the late spring breezes. Then she collected eggs from the hen house and milk from the dairy cow before briskly returning to the kitchen. She sifted and diced and measured and kneaded. The breeze from the windows softly blew flour and cinnamon in the air, dusting the tops of Moriah's baking. Moriah breezed about her kitchen, happily stirring the pots on the stove with her big wooden spoon as wonderful things bubbled and steamed. She stopped often in front of the ovens, checking the doneness of the luscious fruit pastries, cookies and pies, and she hummed delightedly to herself as the little house filled with the most delectable smells.

The morning was warm and clear, and the leaves in the trees sighed and rustled in the sweet and gentle breezes and the sky was a heavenly blue. In the shade of an old apple tree in the center of the little backyard, Ari set out long wooden tables and white wooden benches. Moriah covered each of the tables with crisp white cloths that flapped in the breeze, and she placed large blue glass bowls filled with sunflowers down the middle of each one. Then she began filling the longest of the tables with the wonderful wedding breakfast she had prepared. Off in the distance, Moriah and Ari could hear the sound of horse-drawn wagons approaching. They could see Molly and Sam walking hand in hand up the path to meet their guests.

"Ari," said Moriah, "this is a very special day. The sky is clear and blue and the breezes are warm and ripe with the smell of spring, our family and friends will be here soon and we will dance and sing and celebrate new beginnings."

"You are right, my dear," replied Ari with joy in his voice. "We will dance and sing and raise a glass to the happy couple. We will take pleasure in the delight of our daughter until it is time for her to leave." A small tear threatened to spill from Ari's eyes and Moriah reached up and wiped it away. She smiled up at him and patted his cheek.

"May Molly be as happy as we are," she said lovingly. Ari smiled softly at his wife, then taking her hand in his they walked up the hill together and out to the road to welcome their guests along with Molly and Sam.

At the top of the hill, Molly stood hand in hand with Sam. He wore his new blue wedding suit and she once again wore her beautiful wedding gown. A warm wind blew at the lace hem of her gown and the edges of her veil, flapping gently on the breeze between them. Family and friends called and waved happily to each other as they came down the road in their carts and wagons. When everyone had arrived and hugged and kissed the bride and groom and each other, Ari and Moriah happily led a very long line of their guests into the yard behind their house where the wedding feast was waiting in the shade of the apple tree. There were so many aunts, uncles, cousins and friends that the little yard was crowded with well-wishers and abuzz with happy voices. Moriah and Molly, and Miranda and Grace filled large silver trays with glasses of sparkling wine and began to serve the guests. Ari took a glass from a passing tray and tapped against it several times with a spoon in order to get the attention of his guests.

"Welcome, dear friends and family, welcome!" he said loudly. The voices that had filled the yard moments before became hushed as he continued. "We are so pleased to have you here to celebrate this wonderful occasion with us today. It is not every day that Moriah and I can watch our daughter be married, and gain a son, too! So please join us as we raise our glasses and drink a toast to the bride and groom. To Mr. and Mrs. Sam Gold!" Ari called out excitedly.

"To Sam and Molly!" replied the guests with much laughter and clinking of glasses. "Now, let's eat and celebrate!" Ari called, finishing his little speech and throwing up his hands in pleasure.

Soon everyone was enjoying the wonderful breakfast that Moriah had prepared. Bowls were filled with thick oat porridge drizzled with golden honey and plates were piled high with crisp potato pancakes and dollops of rich sour cream, sizzling sausages and rye bread, sweet and sour cabbage, and a delicious beef stew in a savory broth with mushrooms and onions. Moriah made sure that everyone's plates were never empty and the glasses always full. The guests were jubilant and their glasses clinked often as everyone wanted to give a special toast to the newlyweds. Molly and Sam were seated at a small table prepared just for them, but they were never alone for long as friends and family stopped by to greet them and wish them well, and they were both kept busy introducing each other to their new friends and family. When the last of the marvelous dishes had all been eaten, Sam's cousin Misha unpacked his clarinet and began to play. There was dancing and singing and a grand celebration topped off with a beautiful white tiered wedding cake covered with rich butter frosting roses and sprinkled liberally with Molly's favorite candied violets, and trays and baskets of Moriah's delectable kuchen and fruit pastries. Then it was time for the bride and groom to leave.

Molly left the wedding party a little while before Sam and returned to her room to change and finish her last minute packing. She placed her wedding bouquet on top of the cabinet next to her bed and put the spectacles in their grey felt bag beside it. In the middle of the room stood her trunk. She and Moriah had placed the sheets and blankets they had sewn together in the weeks before the wedding in the bottom. They were neatly folded and scented with the lavender water Molly had used when she had ironed them. Nestled among the linens, Molly had placed the book that her Aunt Pearl had given her. It would be one of the first things she would place in her new home. Now she held up her wedding gown once more before her. Her hands gently spread the lacy fabric and once again the beauty of this amazing gift thrilled her. Folding the silky cloth carefully, she placed the gown and veil on top and closed the lid. It was still early afternoon and the sun glowed high in the sky. Molly's room was in cool shadow as she turned and went out the door.

In the yard, Ari helped Sam hitch his market wagon to Sam's horse. "I am pleased to let you borrow my wagon," said Ari. "This way I know I will see my daughter again soon. Market day is in two weeks and I'll need it back before then," he continued with a small tear in his eye and a warm smile on his face.

"You don't need an excuse to visit your daughter, sir," said Sam. "I hope you will always feel comfortable in our home." He reached over and patted Ari on the shoulder.

"But if we don't pack up soon we might as well stay forever!" Sam laughed, and Ari laughed too.

When they were done packing all the many wedding gifts on the back of the wagon, there was barely room for Sam and Molly to fit on the front seat. There was a bed frame and mattress, crates of dishes and flatware, and a crate of new copper pots and pans. There were silver candlesticks and assorted wooden mixing bowls, several trunks of clothes and household items, and a table and chairs that Ari had made. And strapped to the side, a large grey metal washing tub. Everyone laughed when they saw the overloaded wagon.

"May you always have lots of good things!" yelled Uncle Fred.

"May you never want for anything!" sang out Aunt May. "May your pots always be full!" piped in Cousin Jake. *May you come home soon,* thought Ari, *and bring my wagon!*

Amid much laughter and good wishes, Molly and Sam climbed up into the wagon and began to wave goodbye. "Wait!" called Moriah, and she handed up a woven basket covered with a checkered cloth. "This is for your new life together. Be happy and take good care of each other, I love you," she said. "You are both in our hearts." Patting her daughter gently on her arm, she looked deeply into her eyes for a moment, and then smiling happily, she stepped back to stand beside Ari.

Sam flicked the reins and the wagon moved slowly forward. Molly turned and looked over her shoulder at the house where she had spent so many happy years. Her eyes began to fill with tears. *That was my beginning,* she thought to herself, *and now I will look to my future.* Brushing away the wetness from her cheeks, she turned to look at Sam and then leaned her head against his strong shoulder. Sam looked down at her beside him and kissed her lovingly on top of her golden head and placed a strong arm around her shoulders. The sun was warm on their backs as they traveled down the path that led to Sam's home. The wagon creaked softly as it bumped along the road and the sky was filled with birdsong.

"Molly," said Sam with a smile looking once again at his new wife beside him, "sing to me, sing to me the song of your thirty-five names. I want to remember each one so that when I call you Molly I will know all of you." Molly looked into Sam's green eyes and gave him her heart with her smile. Then she began to sing ...

"Molly is the girl with thirty-five names ..."

CHAPTER 18

The Future Starts Here

It was still early afternoon when Molly and Sam entered the lane that led to Sam's house. Sam's parents, Stella and Harold Gold, had left the wedding breakfast early and were waiting for Sam and Molly when they arrived. The Golds' house was small and made entirely of wood. Everything inside was shiny and polished and gleamed a soft warm honey color. Stella had covered her kitchen table with a pink cloth that she had embroidered with white and blue flowers, and set a cut glass vase filled with lily-of-the-valley and pink roses in the center. She set the table with the delicate cups, saucers, and creamy white china dishes she had received as a wedding present from her father when she had married Harold so long ago. She placed the teapot on a trivet near the center of the table and laid a large plate of biscuits and cookies along with her best preserves beside it. Then she ushered everyone in to sit around the lovely table. As soon as they were seated, everyone began to talk at once.

"We are so thrilled to have you here," said Stella excitedly, passing the platter of cookies and biscuits and pouring the tea.

"We have much work to do," said Harold. "I am anxious to get started."

"I'm ready to get started too," said Sam. "We must have quite a few orders to tend to."

"I am so happy to be here and help in any way I can," said Molly excitedly. "Sam and I have been making wonderful plans, and I can't wait to begin!"

Harold smiled happily and looked at his wife. There was relief and pleasure in his eyes and Stella smiled lovingly in return and gave him a little wink. After they had finished the tea and most of the biscuits, Harold and Stella rose from the table. "Come," said Stella with excitement in her voice. "Follow us. I have something you might like to see …" And they led Molly and Sam through the back door and out into the yard and the late afternoon sunshine.

Just to the right and behind the Golds' wooden house, next to their herb garden, stood a small stone cabin. There were two large paned windows with crisp white trim on either side of the wooden front door. The shutters around the windows were a deep green, and the slate tiles on the tiny roof were dusted with the same green-colored moss. Inside, everything had been swept clean and polished. The wooden floors and cabinets gleamed, and the small fire in the hearth made everything welcoming and bright.

When Molly and Sam entered the cabin and saw all the hard work that had gone into making this space a home for them, they were overwhelmed. "I never expected anything so wonderful," said Molly, her voice breathy with emotion. "This will be our home, our future begins here."

"Mother!" said Sam, a bit in awe himself. "I never expected you to be able to do this for us. Thank you," he said simply. Stella looked up at her son with tears glistening in her eyes. "It is my pleasure," she replied. "Just be happy and healthy, and make wonderful memories here."

Harold took a large handkerchief out of his vest pocket and blew his nose loudly. "Look at the time!" he said. "Better get to unpacking that cart and get you two settled in." And he turned hurriedly towards the door, tucking away his watch in his vest pocket as he went.

Every time Molly entered her little home with her arms filled with the many gifts they had received for their wedding, she felt a sweet comfort and happiness build inside her. She was thoroughly amazed and awed with the new little home she would now share with Sam. Molly had never expected to have a separate home of her own, rather she had always antic-ipated that when she married Sam, they would just share a bedroom in his parents' home as most of her other friends had done. This gift was truly almost too marvelous to believe.

After the cart had been emptied, Molly began to unpack the crates and suitcases slowly, taking care to put everything away in its proper place. Opening her trunk, Molly unwrapped the leaf-green leather book that her aunt had given her and placed it on a shelf of its own in the corner of the room. She made up the bed with colorful quilts and downy soft pillows. Her white dishes sparkled on the wooden shelves above the kitchen sink, the copper pots and pans glistened by the hearthside, and the floral curtains at the windows seemed to create a garden all around her. In the center of the room stood the carved wooden table and chairs that Ari had made for them. With the unpacking now finished and her new home bright and shiny all around her, Molly placed the wicker basket her mother had given her on the table's dark shiny top. She had traveled to her new home with the basket on her lap and had wondered what sort of special gift it held. Molly lifted the lid of the basket. Inside, nestled in clean white linen, lay a large loaf of bread and a bowl of salt. As Molly removed the items and placed them on the tabletop, she saw beneath a note written in her mother's hand. She unfolded the note and a pair of spectacles rolled into her hand

… the very same spectacles that she had found so long ago in her parents' garden. The note read:

My Dearest Daughter,

Your father and I wish you every happiness in your new home. We have sent you the bread so you will never go hungry and the salt for a life well seasoned. May the winds blow softly and your life be blessed with the promise of good things to come. This is our blessing for you and Sam.

I have sent you the spectacles for your safekeeping. I am not the one who should have them, since they hold some insight for you alone. You may not always need them but only you will know when that may be.

I wish you great joy of life my precious daughter, and we look forward to seeing you before market day.

Mama

Molly pressed the note to her heart, holding it close for a moment. Then she folded it carefully and put it down on the table next to her. Picking up the felt bag that held her great-grandmother's spectacles, she unwrapped them and held them lovingly in her palm. They glinted and sparkled just as they always did, beckoning her to try them on again. It made Molly happy just to hold them and she thought back to what she had seen when she walked down the aisle to marry Sam. She could still see the colors and remember the emotions she had felt at that moment. They had only been married for such a short time but Molly had no doubt that she had chosen well. She was no longer afraid of the future; she welcomed it openly. Now as she gazed at the spectacles in her hand, she thought how wise and knowing her mother was. *Even though I don't need them right now,* Molly thought, *they belong with me and safely kept.* Then she rolled the spectacles and the note together, returned them to their felt bag, and tied them up with a red string.

That evening, to celebrate her new home, Molly prepared a small supper for her in-laws. She had placed the bowl of salt in the middle of the table and placed the bread her mother had baked next to it. A copper pot filled with meat and carrots bubbled slowly above the flames in the hearth, and as it cooked, it filled the little cabin with a rich and spicy aroma. As they all sat comfortably around the table together, they talked about the tailor shop that Harold owned and the new sewing machine that had arrived a few days before. Harold had big plans for the new machine.

"We will be able to make garments so much faster," he said excitedly. "The faster we work the more we can earn!"

"Yes, yes, Harold Dear," said Stella. "But please, remember your heart. Try not to get too excited," she reminded him and patted his shoulder affectionately.

"But I am excited," replied Harold. "For the first time in my life I see a real opportunity. We are getting much too old, you and I, to sit and sew by hand." And as he said these words, he leaned across the table to take his wife's hand in his. Molly and Sam exchanged glances and their eyes met. Then they both reached out and joined their hands with Stella and Harold Gold.

CHAPTER 19

Mrs. Kinder

The village of Pushkin, where Molly now lived, was much larger than the little farming town of Zhitomir in which she was raised. Although the roads were still made of hard packed earth, there were several roads that led directly to Pushkin. The village was always busy with people and animals, coming and going. It was all very new to Molly and very exciting to see. Mr. Gold's tailor shop was located in the center of a long wooden building that had been divided up into small store fronts. Each store had its own large plate glass front window, and it was here, in his front window, that Harold had placed his beloved sewing machine.

When Molly and Sam entered the front door of the tailor shop, the sound of tinkling bells greeted them. "Hello," they called. From the back room, Stella and Harold came into view.

"Welcome to Harold and Son!" said Harold with an enormous grin as he reached out to shake his son's hand.

"Dad," said Sam, "I am so happy and grateful, what an honor to be your partner." And he reached around his father's shoulder to give him a hug. "But you'll have to teach me how to use that machine before I'll be your real partner, and Molly is here to help too, so this will be a true family business venture."

"Alright then," said Harold with new authority. "Stella, you take Molly and show her what she can do to help, and I will take my new partner and show him how to get started." Harold had never been happier or prouder and his step was quick and light.

Sam was delighted, too. They had always sewn everything by hand and he was eager to please his father and learn quickly to use the new sewing machine. It wasn't long before the humming of the spinning bobbin filled the little shop with sound. At first it was Molly's job to sweep out and tidy the shelves in the shop and while she did, she watched and learned. It was now Harold's job to work the front counter and do the ordering of fabrics and threads while Stella worked with the customers who came and went throughout the day. She was adept at measuring, so there was always very little waste of material and when she was not measuring, her hands were always busy crocheting lace for collars, cuffs, and tablecloths.

Since the little shop took very little time to sweep out, and the shelves very little time to organize, Molly had asked her mother-in-law to teach her to make lace. In the beginning, Molly had struggled with the complicated stitches and thin thread that Stella used to make her lace. Everything seemed to just come out uneven and hopelessly knotted; it was difficult not to become frustrated. More than once Molly had fought hard not to throw the threads she endeavored to work with across the room, but then she would look over at Stella, who sat calmly and serenely at her work, and Molly, while taking a deep breath to calm herself, would resolve once again to do better. Over time as she sat in the sunny front window next to Sam and struggled with the twisted mess of thread in her hands, things began to change. Her fingers began to lose their tension and she pulled less hard on the thread, and as a result, her stitches became smooth and even. She was becoming proud of her handiwork and it felt good to learn a skill that could help her new family.

Each day, at first light, Stella and Harold would wake in their house and Sam and Molly would wake in theirs. Harold was always the first to arrive outside, anxious to begin the day. Tapping his foot as he looked at his watch, he impatiently waited for the others to dress so they might walk into town together to open the shop. Monday through Friday from early light until dusk when it grew too dark to see, Sam sewed new garments and repaired old. Stella cut and measured and Molly helped out wherever she could. In the early afternoons, when her work at the tailor shop was finished, Molly would walk back home alone to tend to her vegetable garden and make dinner for the family. Sometimes she would look in on her neighbor Mrs. Kinder as she passed.

Mrs. Kinder was quite old and lived all alone. She had been married to the dairy and egg man. Mr. Kinder had been very successful in his business, and so had built a large home for his wife and the children that they had hoped to have. But alas, as the local villagers liked to joke, the only thing hatching at the Kinders' were the chickens. So, Mrs. Kinder was left all alone after her husband passed away with no one to care for her as she grew older. As a result, the dairy and egg business that her late husband had worked so hard to build became too much for old Mrs. Kinder. She had been forced to fire her last few employees and to sell off all but one cow, and she had kept only a few chickens that even now scratched and pecked for seeds in her front yard.

It bothered Molly terribly that Mrs. Kinder was shunned because of her large home and the money that she was thought to have. "People are just jealous," she had told Sam when she had first met the old woman. "I feel sad for her to be all alone in that big house." So it became Molly's habit to look in on Mrs. Kinder once or twice a week on her way home. Mrs. Kinder hardly spoke to Molly, but her eyes shone with pleasure whenever she heard the soft knock at her front door. Usually Molly only spent enough time to put the flowers she had picked from her garden into a glass vase and make a pot of porridge for Mrs. Kinder's dinner, or to peel some of the potatoes that she had brought from her parents' garden.

Molly would stand at Mrs. Kinder's kitchen sink and through the window above it, she would watch the flowing waters of the river that ran at the back of Mrs. Kinder's property. The river was at its widest and deepest at this point and the speed of the current was always variable. Sometimes it ran fast and choppy and the winds would whip the surface of the river and the land would be covered with mist. Other times, when the soft winds of spring would blow, the river would be still and glassy and flat as a mirror and brilliant blue from the reflection of the sky. On days like that, Molly could see across the river to the opposite bank where the grasses and trees grew thick and tall. She had stopped once in a while to put her tired feet in the river, and several times in the heat of the summer she had waded in near the shoreline, enjoying the coolness of the water that splashed against her skin. Molly grew to love the river, but she also feared it because of its constant changeability. Only when the waters were still would she venture anywhere near it.

Each time Molly would visit Mrs. Kinder, she never knew what she would find. Sometimes the old woman would be happy to see her and other times her wrinkled face would be awash in tears. At times like this, Molly would sit and hold the old woman's hand in silence, seeking to calm her with her touch. Molly thought it must be loneliness and loss that made Mrs. Kinder cry, and she was filled with compassion and tenderness for the old woman. And so, before leaving, Molly would light the stove in Mrs. Kinder's kitchen and heat up the food she had brought along. Then she would kiss Mrs. Kinder goodbye on her cold and wrinkled cheek, and sadly leave the old woman to her thoughts. It occurred to Molly more than once as she walked along the path that led her home *how like the river she is, forever changing.* Molly would often pause along the path and stand in silent reflection as she gazed at the blue water, the whisper of a prayer on her lips as she wished happiness for Mrs. Kinder and expressed her gratefulness for the life she had been given with Sam. Even though she knew the winds of change would always blow, she hoped the breezes would be warm and gentle.

CHAPTER 20

A Life Together

It was early evening in September, several years after Molly and Sam had been married, when Harold and Stella sat together around their kitchen table. There was a small pile of silver coins before them. "I just don't believe it could happen again, we were so busy when we first bought the sewing machine. Now each week, there is less and less. It's not the workmanship, if anything we have improved, our quality is good and we are more efficient than ever!" Without thinking, Harold picked up a few of the coins and dropped them one by one on the table. As the weight of the coins clattered and fell against the wooden surface, a silent fear rose up inside him. His mind was filled with vivid memories and he was, once again, a soldier fighting a war that brought only suffering and destruction. He shook his head to clear the images that were too painful to remember.

"Harold dear, remember your heart," said Stella quietly as she patted her husband's hand. She tried to smile at him, but she was worried, too. Stella looked out her kitchen window at the starry sky. When she was a little girl, her father had brought her outside to watch the darkening evening. That particular night had been crisp and cold and the stars in the sky had shone like an exquisite crystal necklace, incredibly brilliant and perfect. Stella had snuggled against her father for warmth and he had placed his arm around her shoulders.

"My Stella, my star," he had said, with a warm smile that she could see even now.

Then he had pointed skywards and towards the north. "Do you see the brightest star in the heavens, my Stella? That is the star I give to you tonight, may it bless you and guide you and keep you safe from harm."

Through the years, Stella had looked to the night sky whenever she felt in need of her father's guidance and comfort. The star had always before appeared bright and constant whenever she had sought it out, but tonight as she sat hand-in-hand with her husband, she watched as a dark haze seemed to move across the star beam concealing it from view. "There is change coming," said Stella, "or maybe it is here already."

For Sam and Molly, the early years of their marriage were peaceful and happy. The world around Molly was filled with beauty and love. Each morning was a gift that slowly revealed itself throughout the day. Never had she been so happy and so complete. In the spring of each year, Sam and Molly would walk in the lush woods that surrounded their cabin and fill their arms with wildflowers and their buckets full of berries for pastries and pies, and from the garden that Molly had put in behind their house, a bounty of fruit and vegetables grew. Sam and Molly harvested their small garden together in the fall. Then in the late afternoon, while Sam was still at work at the tailor shop, Molly would be busy canning fruits and vegetables for the winter. As she placed the jars of fruits and vegetables into the large vat of boiling water, a steamy mist of pickling spice and honeyed fruit filled the kitchen and turned Molly's blond hair to curls and wisps.

Following the age-old recipes her mother had given her when she married, and smelling the aromas that permeated her small kitchen, Molly was connected to the past and future. As each jar spread its jeweled light across the tablecloth, she was proud to be part of all the women who came before her and proud too that she continued their traditions. Memories of other years and other times when she had watched her mother and aunts in the kitchen preparing their favorite recipes returned to her mind, and it was as if their hands and hers were one, helping her to season everything just right and to mix and fill the glass jars that lined her table.

When Sam came home one chilly evening, his tired eyes went wide as he admired all the jars that glinted from the shelves. "You have worked hard my love," he said. "We will have need of these provisions more than ever this year, I think."

Molly looked up at her husband and the smile on her face melted away. "I know things have changed in the tailor shop, but do you think we really need to worry quite so much? We have each other, and a little more hard work doesn't scare me. We are still young, we can find our way," said Molly fiercely and she moved into her husband's arms and held him close. Sam placed a kiss on his wife's cheek and leaned in closer to whisper softly in her ear, so softly that Molly was not sure she had heard him at all.

"I hope it is only just about hard work, my love."

It was a late October morning and the dew on the grass crunched beneath their feet as Sam and Molly walked along together towards the tailor shop. As they neared the town, Molly noticed immediately that the streets, which at this hour of the day were normally full of carts and people rushing here and there, were almost empty. Instead, she saw gatherings of men in uniforms of fiery red and silver braid. They carried swords and pistols by their sides. Molly's heart gave a great lurch and she grabbed Sam's arm before she realized it.

"We're here!" said Sam with relief as he pulled Molly inside the tailor shop. Above their heads, the little bells tinkled gaily, as if nothing had changed. Behind the counter, Harold looked up from his accounts and glanced at his pocket watch.

"They arrived at seven this morning," he said, his voice tinged with anger and fear. "That is why there is no one about, and I doubt there will be any business to speak of again today." *Or the next*, he thought to himself silently.

Stella came in from the back room. In her arms she carried several bolts of cloth and a basket containing laces and ribbons. Noticing Sam and Molly, she placed the fabric and basket on the counter quickly and ran to her son and daughter-in-law. Stella forced a smile onto her face. "Your father likes to worry," she said, "Don't pay attention to him. Business will improve, you'll see. We will adjust to this. We will watch and wait, and while I wait, I will work." With that, Stella gave Sam and Molly a fierce hug and then she picked up her basket and as she did her hands shook a little. "Come, Sam," Stella said with a strength she did not feel. "We at least have a few orders left to finish."

The buzzing hum of the sewing machine was comforting, and as the day wore on and a few customers came and went and a few more people filled the streets, Molly began to feel her initial fear slip away. Her mother-in-law was right, life must continue. Molly thought about Stella's words as she swept up the threads from the floor and wiped down the counter. As she worked, she made a promise to herself. *I will find the strength to do what I must, even if it is hard to believe I can.* Molly looked over at Stella sitting in the light of the window, her head bent closely over the work in her lap, and she smiled to herself. Stella was the star that lit the way for Harold and Sam, and now as Sam's wife, she was included in that loving sphere. Her mother Moriah, she knew, was the wind that blew gently, always forward and always whispering, encouraging softly behind her husband and daughter. *The stars and the wind are my mothers*, Molly thought suddenly, and she bent down and kissed Stella warmly on top of her silvery head.

Stella was startled and looked up at Molly. "What was that for?" she asked.

"Just to say thank you, that's all," Molly replied.

"Oh, pish tosh," said Stella. "There is no need for thank you. No need at all." And she blushed slightly pink.

Over the next few weeks, life in the village slowly returned to a different normal. There seemed to be fewer people in the town, and more and more soldiers seemed to come and go. Sometimes the soldiers would stop in to the tailor shop for a small repair to their shirts or uniforms. The soldiers were always greeted by the tinkling of the bells as they pushed open the door to the shop. Their grim faces and heavy presence charged the air with tension. They spoke crisply to Harold about what they wanted done and before leaving always bowed stiffly to Stella and Molly.

Although glad for the few extra coins in his cash drawer, Harold hoped for the day when the soldiers would finally leave for good. He had seen enough of war and feared what it would mean for Sam and Molly. When Harold was seventeen, a civil war had been declared. The mighty Red Army was financed by the leaders of the country and it was their mission to seek out, control, and destroy anyone who disagreed with their regime. The Red Army soldiers were from the privileged class, enjoying lives of ease and luxury, maintaining large areas of land and leaving a meager existence for the peasants who worked their fields. The Blue Army, meanwhile, was made up of the starving farmers and factory workers who slaved away at jobs for endless hours with nothing to show for their labors, unable even to feed their children. The disparity was too great. The working people of the country rose up to fight against their intolerable living conditions.

Along with the other young men in his village, Harold had eagerly enlisted with the Blue Army, fighting against the Reds who threatened to invade their small village and the surrounding areas. Harold had been proud to serve along with his friends and neighbors. The men fought fiercely alongside one another, but the losses among his company and the Blue Army at large were great. Over time, the men in Harold's unit began to look to him for the leadership that they needed and it was Harold who had kept his men strong, encouraging them with true stories of valor and heartfelt commitment among their fellow soldiers and commanders. He inspired them with stories of survival that he learned from among his family and friends at home, who also fought in any way they could to be free. Time and again he had distinguished himself with honor, putting himself at great risk to rescue injured Blue Army soldiers, leading his men from the front, and urging them forward against a much larger and more powerful army. His rage at the loss of comrades in arms and the injustice of the treatment of his people propelled him on. He had fought bravely against a seemingly unbeatable opponent until the lack of food and ammunition for his men, as well as the rest of the Blue Army, stalled their efforts and they could fight no more.

After many years of hunger, destruction, and loss, an uneasy peace had come between the two armies. When the armistice between the Red and Blue armies had been signed and implemented, Harold and his soldier friends returned home and began to rebuild their lives, but even so the memories were still as fresh as if they had only just happened. Stella and Sam knew of Harold's past experiences. Over the years, he had shared memories of his wartime experiences. He did not want those same memories for his son. As Harold thought back through the past, he was once again reminded of the decision he had made to destroy his military papers and uniform when he returned home from the war and he hoped again that he had made the right decision. He remembered back with crystal clarity his return home from the war. He had felt sick at heart and defeated, as did all of the friends with whom he served.

At first, he had hung his old uniform away at the back of his bedroom closet, thinking to himself as he did that there may come a time when he would need it again. But the fragile peace that the armistice had created seemed to hold and days turned to weeks and then years, and one day he had decided finally to destroy any memory he could of his time at war and he had taken the Blue uniform and his indoctrination papers and placed them in the fire that burned brightly in his kitchen hearth. He was thoroughly sick of war and all the bloodshed and injustice that inevitably came. He wanted peace and a quiet family life and he had felt strongly then and now that it was far better to move forward and erase past experiences, and try to adapt to a new world, than to look back in anger and fear.

CHAPTER 21

Who Do You Trust

The path that Molly walked on this mid-November day was strewn with the red and yellow leaves of autumn. The air was warm for November, but there was a stiff breeze coming across the river. Molly could smell the tangy mist and feel the dampness on her skin and in her hair as she approached Mrs. Kinder's house. It had been a few weeks when last she had stopped by to visit the old woman. Harold had asked that she stay close to home for a while until things had quieted down in the town. His concern had increased as more and more soldiers from the Red Army filled the streets of Pushkin, causing Harold to once again remember vividly the clashes between the powerful Red Army and the poorly outfitted Blues. Even after many years of peace, Harold was very much aware of the anger of the people of Pushkin and the surrounding area that still simmered hotly under a seemingly calm exterior. Occasional squabbles around the town and the country at large never seemed to be over and so Harold was not very pleased. Or at least that is how Molly felt when she had said that she would be going to visit Mrs. Kinder.

"Be careful, Molly," Harold had warned, concern growing in his voice. He knew of Mrs. Kinder and her husband's service in the Red Army, and the newspapers he read avidly each day were full of reports of violence and angry protests. "Times are different now. Be careful who you trust."

"I won't be long," Molly had replied. "It's just next door." And she had picked up her basket and went out into the sunshine.

When Molly knocked on Mrs. Kinder's front door she received no answer, but that was nothing new. Quite often Mrs. Kinder would be dozing in her armchair by the fire, and would not hear her knock. So this time, Molly knocked again a little more loudly. "Mrs. Kinder, it's Molly!" she called and pushed against the front door. It opened easily as if Mrs. Kinder was hoping she would come again. Molly stepped into the front hall and looked into the parlor. Just as she had expected, Mrs. Kinder was snoring softly in her chair. Rather than disturb her, Molly turned to go into the kitchen, when she noticed something shiny out of the corner of her eye. On the hall table was a silver picture frame that Molly had not seen before. She went over to the table. *I wonder who could have sent Mrs. Kinder such a beautiful gift*, thought Molly. But when she picked up the silver frame, she could see that it was really quite old, and the image that looked back at her was of a young man with flowing mustaches and an unmistakable Red Army uniform.

At first upon seeing the picture, Molly's heart had given a great lurch. The sight of the soldier's uniform frightened her. She knew the stories about Harold's service for the Blues and Mrs. Kinder's husband's service in the opposing Red Army, but seeing the Red's uniform on the man in the sepia-tinted photograph startled her for a moment. *That war was so long ago, and there has been peace for such a long time*, Molly reasoned to herself and, replacing the frame on the table, she turned to go into the kitchen to peel the potatoes that she had brought. The kitchen was chilly and Molly hugged her sweater a little tighter around her as she started the fire in the stove. She placed a bowl on the counter top and took up a knife. The peels slipped quickly into the bowl and Molly's thoughts raced as well. Looking out at the fast-flowing river, she remembered Harold's words. *Be careful who you trust,* he had said, *Times are different now.*

Just then, there was a loud knock on the front door. The knock was so loud that it startled Mrs. Kinder awake. She jumped a little in her chair, and then the knock came again, louder this time. Mrs. Kinder rose from her chair and went to answer the knocking. As she crossed the small hallway she looked quickly at Molly and signaled her to be quiet and return to the kitchen. Then Mrs. Kinder opened the door. Standing in the doorway was a soldier dressed in fiery red and silver braid. When Molly saw him standing in the cold light of the front hall she could feel the blood begin pounding in her ears as her heart beat faster and thundered in her chest.

"Are you the lady of the house?" the soldier asked gruffly. He towered over Mrs. Kinder and looked at her sternly. His eyes were blue and ice cold and it seemed to Mrs. Kinder as he looked at her that he could penetrate her thoughts with the intensity of his gaze.

"I am, sir," replied Mrs. Kinder, trying to speak calmly and stand a little taller.

"Is your husband at home?" the soldier demanded. "My commander would like to speak to him."

"I am sorry, sir. You have come all this way for nothing. My husband died many years ago. But he was a proud soldier with the Reds." And Mrs. Kinder turned to get the picture in the silver frame to show the soldier, moving towards him so that her back was to Molly.

"Ah yes," said the soldier. "That is why we wished to speak to him. We required him to report for duty as soon as possible. My men are in the process of looking for any active Blue Army members who might still be in the vicinity. They are a wicked bunch, causing trouble here and there in nearby towns lately. Do not doubt that our men will easily prevail, with our superior weapons and training. That is why we are in the area, patrolling and looking for agitators. We will not hesitate to shoot to kill if we think we must."

"You're quite right, sir, my husband would most certainly have agreed," Mrs. Kinder replied.

Molly could not believe what she was hearing and she was riveted to the floor in fear. Then she noticed Mrs. Kinder's hand waving frantically behind her back. She knew she should run but where? Her legs felt like jelly as she turned for the kitchen door. The wind took the door from her hands and it banged loudly against the house. Molly ran as fast as she could through the wet grass.

The soldier heard the door slam. "Is there someone else here with you, ma'am?" he demanded and pushed Mrs. Kinder aside roughly. The soldier headed for the back of the house, his pistol aimed and ready. He saw Molly as she ran. The edges of her sweater flapped madly around her and her golden curls spilled from her hairpins and cascaded down her back. The soldier raised his arm to fire. The grass where Molly ran was slippery and she lost control of her feet as she ran and tumbled forward, just as a shot burst from the soldier's pistol, missing her by inches.

Molly rolled over and over in the grass staying low as shot after shot whistled near her head. There was nowhere else to go except the river. The waters were icy cold and rough as Molly reached the edge, but she felt no cold as she dove in and began to kick wildly to the opposite shore. Still the soldier fired his weapon as she struggled against the choppy current. And then all was silent. Molly pulled herself up onto the opposite bank and hid herself among the reeds and bushes there. Shivering violently from fear and cold, she looked down and noticed that the knife she had been peeling potatoes with was still clasped tightly in her hand.

When the soldier returned to Mrs. Kinder's house he found the old woman sitting in her armchair by the fire. The knitting needles she held in her hands shook and clicked against each other furiously as Mrs. Kinder strove to appear calm and unconcerned.

"Who was that woman?" demanded the soldier.

"Forgive me, sir. I am an old woman and I need help here and there, you see I am all alone. I did not know that the girl was on the Blue side. I will be more careful in the future, sir. Please forgive me."

Mrs. Kinder reminded the soldier of his own grandmother and so he said in his clipped and angry voice, "These are dangerous times. Vigilance is the order of the day." And he bowed stiffly and left, closing the front door firmly behind him. Mrs. Kinder waited until she heard the loud clip clop of the soldier's horse as he wheeled his stallion around and rode quickly away. Her heart beat so fast it was hard for her to breathe. She rose from her chair as rapidly as her shaking legs would allow and wrapped a warm shawl around her frail body, and then thinking quickly, she took her purse from its hiding place by the stairs. Then she opened her front door and looked around. There was no one and no sound, as if nothing had happened. But it had happened, and that knowledge propelled Mrs. Kinder forward as fast as she could go to the Golds' house.

CHAPTER 22

The How Not The Why

Mrs. Kinder was breathless and her legs shook beneath her as she banged as loudly as she could on the front door of the Golds' house. Stella turned from the dishes she was washing in the sink and went to answer the repeated knocking. When she opened the door, Mrs. Kinder fell forward into her arms.

"What's happened! Mrs. Kinder are you alright?" Stella cried in alarm.

Mrs. Kinder looked wildly around the room. Sam had heard the banging on the front door and came into the kitchen from the back of the house. "Oh! Sam! You're here!" gasped Mrs. Kinder as she saw him. "It's Molly, Sam! A soldier! Shots! She swam across the river. Help her Sam! Help her! Please!" Mrs. Kinder pleaded. Her throat was dry and her words were raspy and she was afraid that Sam did not understand her. But Sam definitely had heard every word.

"Molly swam the river! My god!" said Sam, incredulous.

"I saw her reach the other side, across from my house. I know I did. She hid in the bushes, go! Sam, go!" Mrs. Kinder breathed heavily and she reached for the nearby tabletop to steady herself.

Sam hurriedly grabbed some blankets from a nearby cabinet and turned to his father who stood in the doorway. "Ride to Molly's parents' house," he ordered. "Tell them what has happened and to be ready to move as soon as possible." And he ran quickly out the door.

Stella helped Mrs. Kinder to a chair and looked up at her husband. She was worried to the bone and there were tears in her eyes. "What now?" Stella asked, not really wanting to know the answer.

"I must ride to warn Moriah and Ari, as Sam has asked. You must ready the cart and when Sam and Molly return be prepared to leave and follow me as soon as you are able," said Harold as he glanced quickly about the room for his hat and coat. Then he went to the stone hearth where he removed a loose rock just under the mantelpiece. Reaching into the space behind the stone, he removed a green felt pouch then deftly replaced the stone and quickly put the pouch in his pocket. Now he was ready to leave. As he went out the door, Stella followed him. They did not speak as they brought two horses from the barn. Together they saddled Harold's horse and strapped the other into the harness of the small wooden cart that was kept by the side of the house. As Harold made ready to mount his horse, Stella went to him and held him close and placed a warm kiss on his cheek.

"Be careful," she whispered as she watched him ride away. In the house, Stella sat with Mrs. Kinder and waited. The clock ticked the minutes off like hours until finally the knock that they had been waiting for came.

"Mother!" called Sam. "Mother, we're here!" In a flash Stella was at the door. Standing in the open doorway, Sam held Molly close to support her. She was wrapped in blankets from head to toe and still she could not control her shaking.

"Bring her here, Sam!" exclaimed Stella anxiously, indicating a chair she had placed by the fire. Stella quickly removed Molly's sodden clothes and wrapped her tightly again in dry blankets. When she finished she went to her stove and returned to Molly with a steaming mug in her hands. "Here Molly my dear, drink this, it's hot and it will help warm you." Stella handed the large mug into Molly's hands and busied herself again tucking in the blankets around her daughter-in-law. Molly could not speak for shivering, but she sipped the hot liquid in the mug and looked at her mother-in-law with gratitude.

"We must leave quickly," said Sam.

"The cart is ready and your father is on his way to Moriah and Ari's," replied Stella with a tremble in her voice.

Sam looked at his wife covered in blankets, her blonde hair curling about her face as it dried, and he thought how courageous she had been today and how very lucky they all were that she was unharmed. "Molly," he said to her, "You must be brave just a little longer. We must go to your parents' house as soon as possible. I will put you in the back of the cart with my mother and she will watch over you along the way." Molly still could not speak, but Sam could see the fear return to her eyes. He went to stand next to Molly and reached for her hands. They were white and trembling and still icy cold. "Come, Molly," he coaxed softly as he helped her to stand on her trembling legs and then bent down and lifted her into his arms and carried her to the door.

"Wait!" said Mrs. Kinder, "I'm coming too." And she rose as quickly as she could on her still shaky legs, and tottered towards the door as fast as she was able. "I'll ride in the back with Molly," she continued in a voice that held no room for argument.

Sam placed Molly gently in the back of the cart and adjusted the blankets around her. He turned to face Mrs. Kinder and held out his hand to her. "We must hurry, there is no time to waste. Mother, you'll ride with me up front." Stella jumped up on the side board and settled herself on the front seat, while Sam helped Mrs. Kinder into the back of the cart with Molly. The last thing Sam noticed as he walked around to the front of the wagon was Mrs. Kinder taking Molly into her arms and placing Molly's head on her shoulder.

The sky was beginning to darken when Sam drove the cart up to the front door of Moriah and Ari's house. Harold and Ari rushed out of the front door as soon as they heard the wagon enter the yard. They both hurried to the back of the cart to help carry Molly inside. When Harold saw Mrs. Kinder holding Molly, he was a bit taken aback. His eyes grew wide in surprise when he saw the look of love on Mrs. Kinder's face and the protective arm that lay around Molly's shoulders and held her in a close embrace. Harold was still not sure about Mrs. Kinder's loyalties. *Was she no longer a supporter of the Red Army?* he wondered, Nevertheless it was he who reached a hand out to help the old woman down from the cart. Sam stood aside as Ari scooped his daughter up from where she lay in the back of the cart, and cradling her softly in his arms, he carried her quickly and as gently as he could inside.

Moriah followed Ari and held back the quilts on the bed in Molly's old room as Ari placed his daughter down gently and kissed her on the head. "I'll bring you some warm soup and then you must rest," he said and left the room. Moriah pulled the quilts up and around Molly's trembling body and then she sat down beside her on the edge of the bed. Molly looked so small and pale among the covers, but her eyes were clear and alert. "I am so grateful you are safe," Moriah whispered, and bent forward to kiss her daughter's icy cheek. "It was Mrs. Kinder who saved me, Mother. I would be dead if not for her!" Molly explained, the fear returning to her voice. "I was so very frightened I couldn't think, but she waved at me to run and I did. I didn't even know where to run and then the shots!" Ari stood in the door with a bowl of soup in his hands. He had heard every word Molly had said, and his eyes burned with anger. In his rage he was unaware that his hands clenched tighter around the bowl he carried. As his anger grew, the hot soup splashed and ran down the sides of the bowl, scalding his fingers and flaring his rage ever higher. He struggled to keep his voice calm.

Handing the bowl of soup quickly to his wife he said in a gruff and commanding voice, "It is over now Molly, drink your soup and get some rest." And he turned abruptly and left the room, closing the door behind him.

Giant tears filled Molly's eyes as she watched her father leave. He had been so sharp with her; he had never acted that way before. Moriah picked up the spoon and as she slowly fed her daughter the soup, she said, "Forgive your father, he is only worried about you. You have had a horrible experience, it will take some time for it to leave you, but you must reach deep and find your strength. Let's try to focus on how we must go forward from now on, instead of why this terrible incident has happened, and the path before us will become clear." Molly listened to her mother's soothing words. The warmth of the covers and the hot soup made her body relax and her eyes grew heavy, and soon she was asleep. Moriah rose from the bed and there were tears in her eyes. She wiped them away with the corner of her apron. She knew deep in her heart that an even greater change was coming, a change that would require all the strength she could give. Closing the door softly behind her, she went to join the others.

Moriah entered the kitchen quietly and Ari stood up when he saw her and gave his wife his chair at the table. His thoughts were raging wildly in his head and he wondered, not for the first time, if there would be war once again and if he would be needed to enlist once more in order to protect his family from the Red Army. He knew without question that he would not hesitate to go if indeed he must. When Moriah was seated, he remained close behind her. She could feel the anger in her husband; it was palpable and strong as he clutched the back of her chair tightly.

Harold, Sam, Stella and Mrs. Kinder were already seated closely together around the kitchen table. They were looking over a map that lay spread out before them. Tracing his finger along several different lines marked in black pen, Harold was discussing with Sam the best possible routes and times of travel. Harold was marking the map here and there with small lines and circles as he explained to Sam, while the others around the table leaned in closer and listened intently.

"In my fabric and tailoring business, I have known people in these few villages along the way. They will all be happy to help you with food and shelter. I think though the best possible route is to go south and through the Great Forest," he said, looking closely at Sam. "Now, if all goes as planned, it should take you two days to reach the port," he continued earnestly. Harold took a folded piece of paper from his pocket. It was a sailing schedule and he unfolded it and placed it on the table over the map. "Today is Wednesday," Harold said. "There is a ship sailing at noon on Sunday for America and the Port of Massachusetts."

"America!" breathed Sam, his voice filling with awe. He had not thought about traveling so far and he sat staring at the map for a moment.

"That means we must leave by Friday at the latest," he said quietly as the understanding of what they would need to do and where they were going became clear, and his thoughts came out quickly as he planned aloud. "I think if we travel by night there will be less danger, and at least we will have a little time to pack a few things." His voice grew softer as he realized that he might never see his home again. The reality of that thought and the idea of all that he would leave behind was overwhelming, and Sam struggled to push those thoughts aside. He knew he must focus on the present situation and try to keep Molly and both their families safe. That was the most important thing, the only thing that really mattered.

Harold put the green felt bag he had brought with him on the table, untied the string, and spread out the bag. "There are forty-five silver pieces here," he said, and looked over at Sam. "A ticket costs fifty silver pieces. I ..." Harold began to say with a sigh.

"Wait!" interrupted Ari, "here is a little more." He placed another twenty pieces of silver on the table.

Moriah slipped her wedding bands off her finger and added them to the pile of silver coins on the table. "You may be able to sell these along the way," she said to Sam, and smiled sadly at him. Stella nodded and started to remove her own wedding bands to add to the pile on the table when Mrs. Kinder held out a hand to stop her.

"This is nonsense!" she said in her raspy voice. "I won't hear of you all giving away your gold rings and silver coins when you may soon be needing them yourselves." With that, she placed her purse soundly on the table and, indicating her bag, she said, "There is more than enough here to pay for Molly's and Sam's sailing tickets, and if they are careful when they arrive, there might be a little more to tide them over for awhile."

"Mrs. Kinder," said Sam in amazement. "This is the second time you have saved my wife's life today."

CHAPTER 23

The Winds That Blow

“Molly,” Moriah said as she knocked on Molly’s bedroom door. “Molly dear are you awake?” Moriah could hear the rustling of the covers and a murmured reply. She turned the knob and gently pushed open the door. In her arms she carried a wooden tray on which were a mug of hot tea, a bowl of thick porridge, and the last jar of her best preserves. Moriah placed the tray across Molly’s lap and fluffed the pillows behind her daughter. Then she pulled up a chair next to the bed. “Please eat while it’s hot, Molly,” she said, reaching out to pat her daughter’s hand.

“It’s so very quiet. Where is everyone?” Molly asked. Moriah looked down at her daughter’s hand held in hers and then she looked up, and instead of looking at Molly, her eyes drifted towards the single window in the room. Outside, the day was cold and a blustery wind blew the last leaves off the trees. Moriah looked back at her daughter and let out a deep sigh. It was as if the winds were blowing her along, too. “Molly,” she replied,

"The world has changed now, the peace that was is no more. It has become dangerous for you to remain here, and for a time you and Sam must leave,"

Moriah continued, even though Molly's eyes filled with tears. After yesterday's events, Molly had thought something like this might happen.

"We must keep you safe," Moriah said with a sigh. She patted her daughter's hand again. "Now eat!" said Moriah. "And I will tell you what we have decided."

Molly was amazed by the story her mother told her of Mrs. Kinder's generosity, and the kindness of her actions made Molly's day feel somewhat lighter. The coldness in her body had left, but she still shivered whenever a flash of memory from the day before came into her mind. So Molly tried to keep herself busy while she and her mother waited nervously for Sam and Ari to return from packing up the stone cabin where they had lived so peacefully for the past few years.

Earlier that same morning, while Molly was still asleep, Sam had crept softly from the bedroom and joined the others. Harold, Stella, Mrs. Kinder, Moriah and Ari were waiting for him in the kitchen. "Father," said Sam to Harold, as he entered the room. "I've been thinking, and I think it best if I go to the cabin and pack what I can and then join you later at the shop if you need me today."

"Agreed," Harold replied. "I think it is best if we try to remain as normal as possible until it is time for you both to leave."

"I'll go along with you, Sam," said Ari, "We can take my wagon, and it will be faster if I help you."

"We'll take Mrs. Kinder along with us and drop her home," said Stella. "And this time you will sit up front with Harold and me," she said with a warm smile to Mrs. Kinder.

And so it was that Harold, Stella, and Mrs. Kinder sat close together on the front seat of the cart as they headed back towards Pushkin. Harold held the reins loosely in his hands, but his mind was tense with memories and plans. Who was this woman seated next to him? She had been so kind, but could she still be trusted, or was he sending his children into some kind of unknowable trap? Did Mrs. Kinder still carry an allegiance to the Reds? Mrs. Kinder had been thinking too, and as the memories of that long ago war between the Reds and Blues came flooding back, she began to speak. She felt it was important now to share her story with Harold and Stella and allay their fears.

"My husband, Helmut Kinder, was a happy man when we first married," began Mrs. Kinder, almost to herself. "Proud and happy. His family had been part of the Red government for years. Then came the war. A stupid war like every other, filled with animosity and fear and misunderstanding. The Reds feared the Blues because food supplies had become dangerously low, people were starving. You remember, Harold, how it was? There were so many Blue Army supporters who were unhappy with the Red government; people were marching in the streets. The Reds sent in their armies to control the Blue uprising and Helmut went with them. He was from an important family, and because of his knowledge in languages he was trained as a spy. He survived the war but barely. When he returned home he was a changed man. The happiness was gone from him and he became angry and distrustful. He let the hatred of the Blues seep deep inside him. Our business was doing very well, even though Helmut took very little interest in it as time went on. Then when it became clear we could not have any children, he became empty inside, as empty as the house he had built for a family we would never have. I think that is what sent him to an early grave. Kinder means 'children' you know," Mrs. Kinder said with a sigh.

"I did not know of all this," said Stella with compassion.

Harold looked at Mrs. Kinder. He was ready to protect his family at all cost and he was tense and wary. "What about Molly?" he asked gruffly and with great concern in his voice.

"I was so alone," Mrs. Kinder continued as if she hadn't heard Harold's question.

"In that house with no one. I had lost everything and the bitterness that my husband had brought to our lives began to seep into me. Even though we have had years of peace, I still cherished my anger and could not let it go. I became more and more isolated. Then one day, a lovely young woman with the most beautiful golden curls knocked on my door. There was sun shining all around her and she carried a wicker basket on her arm. 'I've brought you some potatoes from my parents' garden,' she said. 'We have so many, we can't possibly eat them all ourselves. I thought you might enjoy some for dinner.' I remember smiling at her. I hadn't smiled in ages. She did not seem to know who I was or even care. She looked like an angel. How could I say no? So I let her come in and showed her into the kitchen. I watched her as she peeled the potatoes and placed them in a pot on the stove. Then she turned to me and said, 'There you are. I hope you enjoy them. If you like, I will stop by again.' I just nodded and smiled. No one had done anything like that before for me.

"I grew to look forward to her visits. Molly listened to my stories of the past. She knew of your service in the Blue Army, Harold. We hoped that the fragile peace between the Red and Blue armies would be forever. She knew what my husband had done during the war, and still she continued to care for me. I learned to see the folly of what the Red Army was trying to accomplish and I grew to find love in my heart again. Molly gave me a great gift," she said, as she reached out to put her hand on Harold's arm. "When the soldier began firing I was so scared, not for me but for Molly. I forced myself to be calm!" With that, Mrs. Kinder put her head in her hands and her shoulders slumped forward. "The soldier had seen her," she continued through her trembling hands. "I knew that he would remember her beautiful golden hair. I knew then that Molly was in very grave danger, that she had to leave before more soldiers would come to find her." And she gave a deep sigh and looked up. Stella patted Mrs. Kinder gently on the back.

"We're here," said Harold as he pulled the reins up tight in front of Mrs. Kinder's front door. Then he jumped down from the cart and went to offer Mrs. Kinder his hand to help her down. The story Harold had just heard helped soothe his distrust of the old woman and as he walked her to the door, he began to express his gratitude. "I can't thank you enough for all you have done, Mrs. Kinder," said Harold simply. "Please," said Mrs. Kinder, "It is my pleasure to be able to help. And please tell Molly not to worry, I will do whatever I can to help her family while she is away."

"Mrs. Kinder," began Harold.

"Please," said Mrs. Kinder, "call me Mildred." She smiled up at Harold and Stella, then she went inside and closed the door.

CHAPTER 24

The Thirty-Five Women

The door to the little cabin that Molly and Sam had lived in pushed open easily when Sam and Ari entered. The flash of memory that came to Sam as he entered his home and looked around was sharp and sweetly painful. He could see in his mind's eye Molly standing at the hearth, setting the table, arranging the wildflowers they had picked in the woods, canning her vegetables and fruits, and the glow of happiness that lit her face when he came through the door after a long day at work. Remembering was difficult and Sam struggled with the emotions that threatened to overwhelm him. He looked around the small room again and scratched his head: *Where to start, what to take?* he wondered. *When you are leaving, perhaps forever, traveling far and carrying little, what do you take?* He knelt down beside the bed and pulled out an old leather suitcase that had been stored from underneath and clicked open the metal hinges.

Ari had set the large trunk that Molly had brought to the cabin with her on the day of the wedding in the middle of the kitchen floor, and he busied himself filling it with as many of the gifts as he possibly could. In the bottom of the trunk he placed some of the copper pots and pans and dishes and silverware from the kitchen, then came the sheets, blankets, and pillowcases that Molly and Moriah had sewn, then the colorful quilt from on top of the bed. He took all of the family pictures off the walls and placed them carefully on top, adding at the last the leaf-green leather bound book that Molly so cherished. Then he closed the lid firmly and clicked the locks. Sam had finished his packing by this time too, and after a last quick look around, it was time to leave. Sam put the suitcase and several boxes in the back of the wagon and then returned in order to help Ari with carrying the heavy trunk.

While Sam was outside, Ari stood in the middle of the room. He felt he was missing something, *what could it be?* he thought to himself. When Sam opened the door to enter the cabin once again, a bright light flashed into Ari's eyes and instinctively he reached up to shield them from the glare. When he did he was instantly reminded of what it was he had almost forgotten. There, in the bedside table wrapped in grey felt and tied with a red string, were Molly's spectacles, just as Moriah had told him they would be. *They are a gift from Great-Grandmother Ethel*, she had reminded him, *a connection that Molly should carry wherever she may go.* Ari remembered how Moriah's eyes filled with tears as she spoke and he placed the spectacles carefully in his shirt pocket and gave them a soft pat.

After finishing the packing, Sam and Ari stopped by the tailor shop, as Sam had said he would. Harold got up immediately as they came in and, taking his hat and coat from a hook on the wall, he pushed Sam and Ari towards the door. "There is talk in the town about yesterday's shooting," he warned them. "It is not safe to talk here. Let's go home."

When Sam entered his parents' house early that evening with his father and Ari, his mother ran to him and held him close. There were tears in her eyes as she ushered him to the table and made him sit down. She gently kissed the top of his head. "It has been a difficult day," she said, "You need to eat. I'm sure you all must be hungry and thirsty. Please come, sit down." And she busied herself at the stove.

Over dinner, Harold and Stella told Sam and Ari the story of their conversation with Mrs. Kinder, and the promise she had made to them all. Sam's heart filled with relief and gratitude. He had been so worried about leaving both Molly's parents and his own behind. His eyes filled with tears. "Please," he said, "tell her how very grateful Molly and I are for her incredible generosity, and of her promise of protection. It will make leaving a little easier for us both." Sam rose from the table and the others followed. Harold went to his son and shook his hand then pulled him into a tight embrace. "We will see each other again," he said softly.

Stella went to her son and reached up to put her arms around his neck. She kissed him twice on both cheeks then, stepping back, she looked into his eyes. "You are my son, my moon and stars. America is a place of golden promise. There are freedoms there we can only hope to imagine. Make a good life, work hard, and care for each other. I will follow my star in the heavens and I will know you are safe and I know without a doubt that someday we will see each other again." Stella held her son close after that as if she would never release him and her tears fell slowly down her cheeks.

It was late at night when Sam and Ari returned to the little house where Molly and Moriah were already asleep. The sky held no stars as they drove the wagon through the inky darkness up the road and into the barn. Then together they unsaddled the horse and carried the trunk and suitcase into the darkened house. Moriah had left a small candle burning in a lamp on top of the stove. By its dim light, Ari reached into his pocket and handed Sam the grey felt bag that held Molly's spectacles. "These belong to Molly," Ari whispered softly, not wanting to wake his wife and daughter. "Something from her childhood; I thought she would like to have it."

Sam took the bag from his father-in-law and smiled. He knew exactly what it contained. "Thank you sir and good night," he whispered back and shook his father-in-law's hand. Then he turned and went into the bedroom that he and Molly now shared. He could hear his wife's slow gentle breathing, and not wishing to disturb her he placed the felt bag on the table beside her bed so she would find it in the morning. Then Sam undressed in the darkness and crawled beneath the sheets. He was instantly asleep.

Soon after Sam had gotten into bed, Molly was awakened by a dream memory. In the dream Molly saw herself running and heard again the *pop! pop! pop!* of the gun shots. Her heart began to race with terror. Molly forced herself awake and sat up in bed. She saw Sam lying peacefully beside her, and the sight of him calmed her a little. She reached for the water glass on the bedside table and her hand brushed the felt bag that Sam had left there. Molly knew at once that the bag held the spectacles she had found in the garden so many years ago. It had been a very long time since she had last put them on. She hadn't needed them, but everything was different now and after tomorrow nothing would be the same again.

Molly untied the red string, opened the grey felt bag, and removed her great-grandmother's spectacles. The silver metal gleamed softly in the velvety darkness. They felt cool and light in her hand. Then she slipped the spectacles on her nose and looked intently through the lenses. At first she could see nothing; the bedroom was so dark. Then things began to shift. The deep blackness of the room lightened to a misty dull grey and in the center of the grey a small yellow light began to appear. As Molly watched, the yellow light began to grow larger and slowly change color turning to orange then red, blue, green, and purple.

What does it mean? thought Molly as she watched the kaleidoscope of color before her eyes. Then she heard her names said in thirty-five different female voices. *Malkah Hannah Laurie Judith Phyllis Elaine Beth Bella Esther Chaya Dobrisha Elishah Alicia Marsha Pearl Sally Edie Sylvia Maria Raina Sophie Sarah Lily Francis Miriam Bette Rachel Evelyn Agnes Lucy Sadie Mary Ethel Goldah Ann ... We are part of you,* they whispered, *Our strength is your strength.* They sighed. *Remember us and you will find your way,* the voices said in unison. Then all was quiet. Molly removed the spectacles from her nose and held them to her heart. The rapid beating had eased and she breathed more calmly. She knew now that there would be difficult days ahead but that somewhere a tiny light would grow, and that wherever she went, she would always be connected to the women whose names she bore. Molly nestled down in the covers next to Sam, and still holding the spectacles next to her heart she fell asleep.

CHAPTER 25

A Gift of Goodbye

The following day was a flurry of activity. After a hasty breakfast of porridge and coffee, Molly and Moriah repacked the trunk and suitcase, deciding as they went what necessities to take on board for the journey and what to store in the ship's hold for when they arrived. Before anyone had noticed, the sun was beginning to set and it was time for Sam and Molly to leave. Ari brought a small pushcart up to the front door and he and Sam loaded up the trunk and suitcase. Inside the house, Molly looked around for the last time, committing every detail of the space to memory. Then she picked up her scarf and tied it securely under her chin, making sure to cover her blond curly hair completely. Then she put on her coat and began to walk slowly toward the door.

"Molly," said Moriah, "wait a moment please." Moriah walked towards her daughter, and as she did, she unclasped a strand of pearls from around her neck and placed them lovingly around Molly's. The pearls were smooth and warm against Molly's skin and she raised her hand to feel their silky hardness. "You know that my mother gave these pearls to me on my wedding day," Moriah said. "When my mother passed them on to me she told me that they had been a wedding present to her from my father and that since that day she had always worn them and so she felt that part of her essence, her spirit, was imparted into the necklace. Then she put the pearls around my neck and said, 'Now that you will be married and moving far away, wear these and I will always be with you.'

"When you married," Moriah continued and looked tenderly into Molly's eyes, "you left us as you should, but not so far that it would be difficult for us to see each other. And so I hesitated to give you the necklace, but now ..." Moriah's voice trailed off and she reached up and adjusted the pearls around Molly's neck, hiding them beneath her dress. "Part of me will always be with you, my darling daughter, with or without the necklace. But if you are ever in need you must sell them!" Molly struggled to keep the tears from falling as she caressed the pearls around her neck. They were warm and smooth and carried the sweet scent of lavender and vanilla, her mother's scent. She would always wear them. She would never, ever sell them. Moriah held her daughter close and kissed her. It was so very hard to let her go.

"Molly!" called Sam from outside in the yard. "It's almost full dark now and we really must be leaving." Sam's voice was strained with emotion. "It's time to go," he called again. Molly held her mother tighter, wanting nothing more than to remain here in the moment forever. Her eyes stung with tears that ran freely down her cheeks. Moriah kissed her daughter once more.

"I love you more than I can ever say. Please, take care of one another and be safe, now go and say goodbye to your father," she whispered, and gave her daughter a soft little push in the direction of the door. "I'll be right there." Moriah watched for a moment as Ari held Molly tightly and kissed her. Then she took a few things from her cupboard and placed them in a wicker basket covering the contents with a red-checkered cloth. She carried it outside and handed it to Molly. "For the ship," she said, "I have a feeling this will come in handy."

Molly hugged her mother once more and the tears that she had struggled to control all day stung her eyes once again and rolled down her cheeks. Ari patted Sam heartily on the back then shook his hand. "I hope you are able to return my push cart soon," he said with a tearful smile. Then he hugged his son-in-law close for a moment. "Take good care of our little girl, and yourself," Ari said with true affection.

"I promise to care for your daughter, sir, and I look forward to returning your cart someday soon," Sam replied, and his voice was tender with emotion.

"I look forward to it, too," said Molly, kissing her father one more time. Sam picked up the handles of the pushcart and Molly joined him, taking one of the handles, and slowly they began to push the cart forward together along the darkening path and to the road out of town.

Ari and Moriah stood silently in their front yard and watched as their daughter and son-in-law walked away. Each of them was filled with separate memories of the little girl they had cherished and adored. In the growing darkness, they took strength from each other as they watched until Molly and Sam began to disappear from view. Ari put his arm around his wife's shoulders and as they turned to go into the house, the last thing that Moriah could see as she looked back once more was a flash of red-checkered cloth and a golden wicker basket.

PART THREE

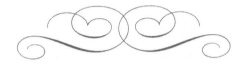

CHAPTER 26

Friends Along the Way

Molly and Sam's plan was to travel as far as they could throughout the night, pushing the heavy wheelbarrow before them and keeping to the side roads in order to avoid contact with any Red Army soldiers in the area. They walked in silence through the blanketing dark, listening intently for any sound of trouble. The path they followed went through deep woods and was uneven and rutted. The going was difficult with the ungainly weight of the wheelbarrow, and they worried that the sounds they made would alert soldiers of their presence as they struggled along the dark and bumpy forest road.

Around them, giant eagle owls shrieked as they soared in wide circular arcs far above the treetops hunting for food. They could hear the horrible yelps and howls from a pack of wolves as the hungry animals tore at their prey in the distance. Then suddenly, from somewhere close by, they heard the wild sounds of people screaming and rough commands, quickly followed by a volley of shots. A few seconds of silence and then more shots erupted, blasting and popping and spitting fire as they hit their intended targets and careened off the trees and forest brush.

Sam grabbed Molly's hand and motioned to her not to speak. Sam knew immediately that the soldiers were Red Army. The loud and angry commands, the rapid popping sounds, and roar of the guns that the Red Army used told him so. His eyes were wide and glowing with fear, and marking the direction of the shots, he pushed the wheelbarrow as quickly as he could deeper into the forest and away from the path they had followed, searching for a place to hide. Sam stopped abruptly among a tight grove of aged oak trees and bushes and quickly parked the wheelbarrow among them, hiding it and its contents as best he could and covering it with leaves and branches. Then, pulling Molly behind him, he ran with her, deeper and deeper into the woods and away from the horrible sounds they had heard. The ground they ran through was plastered with a thick covering of damp fallen leaves, which littered the path where they ran and made the ground slippery and dangerous.

Sam pulled Molly down roughly next to him as he sat down hard at the base of a large oak tree. He held her close for a moment, and when he did, he could feel her ragged and panicked breathing against his ribs and his heart thumped in his chest and matched hers beat for beat. Using the fallen leaves that surrounded them, Sam covered Molly and himself as completely as he was able. Then he lay back down with Molly clinging to him desperately, amid the great gnarled roots of a massive oak tree and waited for the shots that still rang out to stop. The seconds seemed to pass like hours and, once, the heavy thud and crunch of running boots came close enough that they could feel the vibration in the earth where they lay hidden.

Finally, they heard a loud and persistent call of orders being shouted and the footsteps that had come so near retreated rapidly away from the spot where they were hiding. Soon they could hear the revving of truck and jeep engines and the crunch of leaves and gravel as the soldiers prepared to move out. It seemed as though the army of men moved along and packed up their gear in slow motion while Molly and Sam shivered in the cold dampness of their hiding place and waited in agonizing fear, not daring to move, while the loud bangs of occasional pistol shots could still be heard from somewhere close by. They lay rigid and silently hidden, barely breathing among the damp leaves and twigs that covered them, clinging to one another until they were certain that all the soldiers had left the area.

After a long while, when they had heard no sounds other than the birds and animals of the night, Sam stood up slowly and looked around as best he could. Peering through the darkness and listening intently, he brushed the leaves and dirt from his clothes and hair. When he was as sure as he could be that all was safe, he reached down for Molly and helped her to her feet. Immediately, as she rose stiffly from the ground, Molly adjusted the scarf she wore around her head and tucked her blond curls carefully underneath so that they were completely hidden from view. She was damp and chilled, and her hands shook uncontrollably and her legs felt as if they could not support her. Leaning against the oak tree, they stood there together listening closely and then Sam indicated with his hands that it was safe to continue on. Molly's nerves were on edge and she struggled to control the trembling she felt inside. She could tell that Sam was nervous too and she worked hard to keep up with his rapid footsteps. Molly's heart was still racing and her legs grew tired and sore and she slipped several times on the wet leaves at her feet but she did not complain, she only walked faster alongside Sam and tried to control her nerves and racing heart.

The night seemed to last forever, but there was no rest, only the deep unrelenting darkness that surrounded them and kept them hidden. Sam listened carefully and his senses were alert for any sound that did not belong in the forest. Retrieving the wheelbarrow from where he had hidden it among the trees, he led Molly not along the path that he had initially planned but along a secondary side path that he knew of through the deep forest. The night that blanketed them was pitch black and they could see no stars in the sky to light their way. It was slow going avoiding the roots and stones that tripped them up and made their progress difficult. They walked on and on endlessly through the brush and tangle of the dense forest, until just before dawn the groupings of trees along the narrow path began to thin out and then abruptly ended. They stepped out of the forest and into an open area of short grass and bramble.

In the dim light of early morning, Sam looked at the map he carried and Molly sank down on a nearby rock to rest for a moment. "Come Molly," Sam said encouragingly and offered her his hand. "Only a little more, I think we are almost there."

Molly stood up slowly and Sam began to push the wheelbarrow forward. Not far ahead, he turned it onto a narrow dirt lane that fell away sharply on their left into a deep green mist-filled valley. As the sun began to rise a little higher in the sky, they could make out the distinct lines of rooftops in the near distance. Soon, as they walked, the path widened and they were joined by other carts and wagons on their way to work or market in the town ahead. Molly and Sam spoke to no one and kept their eyes on the ground. Molly adjusted her headscarf often to make sure that her blonde hair was not visible. In the town, the press of people continued to grow and Molly and Sam were bustled along the busy main street as they searched for the first of two addresses that Harold had provided. *In case the people have moved away or are not at home*, Harold had told Sam when he had handed him the names and addresses for contacts along the way.

Over the top of the crowd, Sam could see the tall bell tower his father had described and headed in that direction, pushing the wheelbarrow carefully through the crowds. They stopped in front of a one-story red brick building covered in ivy and with tall black shutters that were closed tightly against the bright morning sun. Sam looked at Molly questioningly and shrugged his shoulders while he consulted the address on the paper once again.

"Wait here, Molly," he said with concern in his voice. "I am not sure about this. It looks to be boarded up. My father said he had not been here for a while. I am not sure what we will find."

Molly grabbed at Sam's coat sleeve. "Please be careful, Sam. Maybe we should just continue on." The anxiety showed in her voice and in her eyes.

"We need to wait for evening before we can travel further and we need rest and food," Sam replied with determination. Taking Molly's fingers in his, he released himself from the tight grasp she had on his sleeve. Then he turned, walked towards the front entrance to the building, and reached up to pull the bell rope that hung from a hook in the entryway. It was not long before the door opened a crack and in the darkness of the hallway, a small man in a shabby coat peeked around the side of the door.

"What do you want," snarled the man. "Can't you see that we are closed? What do you people think I am, a charity ward? Go away, go away! I have enough to do trying to take care of myself without being bothered by the likes of you!" he yelled, and spittle flew from his mouth. Then he stepped back and slammed the heavy wooden door in Sam's face.

Sam walked slowly back up the front path. He was filled with anger and rejection and he clenched and unclenched his fists as he returned to Molly. Molly had heard the horrible man's tirade and she said nothing even though she was frightened and angry and so very tired. She reached out to Sam and caressed his face, then in silence she handed Sam the map.

The second address Harold had given them proved to be a large and imposing factory built of grey stone with wide windows facing out onto a very busy street near the center of town. There were so many people coming and going along the streets where they walked that no one paid them any notice as they maneuvered slowly along the cobblestone road and into the drive that led to the factory. When they arrived at the address they had been looking for, Sam went up to the factory door and rang the bell. Quite soon, a smartly dressed young man arrived. "May I help you?" he inquired.

Sam tried to smile as he removed his cap and introduced himself. "I am Harold Gold's son, Sam," he explained. "Mr. Chernov will know my father and I have a note for him." Sam reached into his vest pocket and handed the young man an envelope.

"Wait here," said the young man, taking the envelope from Sam. Then he closed the door behind him. Several long minutes later, the factory door was reopened by a portly older man with a shining bald head. Next to him stood a tall thin woman with her brunette hair swept up into an elegant bun.

"Hello," said the older man reaching out to shake Sam's hand. "I am Peter Chernov and this is my wife, Agatha. Come in! Come in!" He stepped back allowing Sam and Molly to enter.

"You must be exhausted," Agatha said with concern. "Peter tells me you have walked all night."

"Agatha," said Peter, "you can ask all the questions you want later, for now let's get these two settled."

"Right, right," Agatha said with a blush, and smiled shyly at Molly.

"This way," said Peter, and he led them down a long corridor and through an intricately-carved wooden doorway. "Welcome to our home," he said as he ushered them in. The room they entered was warm and cozy. There were thick rugs on the shiny wood floor and lovely paintings lining the walls. A fire burned brightly in the fireplace and the large windows on either side of it were hung with heavy draperies. Molly and Sam followed Mr. Chernov through the room and out into a wide and sunlit hallway. Leading them to the staircase at its center, he pointed upward. "We have a small bed and sitting room upstairs and we have just had it readied for you," he said with a smile and waved Molly and Sam along in front of him.

"We hope you will be comfortable here," Agatha said following them up the stairs, and opening the door of the bedroom she invited them through. "This will be your room, your father has stayed in this room once or twice. He is such a lovely man. It is our pleasure to have you here, and we hope you will make yourselves comfortable." The room was bright and lovely. The walls were papered in creamy white sprinkled with soft pastels of sky blue flowers and moss green leaves and a small green-striped sofa took pride of place, nestled in a sunny bay window draped with cream-colored curtains that opened out onto the street below. The bed stood opposite the window and was large and inviting with blue and green down feather pillows and a comforter in the same green stripe as the sofa. Molly looked longingly at the bed.

"Thank you so much, for everything," she said, stifling a yawn as she removed her coat and sank down on the sofa.

"Your father explained everything in his letter. I know what an ordeal you have been through, you must rest now," said Peter. "We will see you later at dinner." And he ushered his wife from the room.

Molly and Sam slept the whole day through. When they awoke, the sun was already beginning to set. They washed and dressed and soon after, at six o'clock, a young maid dressed in black with an immaculate white apron and a frilly white cap perched on top of her head knocked softly on their door. Sam rose from the sofa and went to answer the knock. "Dinner will be served shortly, sir," she said and bobbed a little curtsey and closed the door behind her.

Molly and Sam, now well-rested and refreshed from their long nap, descended the stairway from their bedroom. As they did, they could smell the delectable aromas of roasting meat and the sweet smells of pies baking. "I hadn't realized how very hungry I am," said Sam.

At the bottom of the stairway stood Peter Chernov, who laughed when he heard what Sam had said. "You're in luck then," he answered. "My Agatha is a most wonderful cook. Come let's go in for dinner. I know it is almost time for you to be on your way. Let's get you fed and ready for the journey you must make," he added, and then, offering his arm to Molly, he escorted them into the dining room where a most wonderful meal was waiting to be served. The meal Agatha had prepared for them was indeed delicious. Thick slabs of roasted beef and gravy, mashed potatoes and buttered carrots and peas were piled on plates and passed around. When they had finished, the young maid removed the dinner plates, and Agatha returned from the kitchen carrying a warm berry pie and a bowl of thick whipped cream for dessert.

Molly and Sam felt revived and much more relaxed as they ate and they kept the conversation light and the details of their previous night on the road to themselves and the talk at the table was lively and warm.

"Do you know where you are headed?" asked Peter.

"A place called Peabody in Massachusetts," answered Sam. "Do you know of it?"

"I think I just might," replied Peter, "I think I just might at that." The name of the town sounded familiar to him. Suddenly remembering, he took a pencil from his coat pocket and a small folded piece of paper.

"Do you speak the language there?" inquired Agatha, who looked from Sam to Molly and back again.

"As a matter of fact we both do," said Sam with a proud smile. "I have studied several languages during my schooling and Molly has a love of books and reading and has learned quite a lot from her studies as well. That is not to say that we are experts," laughed Sam, "but I think we can make ourselves understood."

"I am so glad to hear that. It should be a little easier for you both then," replied Agatha with a grin, "and I wish you both so much luck as you travel along your way."

"Thank you so much," Sam and Molly said together. Then Sam pushed his chair back from the table and stood up and helped Molly to her feet. The two turned to their hosts and Sam said, "We are so very appreciative of your wonderful hospitality, but it really is time for us to be on our way."

"Yes," Molly added, "we can't thank you enough."

"You are so very welcome," Agatha said, and Peter added, "Yes, that is very true. It has been our pleasure. Your father has always treated me with honesty and respect in our business dealings and I am happy to be able to return the favor. I only wish we could do more," he said as Molly and Sam picked up their suitcase in the hallway and went to the door.

"Wait just a moment. Take this," Peter said to Sam, and handed him the piece of folded paper on which he had hurriedly written. "That is the address of an old friend of mine. I have not heard from him for a very long time, but I know that he owns a shoe and garment factory in Peabody not far from the port where you will be landing, as I understand. He may be able to help you in some way."

"We are grateful to you, sir," Sam said.

"Yes, very grateful," added Molly and she smiled sweetly at them both.

Agatha stepped forward and gave Molly a motherly hug. "Good luck," she said, and kissed Molly tenderly on the cheek.

CHAPTER 27

A Jar of Soup

After leaving the Chernov's home, Molly and Sam followed the road that led out of town. While consulting the map periodically, they decided to stay close to the main road, walking beside it and keeping near to the tree line in case they needed to quickly hide. Once again, they walked all night through the dense fog that grew thicker as the night went on, enveloping them in its heavy blanket and keeping them hidden. They moved slowly and continually forward, remaining unseen. It wasn't until early morning that the heavy fog began to lift and the beautiful spires of the great city of Odessa could be seen through the disappearing mist.

By noon, they arrived hungry and exhausted at the city port. Sam went to get the tickets and left Molly to wait with the luggage. While she waited, Molly watched the crowd grow larger and larger. There was such a press of people that Molly feared that Sam would not find her again. She could not leave her spot, so she removed the trunk and suitcase from the cart and placed them on the ground beside it and climbed up. She almost lost her balance as she stood up, but her head and shoulders were now well above the crowd that pushed and jostled around her. Never had she seen such a crush of people. From where she stood she could see that there were three ramps going up to an enormous black and white ship, the size of which she could never have imagined. There were four huge chimneys that billowed a haze of grey smoke that rose so high Molly had to tilt her head back to see their tops. Around the edge of the upper deck, a white railing circled and a bright steel anchor spread its enormous arms and gleamed like a star at the very front of the huge ship. Along the side, just below the chimneys, row upon row of round windows glistened in the afternoon sun.

As Molly watched, she could see that there were three large entrances standing open dark and wide along the side of the ship, each with a long wooden ramp with metal handrails leading up to them. On the first ramp, white uniformed sailors escorted ladies in magnificent clothes and feathered hats and their cigar-smoking husbands on board. As Molly watched them enter, she could see some of these same passengers waving to people below on the pier while standing along the guardrails at the top of the ship. On the second ramp, in the middle of the ship, the passengers' luggage was being loaded and on the third ramp, located at the very back of the ship, a more ragged and sad-looking group was moving slowly up the ramp and onto the vast ship.

Molly and Sam joined this third group, and when they finally reached the top of the ramp, they showed their tickets to a uniformed sailor standing up at a tall desk just inside the entrance. The sailor looked at their tickets closely and then took a very long look at Molly and Sam.

"You are Mr. and Mrs. Gold, are you not? " he questioned them.

"Yes, sir we are," replied Sam nervously.

With a grunt, the sailor stamped their tickets quickly, and without another word or look, pointed through a doorway and down the hallway where another uniformed sailor stood stiffly beckoning them forward and silently pointing the way to the nearby stairs. Down and down they went in the dimly lit stairwell. Molly was amazed how far down they went, their shoes clanking loudly on the metal stairs. Finally, at the very bottom of the stairway, stood two sullen and angry-looking sailors, each standing ramrod straight and rigidly tall in their immaculate white uniforms and white caps. The taller of the two pointed the way down a long hallway to the crowd of people who had come down the stairs ahead of Molly and Sam, counting each one as they passed by.

"That's it for the forward compartment," the sailor said, stopping Molly and Sam from moving forward. "We will commence with the loading of the aft cabin when this corridor is empty," he said in a deep and gravelly voice to the sailor who stood beside him. "Three hundred fifty souls for the forward cabin, three hundred fifty for the aft," he remarked while the other sailor wrote down the number in a large leather-bound book that he held. "At thirteen hundred we will commence filling the aft cabin." The tall sailor continued and looked down at the silver pocket watch he carried on a long chain.

Molly and Sam had waited patiently while the group before them moved along the corridor to their accommodations. The noise in the hallway was almost deafening as trunks and suitcases banged against the dark grey metal walls and shoes scraped against the grey metal floor. Above the din they could clearly hear the roar of people calling to one another in a variety of different languages filling the tight space. When the last person had disappeared into the forward cabin, the sailor turned to Molly and Sam.

"This way," the sailor said gruffly and pointed to another wide-open doorway several yards ahead. "The aft cabin," he said.

Sam led the way through the doorway and into the wide room, carrying the suitcase with him. Molly followed, carrying the wicker basket her mother had packed for them on her arm. They were the first to arrive in the cavernous space, and the first thing Sam and Molly noticed was a potbelly stove in the middle of the room. The warm glow of the stove drew them closer. Sam put down the suitcase and stretched out his cold hands to warm. As he did, he began to look around for the first time. The room they stood in was enormous and the walls were painted a dull grey, as was the floor. Lining the walls, two-tier bunk beds stood side by side by side and were each covered by a thin grey blanket.

Sam suddenly felt so very tired that his shoulders sagged forward. Emotions that he had not allowed to surface threatened to overwhelm him. They had left so much behind and there was so much that he could not control. His mind raced with questions. What were they to find when they arrived in Massachusetts, would there be work, a place to live? Sam shook his head to clear his thoughts. *I must be strong for Molly,* he said to himself. *Together we will see this through and no matter what, we will stay together and be strong, that will and must be enough.*

Sam bent down and picked up the suitcase he had carried. He could hear the loud chatter of voices coming along the hallway and then the doorway was filled with people pushing and shoving to enter the room. Molly's eyes scanned her surroundings, and then taking Sam's hand in hers, she quickly chose a bunk bed in the last row in the corner by the wall. "There may be a little more privacy here," said Molly, slumping down on the bottom bed. She was suddenly overcome with exhaustion and her head began to ache. She removed her scarf and coat, noticing as she did all the people who were streaming into the already crowded room. The sound of different languages, crying babies, men and women arguing, and children running, created a din of noise. It made Molly's head ache even more. She lay down on the bunk and pulled the flimsy blanket up to her chin. She closed her eyes and felt as if she were floating in a storm of deep grey mist.

Lying there, Molly could feel an achy soreness building up in her chilled body, and her heart and spirit ached too. She missed her parents and her home desperately. *Where were they headed and where exactly was Massachusetts anyway,* she wondered sadly, and *what would it be like there? Would there be work, friends, a decent place to live, would she and Sam ever see their parents again?* Molly's head throbbed terribly and her eyes filled with great salty tears. She pressed her fingers along her wet cheeks and wiped the tears away. She did not want Sam to know that she had been crying. It was her fault that they were here, after all, and so she rolled over on her side and faced the grey metal wall of the ship, pulling the blanket up to cover her ears. Soon exhaustion overcame her and she was fast asleep.

Sam sat on the edge of her bunk and watched Molly as she slept for a while, watching too the turmoil that surrounded him. Thousands of people were packed in tightly on board this ship and the noise was deafening. It would be like this at least for the next few weeks, depending on how long it took to make their crossing. Sam could almost not believe that Molly was able to sleep so soundly with the din as loud as it was, but he knew how tired out emotionally and physically she was and for a short while he sat beside her until he too climbed into his bunk and went to sleep.

Sometime during the early morning hours, Molly awoke. She felt feverish and her body ached. She tossed and turned for a while, trying to find a position of comfort on the thin and lumpy mattress. When Molly looked up, she could see the impression of Sam's body in the sagging mattress above her. She reached and pushed up on the bottom of the mattress and called softly, "Sam, Sam." Sam rolled over to the side of his bunk and looked down at Molly. "I think I may be sick, Sam," whispered Molly. "I'm so sorry." Her eyes filled with tears. The last thing Molly wanted was to be a burden to Sam. After all, it was because of her that they had been forced to make this journey. Molly's head pounded and her throat felt parched and dry. She lay back down and closed her eyes. Sam could see at once that his wife was not well. Her cheeks were red and her brow was hot when he touched her and she was shivering. Taking the blanket from his own bunk, he covered Molly with it.

"I'll get you some fresh water," he said, the concern growing in his voice.

For days and days, Molly's fever came and went, and with the fever came dreams and terrors. Molly tossed in her bunk and pulled at the covers when once again she remembered her escape from the soldier. In her mind she could hear again and again the shots, the pop, pop, pop from the pistol that had come so close. She could feel once more the frigid cold of the river and she thrashed as she tried to kick her way to the other side. She screamed and called out for help. Then the nightmare of what had happened at Mrs. Kinder's blended inseparably with the horrible remembrances of her experience with Sam in the forest. In her dreams she was running and falling and thick, heavy leaves covered her body and grabbed at her legs and mixed into her hair and she swatted at them repeatedly and tried to push them away. Then her dreams would return her once again to the frigid river water at the back of Mrs. Kinder's property and she moved about wildly, fighting the strong current and the pull of the choppy waves, reaching out to grasp the reeds along the shore. She shivered uncontrollably from cold and fear. Through her dreams she could hear repeated pistol shots ringing out loudly all around her and she pulled at her ears to make them stop.

"I'm here Molly, I'm here, I won't leave you. You are safe." Sam would try to soothe her as he sponged her with cool water. Sometimes Molly would hear a woman's voice through her fever delirium. And she would call out for her mother.

"There, there dear," said a strange woman's voice, and Molly would feel the coolness of a damp cloth against her forehead.

Then one late afternoon as Sam sat on the edge of his wife's bunk, Molly opened her eyes and smiled up at him. "I'm hungry," she said. Sam was so happy that he roared with laughter. The people in the surrounding bunks around them heard Sam's laughter and they came over to Molly's bunk to see what he found so funny.

"I see the little Mrs. is doing better," said a short round woman with a knot of grey hair on her head, pushing her way through the crowd. "I'm so glad of that. You've been very sick my dear, and your husband never left your side. You have a wonderful man there, that I know for sure," she said with a smile.

"Molly," Sam said. "This is Mrs. Petrova. She helped me take care of you."

"Thank you so much, Mrs. Petrova," Molly smiled weakly, laying back down on her wrinkled pillow.

"My wife tells me that she is hungry," Sam said happily.

"Yes!" replied Mrs. Petrova in a jolly happy voice. "But there's hardly a morsel to be found around here, and that is the truth."

"Sam," said Molly, "Look in the wicker basket, please." Molly had placed the wicker basket on a hook above her bed when she had first arrived on board, and there it still hung. In his concern over his wife Sam had forgotten all about it. Now he pulled back the checkered cloth and looked inside. There, wrapped in straw so it would not break, was a small jar of soup, and next to it was a loaf of bread and a shaker of salt. "Now all we need is a pot," said Sam, and he tore a large chunk off the loaf of bread Moriah had sent along and handed it to Molly.

"I can do that!" laughed Mrs. Petrova and she toddled over to her bunk and soon returned with a very large pot. "I have five children and a husband," she said with a chuckle. Sam poured the soup into Mrs. Petrova's pot. When he looked into the pot he could see that the amount of soup barely covered the bottom. Sam looked at Mrs. Petrova.

"That's all there is," he said sadly.

"Wait just a minute," Mrs. Petrova replied, and she reached into her apron pocket and took out two potatoes and a small shiny knife. She diced the potatoes finely, the small pieces falling into the pot one by one. "Let's see how that does," said Mrs. Petrova and she toddled over to the potbelly stove in the middle of the room and placed her soup pot on top of the flat lid. She stirred the soup slowly and as the aroma of the soup began to fill the room, people came to stand around her.

"I have an onion you could add," said a woman standing nearest the stove, and she went to her bunk and soon returned with a small onion. Mrs. Petrova diced it finely and added it to the simmering soup. "I have a carrot," said a little boy with a very dirty face. Mrs. Petrova diced that too and into the pot it went. "I have a little meat," said a tall man in the crowd. "I have some celery," said another. Soon everyone was adding to the pot of soup in whatever way they could, while Mrs. Petrova diced and stirred. With each new addition the contents of the pot increased until finally Mrs. Petrova could add no more without the risk of the pot spilling over completely. "It's ready!" she announced, when the soup had finished cooking. "First Molly and Sam, then the rest!" she said loudly. "After all, it was them that started us off with this marvelous meal." She filled two bowls to the top and brought them to Sam and Molly. "To Sam and Molly," she said with a laugh and she saluted them with her wooden spoon. Then she returned to the soup pot and began ladling out the soup bowl by bowl until everyone in the room had some.

There was silence in the room as everyone enjoyed the wonderful soup they had all created. Then, when all the bowls were licked clean and the soup pot was empty, a middle-aged man with a stubbly beard stood up. His name was Constantine Garibaldi. Reaching under his bunk, he removed a small battered case and, placing the case on the bunk, he clicked open the lock. He reached inside and lifted out his prize possession, a violin that Mr. Garibaldi lovingly called "Rosa." Taking a cloth from his pocket, he wiped down the shiny surface of the violin and lifted it to his chin and began to play. At first the music was soft and shy, but as more and more people began to tap their feet, Mr. Garibaldi increased his tempo and soon people were dancing and singing. Molly lay in her bunk and watched the merriment that filled the room while holding Sam's hand tightly as he sat beside her.

"Danke, Molly und Sam," exclaimed a happy couple as they danced by.

"Spasiba, spasiba, thank you," said a very old woman who had come over to Molly's bunk and she had kissed Molly loudly on her head.

"Look at what a marvelous thing you have done!" exclaimed Mrs. Petrova, returning to stand beside Molly and taking her hand. "My goodness! What a happiness you have given us, Mrs.!" and she beamed down at Molly and Sam. Molly smiled back and there were joyful tears in her eyes.

"Oh Mrs. Petrova," Molly said delightedly. "I will never forget tonight. Such a little soup grew to feed so many. I can't tell you how happy I am that we all were able to share together, but I think it is my mother who should be thanked even more than me. When she handed me the basket, she said she thought it would come in handy on my journey. I just never imagined in what way. I never got the chance to look inside, we were moving so fast. But when I woke up and saw the basket still waiting for me to open, I had a feeling what was inside. I have seen my mother do some marvelous things," Molly said, smiling widely. "She has always been a very special person." "It is an evening I will never forget!" Sam said excitedly and he kissed Molly heartily on the lips. "I've never seen anything like this before!" he added, with a huge grin on his face. "I am so thankful you are well again Molly."

Molly smiled warmly, and as she looked at Sam, she thought to herself, *I have*, and she hugged her knees to her chin as the memory of those long ago days when she had visited Mrs. Eos, Mrs. Teresky, Mrs. Lieben, and her wonderful Aunt Pearl returned to her mind.

"Thank you, Mama," she whispered to herself. "Even though I am far away, you are always with me." And she hugged herself a little closer, absentmindedly fingering the pearls she wore around her neck and swaying gently to the music. Her eyes were bright and sparkling with happiness and tears. Mr. Garibaldi was playing a waltz and couples twirled and glided slowly in the center of the room. Sam stood up from where he sat next to Molly and extended his hand to Mrs. Petrova.

"May I have this dance, my lady?" he asked and bowed elegantly. As he reached out for Mrs. Petrova, there was an enormous smile on his face.

"Oh my, sir!" giggled Mrs. Petrova and she blushed a deep pink. "I'd be proud to."

"You don't mind, my love?" he asked Molly, "I won't be long."

Molly smiled, she was so very happy. "Of course not," she said and lay back once again on her pillow.

Sam took Mrs. Petrova in his arms. *One, two, three. One, two, three.* Sam counted the beats of the music. Then to the beautiful sound of Mr. Garibaldi's violin he waltzed Mrs. Petrova gracefully away.

CHAPTER 28

Arrival

Several weeks later on a cold and blustery early December morning, Molly and Sam stood closely together among many other passengers along the crowded guardrail on the top level of the ship. Huddled against the cold, they stared out across a vast and icy Atlantic sea as they passed many hundreds of nautical miles away from New York harbor. They had been told by the officer of the deck that somewhere through the heavy mist, in the deep grey distance and in a tiny protected harbor, stood the Statue of Liberty. They had often heard of this majestic statue from their fellow passengers and they knew it as a mighty symbol of freedom and welcome for all. Behind them in the crowd a loud male voice suddenly yelled, "America! The land of the free!" Another voice yelled out in response, "The land of plenty," and then the clear and strident voice of a young woman, "The land of safety!" Everyone, rich and poor alike, clapped together in excited appreciation.

Many long hours later in the dim light of early morning, Molly and Sam watched anxiously once again as their ship was met at the entrance to Boston harbor by a fleet of tiny tugboats that blew their horns loudly. They pulled the great ship along through a rough sea and the windswept coast, navigating her slowly, to her berth inside the bustling port. In the heavy fog that surrounded them, the blasts of the tugboat's horns and the commotion of the passengers on board sounded muted and far away. Then, suddenly, the engines of the great ship stopped and the constant vibration and mechanical noises that had been ringing in their ears and thrumming beneath their feet for the last few weeks were no more. Just as suddenly they heard another kind of loud metallic banging, as the crew made the ramps ready for disembarkation.

First the luggage compartment was emptied, and men on the pier and along the ramps ran back and forth sorting and piling suitcases and trunks. Then the first class passengers were allowed to disembark and they went down the ramp at the front of the great ship the way they had entered: elegantly dressed in velvet jackets and furs. Mrs. Petrova's five children pushed and shoved in order to be first at the top of the third ramp, and when the gate opened in front of them, they dashed one after the other down the ramp to the pier below. Mrs. Petrova followed as fast as she could, panting and trying to catch her breath.

"Come here to me at once!" she called to her children, her eyes scanning the growing crowd anxiously. Grabbing one of her sons by the collar when he ran past, she turned around to catch another of her children when she noticed Molly and Sam coming down the ramp. Sam held the suitcase and the wicker basket that Molly carried on her arm bounced between them.

"Stay right here Sergei and don't move an inch!" Mrs. Petrova hissed to her son. Releasing his collar, she then opened her arms wide as she turned to greet Sam and Molly. "Oh, my dears, I guess that this is goodbye," she said sadly, giving Molly a kiss on the cheek.

"We wish you the best of luck. You know we do," Mrs. Petrova continued, a small tear in the corner of her eye.

"Thank you, Mrs. Petrova, for everything," Molly said, returning the older woman's motherly kiss. "I hope we meet again."

"May the rest of your journey be an easy one," said Mrs. Petrova with a sniffle.

"Yours as well," said Sam, "and thank you." And he gave Mrs. Petrova a quick hug. Sam picked up the suitcase and took Molly's hand. "We must be going now," he said.

"Well goodbye my dears!" Mrs. Petrova called as Sam and Molly disappeared into the crowd. The last thing Molly saw of Mrs. Petrova was her waving goodbye with one hand and frantically grabbing for her children with the other.

Sam and Molly fought their way through the crowd to retrieve their trunk. Nearby the luggage area stood a barn-like structure with an open front. The sign over the opening read *Livery Stable* in faded gold letters. Inside and at the far end of the building there were several lovely carriages. In the middle were large wagons and farm carts, and piled in a corner were several small wheelbarrows. Sam approached the front of the building and took a blue leather money pouch that Mrs. Kinder had given him out of his pocket and counted his remaining bills and coins. He stood there for a moment and then, with Molly following close behind, he entered the livery stable and looked around carefully. He wondered what it would cost to purchase a small wheelbarrow like the one they had left behind when they boarded the ship.

From the back of the stable he heard, "Hello, what can I help you with?" Sam turned towards the sound of the voice, which belonged to a tiny man with bulging muscles and a huge moustache. He was walking towards them out of the shadows at the back of the large room.

"Is it possible to buy a small wheelbarrow?" asked Sam hopefully.

"Well let's see," replied the little man and he twisted his moustache with his fingers.

"We're not really in the business of selling things," he went on a bit gruffly. "Mostly it's just rental we are known for, you know, but as you can see we do have a few more wheelbarrows than we may need ... make me an offer," he said hesitantly, and he stepped in a little closer to Sam.

"Well," Sam hesitated, "What do you think is fair?" he asked.

The little man continued to twist his moustache as he thought, and then he said, "I paid five silver pieces for each of the wheelbarrows you see here," and he pointed to the corner of the room where the wheelbarrows were stored. "I need to make some profit. How's about nine?"

Sam looked intently at the tiny man. "What about seven?" bargained Sam.

"What about seven-fifty?" returned the man, starting to twist his moustache more violently.

"Done!" said Sam and he reached inside the pouch his father had given him and handed the coins over to the little man and shook his hand. "Thank you," he said sincerely.

"Come with me," replied the man, "and I will help you pick one out and see you on your way. Call me Tony."

"Thank you again, Tony," replied Sam, and he followed the man to where the wheelbarrows sat in a corner.

"This should work well for you," Tony said. "I actually just oiled the wheels on this one last week, musta guessed somehow I would be doing business with it one way or the other, and now it works like a charm." Tony took the handles of the wheelbarrow and pulled it smoothly and easily back and forth across the dirt floor. "See what I mean," he said, and he offered the handles to Sam. Sam pushed the wheelbarrow easily out the door of the building and into the yard in front of the livery stable and began to load up the trunk and suitcase. Then he turned and handed the little man a folded piece of paper. "Can you tell me how to get to this address?" he asked, pointing to the paper.

"It ain't too far," said the man. "Just a few miles or so. Follow the main road out of town and head south, you'll soon see the signs that will lead you to Peabody. Once you're there you'll need to ask for more directions. I've never spent much time there before, you see. Good luck," said the man and shook Sam's hand again. "Pleasure doin' business with ya." Then he turned away and walked back inside the building.

At first the main road led Molly and Sam along the waterfront, and it was a struggle pushing the wheelbarrow through the remaining crowds. The winds that blew off the water were bitter and the waves sent salty spray in the air. Molly pulled her coat tighter around her and drew her collar up to cover her ears. Sam stopped for a moment. He let go of the wheelbarrow's handles and placed his arms around Molly's shoulders. Looking deeply into her eyes, he brushed a soft kiss against her lips.

"Well, we are here," he said with a small laugh. Molly nestled closer, gathering courage from being in Sam's embrace.

"We are here," she replied. "I wonder how far it really is and what we will find when we arrive in Peabody."

"The man in the livery stable told me that it is only a few more miles or so from here. We should find it easily as there are road signs along the way that we can follow," Sam said encouragingly. But deep in his heart, Sam wondered the same thing, *What would they find in Peabody?* At least he hoped that there would be a place where they could stay for the night. As the thoughts came to him, large and heavy snowflakes began to fall. He looked up at the sky overhead and then he turned to face Molly, giving her hand a squeeze and reaching down to pick up the handles of the wheelbarrow and pushing it forward again slowly. For some time they did not speak, both lost to their own private thoughts, not ready or willing to share their deep worries and fears of the unknown. They followed the road for quite a while, and as they walked, a heavier snow began to fall, clinging to the damp grey trees and making the going harder. Sam noticed the signpost first: *Peabody 1 mile*, it read. "We're so close Molly, only a little bit more," said Sam encouragingly. Molly smiled at Sam as her eyelashes twinkled with the sparkling snowflakes. "So close," she said. Then taking one of the wheelbarrow handles as Sam took the other, they pushed it together towards the town of Peabody.

CHAPTER 29

Peabody, Massachusetts

The streets of the town of Peabody were almost deserted when Molly and Sam arrived. There were piles of dirty snow along the gutters that had been shoveled from entrances and sidewalks, and the main street was a sea of mud and ice. The buildings that lined the rutted road where they walked were shuttered against the winds and built closely together. They appeared dark and foreboding in the dim and misty light of the day. Molly and Sam huddled together against the frigid air as they walked slowly along, struggling with the heavy and ungainly wheelbarrow that they pushed before them. It was a while before they were able to find anyone to ask directions of and so they walked the icy streets for a time, hoping to find someone to talk to and wondering over and over if they were going in the right direction. Through the swirling snowdrifts they could see, not far ahead, a front door open and an old woman in a wool shawl began sweeping away the snow from her tiny front porch.

When Sam called out to her and asked her about the address he and Molly were looking for, she pointed over her shoulder and peering at them through the fast-falling snowflakes, she quickly replied, "At the end of the road, can't miss it." Shivering, she pulled her shawl tighter about her, then took her broom and went inside and closed the door.

The road they followed veered to the left and, as Molly and Sam turned the corner, they could see an imposing grey brick building at the end of the street. The sign over the doorway in black letters read *S. Pimms Garments and Shoes.* Sam and Molly went up to the door and knocked. The humming and buzzing coming from the factory was so loud that Sam and Molly were sure no one could hear them, so they pushed open the door and went inside. The air inside the building was hot and stifling when they entered and filled with tiny dust moats of lint and thread. They stood inside a long and dimly-lit hallway. It took a moment for their eyes to adjust to the change of light inside. Sam brushed the snow from the shoulders of his wool jacket and removed his knit cap and gloves, then went up to the secretary who sat at a tall desk just inside the doorway. The secretary was a very skinny woman with silver grey bobby pins sprouting out of her untidy bun. She was busy writing in a ledger and did not hear Sam and Molly when they came in.

"Ahem," said Sam, then a little louder, "*Ahem.*"

The secretary looked down at Sam from her tall desk. He had startled her by this different sound and she looked at him irritably. "Yes?" she said in an unwelcoming voice. She stared directly at Sam and began pulling her black-rimmed glasses down her very long nose. "What do you want?" she inquired angrily. The secretary did not like being disturbed at her work, particularly by strangers.

Sam reached into his pocket and handed the note he carried from Mr. Chernov to the secretary. "For Mr. Pimms," he said simply. The secretary took the note from Sam and looked at it closely.

"Wait here," she said in an aggravated tone. Then she stood up, turned on her heel and walked away, her shoes making clackety noises across the dusty wooden floor. She vanished into the darkness of the hall beyond. Once again, Molly and Sam waited. Would Mr. Pimms be able to help them, they wondered, and if not, where would they go?

Mr. Pimms approached them from out of the dark shadows of the hallway. He proved to be a man of medium stature, slightly paunchy with dull silver hair circling the sides of his head. He was wearing a grey shirt and black pants held up with black suspenders and his black leather shoes were covered with a fine dust.

"Well hello," said Mr. Pimms in a somewhat annoyed tone. "I just read the letter you brought from Peter Chernov. He was a business associate of mine, but I have not been in contact with him for a very long time," he continued. "He speaks very highly of you and your father."

"Thank you, sir," replied Sam. Molly looked at Mr. Pimms and smiled shyly.

"So," he went on, not really listening to Sam or noticing Molly where she stood beside her husband. Mr. Pimms consulted the letter he held in his hands again. "You are a tailor by trade and familiar with the use of a sewing machine." He went on ignoring Sam's responses.

"It just so happens," Mr. Pimms continued, "you are in a bit of luck. I have recently lost my best stitcher in my garment factory. I wouldn't normally take such a chance on someone I really don't know, but since Peter spoke so highly of you, I am willing to give you a try. I can't promise you anything, just that we'll try you out and see how you do. In the meantime, you can stay at this address." He handed Sam a card. "It is not far from here, just around the corner. Out the front entrance and head right. Ring the bell of number three and someone will let you in."

Molly was so relieved. Sam would have work and they would have a place to stay, at least for a while. Sam reached his hand out to Mr. Pimms. "I won't let you down, sir," he said, smiling widely with relief and happiness.

"I'll see you on the sewing room floor at six a.m. sharp tomorrow," said Mr. Pimms and he gave Sam's hand a very quick shake. "Be prompt," he said gruffly, "or I will fire you on the spot." And he turned away abruptly, disappearing into the shadows of the hallway.

Sam was thrilled with the prospect of a job and eager to get started, but he wondered to himself about Mr. Pimms and what type of boss he would prove to be. *I'll never be late or give you cause to fire me. No sir!* Sam thought to himself while he replaced his cap and gloves. The secretary took no notice of Sam and did not respond when he thanked her quickly as he passed her desk. Then taking his wife firmly by her hand, he opened the factory door for her. They were immediately met by a rush of wind and snow that swirled around their ankles and blanketed the entry floor. Sam closed the door quickly behind them and once again they found themselves alone in a white and frozen world. Molly paused for a moment on the factory stairs and reached for her husband. There was a look of pride in her eyes and she placed her arms around Sam's neck and held him close.

The address that Mr. Pimms had given them was several long blocks away from the factory. In the neighborhood that Molly and Sam walked through, they could not help but notice that all the houses looked exactly the same with peeling paint and sagging front porches. The houses were very tall and built so close together that there was hardly any space between them at all, and their pointed roofs seemed to block out the sun. "This is it," Sam said to Molly, stopping in front of one of the houses that stood in the middle of the block, and consulting the address on the card Mr. Pimms had given them. "Number three," he said with relief. "We are here." Together they pushed the wheelbarrow through the deep snow of the sidewalk and up the uneven front walkway. Leaving it hidden in a clump of snow-covered bushes for safety, they went up the front stairs of the peeling four story wooden building and rang the bell of number three. The building was so very old that the snow-covered floorboards groaned from their footsteps as they climbed the sagging wooden steps. Sam knocked loudly on the front door. Several minutes later, the front door creaked open and a young girl with a mop of curly brown hair looked up at them with wide eyes. She held a baby on her hip.

"We are here about the room," Molly said, bending down slightly to speak to the girl.

"Just a moment, I'll get my mom," she replied without a smile, and went up the stairs to the third floor carrying the baby in her arms. Molly and Sam heard the girl call to her mother loudly when she had entered her apartment, then they heard the baby start to scream.

"Give that child some milk will you, and then put her down for her nap while I go answer the door! Oh what a day, what a day," moaned a woman's voice from three floors above.

Molly and Sam could hear the woman's heavy tread as she came down the stairs. First to come into view were the woman's dingy black boots, then her long grey dress covered by a stained apron with very large pockets. "Are ye come about the room?" the woman asked. She stood on the bottom step and although she was very short, her girth seemed to fill the stairway.

"Mr. Pimms sent us," said Sam, removing his hat and holding it in his hands. "I am Sam Gold and this is my wife, Molly."

"Well come along, come along. I haven't got all day," the woman said. "If Mr. Pimms sent you, that's all I need to know." She turned around abruptly and led them down a short dark hallway. "Here 'tis," she said, and reaching into her deep pockets she pulled out a dull brass key and handed it to Sam. Sam placed the key in the lock and with a click and a push the door opened. From where they stood in the darkness of the doorway, the apartment looked tiny and cramped. The woman stood just behind them in the hallway and reached into her pockets once again. "Here, Mrs.," she said and handed Molly several candles, a small loaf of bread and a piece of cheese wrapped in a cloth. "Not much I reckon," she said with a sigh.

"We are very grateful," said Molly, "We have come such a long way ..."

"Now, now dear. I wish I had a penny for every time I heard that tale," said the woman. "I am the caretaker here for Mr. Pimms. My name is Mary, Mary Begley. I've been taking care of things around here for as long as I can remember. I've seen many like you come and go. Most likely I will again. Now I'll let you two get settled." Without a further word she walked away, her heavy tread echoing down the hallway. Molly was a bit stunned by the briskness of Mrs. Begley. She had been hoping that she would be warmly welcomed to her new home, but that was clearly not the case, and her hands shook a little as she stepped in front of Sam and pushed the door of the apartment open a little wider. She stepped tentatively inside what would be their new home.

While Sam went to get the trunk and suitcase, Molly looked around. Her eyes had to adjust to the darkness and she could barely make out the outlines of the windows and door. She lit one of the candles that Mrs. Begley had given her and placed it on the wobbly table that sat in the center of the room, her surroundings coming into focus. From where she stood next to the table, Molly could see the entire apartment. It was narrow and rectangular in shape. To her immediate left were an iron bed frame and a small chipped metal cabinet. There were two mismatched wooden chairs tucked around the table. In front of her was a window that looked out on the dirty painted wood siding of the house next door, and pushed up against the window frame stood a black wood-burning stove, its surface caked with grease. In the corner stood a cracked and pitted grey stone sink.

The room she had entered was not the home that Molly had foolishly hoped for; it was old and well worn and the air inside it smelled like cooked cabbage and dirty clothes. She struggled with the childish feelings of disappointment that rose up inside her and threatened to overwhelm her. She added several pieces of kindling to the open stove and then some rolled up newspaper that lay in a crumpled pile next to it on the floor, and began to light the stove with matches that lay on the counter. She filled a pot with water from the tap for tea, and while she waited for Sam and for the water to boil, Molly set about dusting off the table and chairs. She placed the bread and cheese in their wrappings on the table. Salty tears filled her eyes. She pulled her wool coat more tightly around her and sank down onto a chair at the table. She was tired and cold and suddenly so very sad that her heart ached to return home to her parents and the life she had known. Everything was new and different and the future was once again unknowable, would she ever see her loved ones again? Her cheeks were wet with the tears that seemed to be her constant companion, but she brushed them away upon hearing Sam in the hallway. When he came in, his cheeks were red and his coat was covered with snow. He pushed the trunk and suitcase inside.

"Well," he asked, "What do you think?"

Molly's eyes glistened and she smiled at her husband. "We are here, we are safe, and the rest will come." Molly helped her husband remove his coat and hung it on a hook by the door. "Come," she said and led him to the table.

CHAPTER 30

The Factory

Sam rose early the next morning well before first light. He shaved his scruffy beard and combed his hair. *First impressions are important,* he thought, as he checked his reflection in the cracked mirror above the sink. Then with a quick glance at his pocket watch he kissed Molly goodbye and went out the door.

For a long while after Sam had gone, Molly lay in bed with the covers pulled up to her chin. She almost could not move. For the first time in her life she felt all alone and once again tears filled her eyes and ran freely down her cheeks. The sadness and loneliness that she felt threatened to overwhelm her. *I can't let myself wallow in self pity,* she thought. *I must get up and get busy and not allow myself time to think.* She forced herself to sit up and wiped her eyes with the corner of her coverlet. As she did she remembered the voice of her mother-in-law that last day in the tailor shop. Stella had said bravely, *While I wait, I work.* Molly looked around her and knew what she must do. In the dim light of the early morning she could see spider webs in the corners of the ceiling above her head and the windows and stove were dull and dingy with grime. Getting out of bed, Molly dressed quickly and made herself some hot tea. She finished the last of the cheese and bread that Mrs. Begley had given her and then she walked down the hall in search of the bathroom that all residents on the floor shared. Outside the bathroom door was a broom, mop, and bucket, and on a shelf in a closet nearby she found a stack of cleaning cloths and soap.

Molly placed the soap and some of the cloths in the bucket and carried the broom and mop with her when she returned to her apartment. She stood in the doorway and looked around the narrow room. *Where to start*, she thought to herself, *everything needs a good cleaning from top to bottom.* She looked slowly and critically at the walls, floor, and ceiling once more. *So that's just where I'll start.* Molly covered her hair with a scarf and then she dragged a chair over to the middle of the room and stepped up on the seat. She could just reach the ceiling with the broom and she swept it clean of dead spiders and dust. Filling the bucket from the sink, Molly added the rest of the hot water from the kettle and began washing down the walls with a rag.

The wallpaper that covered the walls had at one time been a pattern of red roses and green leaves. Molly could tell it had once been fairly pretty but the colors had darkened and faded over time and now all her cleaning did was make the roses look brown and wilted and even worse than they had before. She replaced the filthy water in her bucket over and over as she washed the window and floor. Little by little the color of the water in the bucket grew lighter. Eventually Molly was satisfied with her work, and everything in the little apartment had been swept and washed. Sliding the trunk into the tiny kitchen, she put her dishes on the shelves, hung her pots on the wall above the stove and made up her bed with the linens and quilts she had brought from home. Even though the colors of the quilt were bright and vibrant, they looked dull and dreary and washed out in the dim light of the room, as if all her efforts had been for naught. Even so,

Molly was satisfied that everything in her home was as clean as could be and now with her work finished, she put on her coat and wrapped a clean scarf around her head. Taking up her wicker basket, she left the apartment, closing the door behind her.

Her short list of errands and her natural curiosity drew Molly outside to see the neighborhood where she now lived. The cold air felt refreshing on her sweaty skin as she walked down the path. It was good to be out of the apartment, even though the sky threatened another snowfall. Mrs. Begley's children were outside playing and throwing snowballs at one another in the yard, their bare hands red and chapped as were their exposed knees and dirty cheeks. It was still early afternoon and as Molly walked away she looked back over her shoulder once more, making sure of the house numbers so she would not lose her way when she returned. She followed the main road into town, her wicker basket swinging on her arm. There were very few people on the streets, and Molly thought it must be because all the people who lived in the town seemed to be working one way or the other for Mr. Pimms.

Turning the corner and crossing the muddy wide street, Molly pushed open the door of the post office. Going up to the counter, she bought a three-penny stamp and a postcard. The employees behind their desks looked sad and overworked and even though she tried to be friendly, her attempts were totally ignored. So she put her purchase in her basket, said thank you to no one in particular, and went out the door. A few blocks away, Molly heard the tinkle of bells over her head when she pushed opened the door of the grocery shop. For a moment her heart gave a little leap as she imagined herself entering the tailor shop again. Then she heard a sharp voice.

"Close the door, it's freezing in here!" said a very thin old man with a tattered wool scarf around his neck and a flattened grey hat on his head. "Oh! Excuse me. I'm sorry!" exclaimed Molly, awakening from her short daydream. Molly stepped up to the counter. "Please," she said to the old man somewhat shyly and speaking a bit slowly, "I would like a pint of milk, six eggs, one pound of flour and one small chicken."

The thin old man brought Molly her order quickly and without speaking. She placed a few silver coins on the counter and hoped it would be enough. The new money was strange to her and she was a bit uneasy with it. The old man counted out the coins and dropped them in the register, shutting the till loudly, then he picked up his newspaper, and without saying another word or looking again at Molly, he disappeared behind its pages.

CHAPTER 31

An Unexpected Explanation

Molly walked slowly back to the apartment building. Her basket was filled with her purchases, but she felt empty inside. *How strange to be in a new country*, she thought to herself. *Everything is so different from home. Will I ever find a place for myself in this cold grey place?* Molly's thoughts were drawn back to her village of Zhitomir and those she loved. Reaching inside the neck of her dress for the pearl necklace that her mother had given her, she felt their warm smoothness against her fingers and their presence around her neck helped calm her racing mind. The wind began to blow stronger, swirling large snowflakes about her ankles. Molly could almost visualize Moriah standing before her, her long brown hair flowing in the breeze. *You are like the wind always pushing me forward. Your strength holds me up, you have given me wings to fly and have kept me safe,* Molly whispered to her mother with her heart. *I love and miss you more than I can say.* Listening closely, she could almost hear her mother's voice calling back to her through the icy wind: "We are together, we are safe, we will be together again," her mother's voice seemed to whisper.

Molly's thoughts then flew to the memory of the voices of all the women who had called out to her when last she had worn the spectacles. She could almost hear them again calling out to her on the growing wind. "I am not alone," she said aloud to the empty street; the sound of her own voice gave her courage. She pulled her coat tighter around herself, bent her head into the gusty breeze, and headed back in the direction she had come towards her new home. Molly was almost happy preparing dinner in the tiny kitchen, the memories of her mother and the voices of thirty-five women had helped buoy her confidence and gave her the strength to go on.

When Sam came in from work they enjoyed a hot meal together and, that evening, as Molly washed the dinner dishes in the sink, Sam told her about his day. He was very happy to have a job and grateful to Mr. Pimms for trying him out. "They started me out in the sewing room. There are rows and rows and rows of sewing machines … and the noise!" said Sam. "There are at least one hundred people who work in that room. Mostly I work finishing the garments that come from the basting room, and before they reach the basting area, the fabric is cut in another enormous room, and that is just the clothing factory! Next to the building I work in there is another factory also owned by Mr. Pimms, where the shoes and boots are made. It seems to me that all the people in this town are employees of Mr. Pimms in one way or another," Sam continued.

At the sink, with her back to Sam, Molly smiled to herself. *I had a feeling that was why the streets were so empty; maybe that's why everyone seems so sad here. Can it be that one man can affect the lives of so many people?* she thought, her eyes growing large with the realization.

"It's funny," Sam continued, "all the clothing that Pimms manufactures is grey and all the shoes they make are black. I wondered why, so when the bell rang at the end of the day, I walked home with the man who worked beside me. His name's Schroeder, Thomas Schroeder. He had been helpful to me during the day with any problems I had, so I was comfortable asking him a few questions. He told me that many years ago, Mr. Pimms's father had a shoe factory here, and when he married, his wife's family let him run the garment factory they owned as well. That Mr. Pimms, I believe his first name was Simon, became very prosperous with his two businesses. He employed large numbers of people and those people needed places to live. So he began buying land and building housing for his employees. He established a bank, a school, a grocery store, and a post office and more. Then he built a large mansion on top of the hill for his wife and son. From what Thomas told me, the elder Mr. Pimms took pride in the town he had built, and he maintained it well. He was also very proud of his son and trained him to take over his businesses one day. It was a good time then, the factory prospered and people were happy.

"Then one day the luck of the Pimms family seemed to run out. The elder Mr. Pimms died suddenly and then his wife a short time later. Within that same year, the younger Mr. Stewart Pimms's dear wife died in childbirth and their baby too. Mr. Stewart, who had always been sunny and carefree, Thomas told me, retreated to his mansion, and when he finally emerged many weeks later, he was a changed man. Because the younger Mr. Pimms had inherited the whole town, everything changed around here as well, Thomas said. All the younger Mr. Pimms cares about now is money. He holds on to everything he can to make a profit and never spends a dime. Since all the color went out of his life, he refuses to make anything in his factories whether it be garments or shoes that is not grey or black."

Molly returned to the table carrying two cups of tea. She put one down in front of Sam, then took a seat across from him. "What a sad story," Molly said, "two men who affected the lives of so many people, one who shared his prosperity for the good of everyone, and the other who has lost the will to give and so those around him suffer."

"You are wise beyond your years, Molly," said Sam, looking closely into the depths of his wife's beautiful blue eyes.

Molly took a sip of her tea and placed the cup down in its saucer. "Is it wise to stay in such a place, Sam? Do we really want to live here forever?" Molly's eyes glistened and she dabbed gently at them with the corner of her apron. At that moment, Molly felt a deep longing for the feel of her mother's arms around her once more. Seeking comfort, she reached out to hold Sam's hand and held it tightly.

Sam looked at Molly intently as he searched for the right words. Really, there was nothing to be done about the circumstances in which they were living; only the passing of time would unveil what their lives would be. "Let's take each day, Molly," he said and smiled at her tenderly. "It may not be forever, my love," he added softly, "but for now."

CHAPTER 32

Mr. Garibaldi

The winter days passed slowly for Molly. Each day Sam left early for work and did not arrive home until evening and, as there were still no jobs available at the factories, Molly spent most of the day by herself. After tidying up the small apartment, she would put on her coat, take up her wicker basket, and go about her few errands. This particular morning, Molly had a postcard to mail, but she debated even going out because of the snow squall she could see out her window. However, the thought of staying inside all day was not something she cared to do. *I'll just go out for a little while*, she thought to herself. She opened the door of the little metal cabinet next to her bed and reached in for a pair of woolen socks. At the very back of the drawer was the felt bag that held the spectacles. Molly took out the felt bag and held it in her hands. The material was soft and warm and Molly could feel the hard metal of the spectacle frame beneath. She slipped the spectacles in her apron pocket, finished dressing, and went out the door. As usual, the streets were mostly empty. The deep snow muffled Molly's footsteps and the sky was a deep pearly grey, and it seemed as if she walked in a silent world.

Entering the post office, Molly said, "Good afternoon" when she reached the counter. Other than the sound of typing, there was no response. Molly placed her postcard in the mail slot, pushed open the front door, and went out. The door to the post office closed slowly behind her with a loud click. Molly stood in the covered entryway for a moment and adjusted the collar of her coat. *It is cold here in every way*, thought Molly once again. *Can the sky get any darker, will there ever be sunshine again?*

Almost without realizing it, Molly reached inside her coat and drew out the felt bag from her apron pocket. She untied the red string and slipped the spectacles from the bag. She looked at them for a moment as they lay glinting softly in her palm, beckoning her to try them on. Then she slipped them slowly on her nose. Still standing in the entryway of the post office, she looked left in the direction she had come. Nothing happened. The shift of focus that Molly was expecting did not occur. She removed the spectacles and wiped them off on her apron. *Maybe I'm too old for them any more*, thought Molly sadly, but instead of returning the spectacles to their bag, Molly put them on again and this time she looked right. The change was rapid and dramatic. Molly saw a kaleidoscope of swirling colors and heard sweet angelic music that invited her in and propelled her forward. Her heart swelled with happiness, a happiness that she had not known for a long time, and she was drawn away from the post office and down the street in the direction of the music.

Crossing the muddy road, Molly could see a tall man with a stubbly beard and a long tattered coat standing on the corner. He was playing the violin and before him on the ground was a battered old case, its lid left open for tips despite the almost completely deserted street. The music that he played was lovely, sweet, and entrancing. Molly's feet fairly floated along the pavement and as she drew nearer the vividly bright colors she had first noticed seemed to swirl around the man, encircling him in long thin ropes and large thick strands of rainbow colors as he played. Molly removed the spectacles and put them in the felt bag as she listened to the strains of music wafting in the cold breeze. She had a few pennies left in her pocket and she could see that even though the man played so beautifully, he had very little money. She walked up to the case and dropped in her pennies. "Thank you, sir," said Molly, "your music is so lovely." She looked up at him for the first time. She recognized him at once.

"Mr. Garibaldi!" exclaimed Molly, "Do you remember me? From the ship and the soup?" Molly asked.

"How could I ever forget, Missus. That was a truly special night. I will remember it for a very long time," said Mr. Garibaldi.

"How do you happen to be here in town, Mr. Garibaldi?" inquired Molly smiling up at him.

"I am a traveling musician, Missus. I have a wanderlust and it takes me far and wide."

"I envy you," said Molly sadly. "Your travels allow you to see all the colors in the world. All I see is grey, and it is icy cold and so lonely here." Mr. Garibaldi bent down and removed Molly's few pennies from his violin case. He tried to place them in her hands, but Molly refused. "Those are for you," she said.

"Missus," said Mr. Garibaldi, "when life is grey we must find color wherever we can." He picked up his violin and began to play.

"Thank you," said Molly and she stood there for a short while listening to the beautiful music and thinking about what he had said. Mr. Garibaldi was immersed in the music he made and he just nodded and continued on with his playing. "Goodbye," said Molly, "safe travels." It was difficult to leave; the music touched her heart and filled an empty space deep inside. Mr. Garibaldi was lost to his music and did not seem to see her anymore and so she slowly turned away and began her walk back home.

Preparing dinner that evening, Molly thought about what Mr. Garibaldi had said, and she wondered (not for the first time) how to create color in this dark grey world in which she now lived. *Happiness is a kind of color*, she thought. *My happiness is the warm amber of honey, the very color I saw when I first met Sam. The sadness I feel whenever I miss my family is a deep stormy violet, and my memories of home are rosy pink. That is my rainbow, and for now I guess I have to make that enough.*

Molly had told Sam about meeting Mr. Garibaldi in the street and the delightful music he played, and they had laughed together as they remembered that special evening on the ship when everyone had added something to the pot of soup and listened to the simple beauty of Mr. Garibaldi's wonderful music that made people sing and dance. Sam stood up and took Molly in his arms and hummed a little tune as he danced her around the apartment floor. Then he bent down to kiss his wife and noticed that there were tears in her eyes.

"I wish we could stay in each others' arms like this forever," Molly whispered and kissed her husband deeply. "I am so alone here."

"I know it is hard for you here Molly, but we can't leave right now. We need money and a place to live. Be thankful it's me working in that factory and not you. Mr. Pimms is a tyrant. He walks the entire factory each day with his supervisors, up and down the rows with his hands behind his back, checking and rechecking and never satisfied. My quota seems to increase weekly, but it's Mr. Pimms who makes the money, not me." Sam was bitter and after only such a short time at the factory.

Molly felt guilty for burdening him. She knew how hard Sam worked and she ached to help him in any way she could. "I wish I had something to do that could help in some way. I just don't know what it is right now since there is nothing available for me at the factories or in town," Molly said apologetically.

"Molly," replied Sam, "you have always been a hard worker and quick learner. I don't know what your path is while we are here in this place, but

I do know that it will become clear as you go along." Sam wished with all his heart that he could ease his wife's sadness and take away her loneliness. He hoped that whatever that answer was, it would come soon; he wanted so much to make her happy. He reached out for Molly once again and held her close.

Molly snuggled deeply into his arms, enjoying the warmth of his embrace. Then she smiled up at him and laughed softly through the tears that made her eyes shine brightly. "You know," she said, "you sound just like your mother!"

"I guess I do!" Sam replied with a grin and he wiped away her tears and caressed her cheek. "I knew I had heard it somewhere before!" And then they laughed together, the tension they both had felt evaporating as they shared a happy memory.

CHAPTER 33

Rainbows In a Paper Bag

At the crack of dawn each day Sam would rise quickly, take his lunch pail from the window sill where Molly had left it to keep its contents cold overnight, and be out his front door by five-thirty in the morning. Sam was punctual like his father Harold, and now his boss Mr. Pimms. There was always a line at the factory entrance as Mr. Pimms's employees raced to be at their stations before the bell rang. When the clanging of the bell stopped, the ear-splitting din of the sewing and cutting machines filled the factory. All day Sam would sit at his machine, finishing one grey garment after another.

Each time Sam would complete one basket, it would quickly be removed and replaced by another. Sam worked as fast as he could to keep his basket as full as possible, sewing hems and inseams one after the other in a seemingly unending line of grey garments. He had learned that if Mr. Pimms noticed an empty basket as he marched his way down the factory floor, the unfortunate sewing machine operator would have his quota raised. Mr. Pimms was never satisfied, and his anger lay ready to boil over just beneath the surface. It was unwise to make Mr. Pimms angry, so Sam kept his head down and sewed and sewed as fast as he could.

One bleak morning in February, Sam opened his apartment door to leave for work and almost tripped over a large brown paper bag that had been left in front of his door.

He reached down and picked it up. The bag was old and well used, and felt almost like it was full to the brim with large potatoes when he touched the bottom. Sam looked at his watch. It was almost five-thirty, and if he didn't leave at once, he would be late. So he placed the paper bag on the table and left as quickly as possible.

When Molly woke up a short time later, she immediately noticed the large brown paper bag sitting on the table. *Had Sam left her something special?* It had just been her birthday, but they had both agreed that there would be no presents this year since they were saving every penny. Had Sam changed his mind? Molly was very curious. She pushed the quilt quickly aside, rose from the bed, and went to the table. She unfolded the top of the bag and looked inside. When she realized what filled the bag, she gasped with pleasure. She reached in and pulled out a pair of knitting needles, a crochet hook, and ten large balls of yarn in every color Molly could think of, and more. She was delighted with her gift and her hands itched to get started. "Oh! Thank you, Sam," she said aloud to the empty room. "What a perfect gift."

Molly spent the rest of the day sitting in a chair by the window with a crochet hook in her hands. Her fingers flew through the complicated stitches and her work was beautiful. She knew exactly what she wanted to make and seeing her ideas come to reality as she worked made her relaxed and happy and satisfied for the first time in a very long while. As the sun began to set and the room darkened such that it was too difficult to see, Molly put away her work. She folded each piece away in linen and placed them in her basket. She couldn't wait to show Sam what she had made.

A short time later, Molly could hear footsteps in the hallway and then Sam's key clicked in the lock. Molly had been standing at the stove putting the finishing touches on a stew she was making. She put down her mixing spoon and went to greet her husband and help him remove his coat and hat. Molly reached into a wicker basket on the counter and handed her husband a small package wrapped in a white linen napkin. "What's this?" asked Sam in surprise as he took the package from Molly, "I thought we agreed, no presents this year."

"But you left me the package this morning, I thought you meant it for my birthday," Molly said.

"Yes, I did leave you a package, but it's not from me. It was at the front door when I went to leave this morning. What was in it anyway? It felt like potatoes," Sam asked.

Molly did not know what to think and went to sit down at the table. *If it wasn't Sam who sent her the package, then who?* she wondered. Sam followed Molly to the table and sat down.

"Well, let's see what this is," he said as he placed the package she had handed to him on the table and folded back the linen. Inside, in golden amber hues, was a scarf. Sam could see that Molly had stitched into it their combined intertwined initials in a subtle and intricate coiling design. It was a work of love and beauty.

"Molly," Sam said, "I have never owned anything so fine." He lifted the scarf from its wrapping and placed it around his neck. Molly leaned forward and adjusted the scarf. The wool was so soft against her fingers.

"When I opened the bag this morning I found it was filled with balls of yarn in so many lovely colors, but Sam, if it wasn't you ..." Molly started to ask.

"I don't know who it was, Molly, but it certainly is a timely gift. I can see how happy you are, and I am so glad, glad for you, and glad for me too! It is wonderful to see you so happy. Did you make anything other than my scarf? Your workmanship is truly beautiful and I know it took much time, but I hope you made something for yourself too from all that yarn."

Molly smiled broadly. "Close your eyes," she said secretively. Sam smiled at her but did as she had asked. Molly took a package out of her wicker basket and, unfolding the white linen of the package, she went to stand before the cracked mirror above her sink. She smiled brightly while examining her reflection before turning around. "Ready!" she said. Sam opened his eyes and looked at his wife. Molly had chosen blue, green, red, and pink for her palette, and she had done magic with her yarns. While Sam closed his eyes, Molly had re-pinned her blonde hair and swept it back into a neat bun at the base of her neck, placing the new hat she had made happily on her head.

"Molly," said Sam in awe as she turned around, "You look beautiful." The brim of Molly's new hat was a soft sky blue and she had placed it slightly forward on her brow so that her blue eyes sparkled and reflected the color. The hatband was a forest green that twisted and turned as it went round and round the band, sprouting tiny leaves and pink buds, and to one side a spray of deep red roses and tiny pink buds fell gently against the brim.

"It did come out nicely," Molly said shyly. "I also made these." And from the pocket of her apron she removed a pair of gloves and slipped them on. The gloves matched Molly's hat to perfection. The palms of the gloves were a soft sky blue. Around the wrist, a green vine wrapped and twisted and sprouted tiny pink buds and on the top of her hand in tiny raised stitches was a spray of delicate red roses. "They remind me of my garden and Mrs. Teresky," said Molly.

For a moment her thoughts were far away. Then she continued, "My mother once made the most wonderful shawl and gloves for an old woman in our village. She was one of the women who named me," Molly explained. "When I saw those same colors of yarn in the bag, I remembered that incredible day and now when I wear my hat and gloves I will be reminded of it always."

Sam took Molly's gloved hands in his and he was once again awed by the intricate beauty of Molly's handiwork. Then he noticed that the ends of the vine that wrapped around the wrist were dangling loosely and actually trailing off the gloves. "What is this?" asked Sam, and he looked up at Molly. "I know it's not a mistake," he said with a laugh.

"No, it's not a mistake, just look." She pulled the ends of the loose green strings and the wrist of the glove tightened. "Now they fit snugly and I won't lose them like so many others I've had before," Molly said proudly.

Sam placed a kiss in his wife's palm. "You are truly amazing," he said, "in so many wonderful ways."

The next afternoon Molly put on her coat and stood before the mirror to put on her new hat. It was really most becoming and she smiled to herself as she picked up her wicker basket and went out the door. Once again, she was enveloped in a silent grey world. There was no one about and the sound of Molly's heels clicking against the pavement was the only sound to break the eerie silence. Molly looked down at her gloved hand and the beauty of the colors against the stark white snow lifted her heart with joy. She did not know who had given her this wonderful gift. It had come when she had most needed it, and she was deeply grateful and so very happy. She wanted to share that happiness with everyone around her. That is when she had her idea.

CHAPTER 34

Mr. Travis and the Children

The bells tinkled gaily above Molly's head as she pushed open the door to the grocery. She loved the sound of those bells, their light and airy sweetness was a welcome sound to Molly, but that was where the lightness ended. The grocery was always dark and icy cold and it always took Molly some time for her eyes to adjust to the dim interior. The old man sat behind the counter with a large newspaper in front of him, still wearing his battered hat and scarf. Molly walked up to the counter and waited. The old man slowly put down his paper and looked at Molly with annoyance. Molly was, by now, used to the angry silence of the old man and it no longer bothered her. She only felt sorry for him, so without speaking, Molly passed the man a handwritten shopping list. This was a bit unusual for Molly, as she had always spoken to the man when she placed her order. The old man glanced at Molly with something akin to surprise on his face and then went to get her groceries. He returned presently and placed the items on the counter.

Molly handed him her money, and while the old man was making change, Molly filled her wicker basket with what she had bought. Then she removed a small package from her basket that was wrapped in white linen and tied up with a navy blue yarn. Molly placed the package on the counter and waited. The old man was returning to his newspaper when he realized that this customer was not leaving and that there was a package that he did not recognize sitting on the counter. He looked at the package quizzically and then back at Molly. Molly did not say anything, only pushed the package closer to the old man and gestured to him to open it. The old man scratched his head and his grimy grey cap slid back revealing his shiny baldness.

Without speaking, he pulled the navy blue string and unfolded the linen. The richness of the navy blue against the crisp white of the linen was stunning and the old man could not resist rubbing his hand along the wool. He looked at Molly in surprise. Molly reached across the counter and, without saying a word, smiled up at him then removed the old man's hat from off his head and replaced it with the new one she had made. She took another piece from the package, a thick navy shawl, and draped its patterned stitches of squares and triangles around the old man's shoulders. The old man was so astonished he could not speak. He reached up to the new cap that Molly had placed on his head and took it off, looking closely at the wool and the stitches. Then he replaced it carefully. He ran his hands across the shawl that Molly had draped around his shoulders and pulled it closer around his thin frame. His eyes grew large and his mouth gaped open in surprise as he looked at her. Molly had watched the grocer's reaction closely and was delighted with what she saw, and that was enough. She did not need to hear his words of thanks; she had seen it all in his expression. So without a word or a backward look, she turned and walked out of the store.

Mrs. Begley's children were playing in the snow in front of the apartment house. Their cheeks were rosy red from exertion and cold, their coats unbuttoned and open wide as they ran after each other in the yard. They wore no gloves to protect their cold hands and their knee high stockings had large holes, yet still they made snow angels and threw snowballs wildly at one another. When Molly came down the path, she smiled and waved and called to them. They had seen Molly many times before as she came and went on her errands or along the apartment house hallway of course, but they had never really spoken to her and so they held back in silence.

Molly stopped and watched the children while they played for a short while. Then she put down her basket on the icy sidewalk and opened the lid. The Begley children had seen her open the basket and soon, out of curiosity, one by one the six children came over to see what it was that Molly wanted to show them. They waited patiently and then out of the basket Molly took six white packages tied up with string the color of rainbows and passed them out to each of the children. They stared wide-eyed at Molly and did not know what to say to her; no one had ever given them presents before.

"Go on," Molly said with a laugh and a wide smile, "open them!" The children sat down right there on the icy sidewalk and ripped off the string and opened their gifts. Their eyes popped when they saw the rainbows of color on the socks and mittens Molly had made, and then there was a scramble as six pairs of old socks came off and six pairs of brand new rainbow-striped socks were put on icy feet. The children sighed as the warmth returned to their toes and then Molly showed them the mittens she had made. They were rainbow-striped like the socks and the colors were bright and vibrant and Molly had connected each pair of mittens by a long rainbow string. Molly showed the children how to put one glove on, then she put the string around the back of their necks and drew the other mitten through the opposite coat sleeve. "When you take off your coats, the mittens will be attached to the string so you will be less likely to lose them," she explained happily.

"Oh, Mrs.," said Amy, Mrs. Begley's oldest daughter, her eyes wide with delight. "No one has ever been so kind. They are truly beautiful and I will never lose them, never ever." One after another the children said thank you to Molly and then just as quickly they were gone again, back to their play. Molly stood and watched them for a while with a warm and bright smile lighting her face and her fingers caressing the pearls around her throat. Then she turned and went back up the front walk and into her apartment. Her heart felt lighter than it had for a long time. She had used up all the yarn in the bag, but Molly was delighted with what she had done and pleased that she had shared her special gift with others.

With no more yarn, Molly's life slipped into a dull routine, and the snowstorms that blew ferociously day after day kept her close to home. On evenings such as these, Sam would come in half frozen from his walk home and his coat would be covered with a heavy layer of snow covering his shoulders. Around his neck he always wore the golden scarf Molly had made him. The scarf was not only beautiful, but it was an added level of warmth under his threadbare coat and he was grateful to have it. However, Sam was worried and each day as he hung his coat up on a hook in the coatroom, he made sure that the scarf was carefully tucked away and securely hidden from view.

CHAPTER 35

Oranges and the Post Office

One icy early morning in February as Sam opened the door to leave, his foot banged against something in the doorway. It was so dark in the hallway that Sam could barely make out what it was he had kicked. As his eyes adjusted to the darkness, he could see that it was another large brown paper bag. He picked it up and quickly carried it over to the bed. "Molly, Molly wake up," Sam said shaking his wife on the shoulder. Molly opened her eyes slowly. She saw the bag in Sam's hand and was instantly awake.

"Is it?" she whispered.

"I don't know. Let's see," said Sam and he upended the bag and spilled its contents out onto the bed. A shower of colorful yarn fell from the bag into Molly's lap as she sat in the bed. She clapped her hands in delight and laughed out loud.

"Such a simple thing can make me so happy!" she said, her face glowing with excitement.

"It's not simple for you, Molly. It is your talent, your expression and your enjoyment," Sam said. "That is definitely not simple!" Kissing his wife on her head, he turned quickly and went to the door. "Have a wonderful day," he said and closed the door behind him.

Molly could not wait to get started and she spent the rest of the day, and the day after that, sitting by the window, her crochet hook flying. It did not matter to her at all that the storm winds blew furiously outside her window. Her mind was full of ideas and her fingers were quick to create them. It was still a mystery where the yarn was coming from; Sam and Molly had talked about it often and knew no one in town and certainly no one who would be able to afford to give such a lovely gift. *Except Mr. Pimms…?* Molly had thought, but Sam had assured her emphatically that it was definitely not Mr. Pimms. He of all people would never, ever do such a thing. So Molly and Sam had continued to wonder.

The storm blew itself out after several days and Molly was anxious to be on her way. She put on her coat and her new blue hat and gloves and picked up her wicker basket and went out the door. The snowdrifts were huge and already sprayed with mud as she made her way carefully along the slippery streets. Above her head, the little bells of the grocery store jingled happily when she pushed open the door. She walked to the back and placed her written list on the counter and waited. The little old man put down his newspaper, and when he saw Molly, his wrinkled face crinkled up into a wide smile. He pushed the paper list back to Molly.

"Mrs.," he said, his face aglow with happiness. "How nice to see you again. I wanted to thank you for my gift. It's been so long since anyone has given me anything, I was quite overwhelmed and could not find the right words." Molly smiled at the grocer. He was indeed wearing the cap and scarf that Molly had given him but he had covered them with his old battered ones.

Is he so cold that he needs so many layers or is he hiding them for some reason? Molly asked herself, but she asked him no questions and only reached out her hand to shake his when he introduced himself.

"My name is Jake Travis," said the grocer. "Let me get your order, don't want to keep you waiting." He busied himself with getting the items. He placed everything on the list on the counter and then added four very large and sweet-smelling oranges.

"Oh, Mr. Travis," said Molly hastily, "You must have made some kind of mistake. I didn't order these. They are dreadfully expensive."

"That's just the point," smiled Mr. Travis. "They are from Mr. Pimms's private stock. He owns this store, you know, and most everything else in this town. I'll just tell him a few came in rotten and I threw them away. It will serve him right since he's as rotten as any piece of bad fruit I ever saw!" and Mr. Travis chuckled with glee. "Consider it my gift to you," he said, still laughing to himself. Molly thanked him for the oranges. She felt a little guilty taking the fruit, but Mr. Travis was insistent and he carried her wicker basket for her as he escorted her out of the store and waved goodbye.

The door to the post office creaked loudly when Molly pushed it open, but the sounds of typing and sorting machines were louder still, echoing in the gloom and cold of the enormous room so no one looked up as she entered. Molly had a letter to mail, but instead of placing it in the mail slot on the wall, she walked up to the main desk and waited patiently. There was a small bell on the desk and Molly almost rang it, but she thought better of it and reasoned it would not be heard anyway with such a din. There were ten employees behind the main desk, all wearing dark grey smocks with the initials PPO embroidered in black on their left breast pockets. They worked quickly and efficiently; there was no conversation or laughter.

On a platform at the back of the room behind a high desk sat the supervisor. Molly had never noticed him before, and as she watched him, he stepped down from his desk taking a large ledger with him. The supervisor walked up to a young woman at the end of a row of desks and pointed at Molly, then he took his coat from a nearby hook and left. The young woman rose quickly from her work as she was told. "Can I help you?" she asked Molly.

"Yes, please," replied Molly, "I have a letter to mail." The young woman took the letter from Molly. "And I also have this ..." Molly reached into her basket and took out ten packages each wrapped in white linen and put them on the counter.

"Do you wish to mail these?" asked the young woman.

Molly smiled brightly. "These are for all of you," she said, and she pointed to all the workers behind the counter.

The young woman's eyes grew very large and she said in an incredulous voice, "For us, Mrs.?"

"Yes," Molly repeated, "for all of you." She handed the young woman a package tied with red yarn. "Open it," she said happily. Picking up the remaining packages from the desktop, Molly walked around it and began passing out her packages to the other workers in the room, ten in all—six tied up with royal blue yarn and four with red. Molly had counted correctly. One by one the machines stopped and there was total silence in the room. The workers did not know what to do or say. They just stared at Molly, expressions of wonder and amazement on their faces. Never before had anyone given them a package that wasn't bound for somewhere or someone else. They were shocked into silence.

"Well, what are you waiting for?" asked Molly with a smile, and she went over to the young woman who still held her package tenderly in her hands and pulled the red yarn closure. The linen unfolded softly in the young woman's hands and there nestled inside the white linen was a pair of ruby red wool gloves.

"Oh, Mrs.!" sighed the young woman as she stroked the soft wool. "How beautiful!" When the other workers saw Molly untie the young woman's package, they began to untie their own. There was much excitement and laughter as the workers opened their packages. The six men received royal blue gloves and the four women ruby red. Around the wrist of each glove was a dangling silver string. The young woman was the first to slip on her gloves, then the others followed. Molly stood in the center of the room and watched with delight as the packages were opened and the workers admired her handiwork. Then there was silence again.

"Is something wrong?" Molly asked, and turned to the young woman beside her. The young woman held out her hands and fluttered her fingers.

"Please, Mrs.," she said. "We are all grateful for your gifts, but I think the gloves are not quite finished. Not meaning any disrespect, Mrs."

"No disrespect taken," said Molly with a laugh. "I made these gloves with the thought of people typing, filing and sorting," Molly continued. "That's why the tops of each of the fingers are missing. My father had such a pair for his work; they kept his hands warm and still he could do his work easily without having to take them off." Molly explained, then she showed them how to pull the silver cords to tighten the gloves.

"How very nice of you, Mrs. We've never seen such a thing before," the young woman said gratefully.

"It's surely true," said a man standing near. "We've never seen the like. Not the gloves or the caring."

Molly blushed slightly. "It's my pleasure," she said simply. "Wear them well." Then she picked up her basket and walked to the door. Before opening it, she turned to wave goodbye once again, and saw behind the counter all ten people standing together watching her in amazement.

Molly's heart was light and she hummed a tune to herself as she walked back home along the icy streets. She had used up all the yarn. She had no idea if there would ever be more, but she had used her gift for good, and that was enough.

The four oranges glowed in the candlelight. Molly had placed them in her best china bowl in the center of the table and continued to sing to herself as she went about fixing dinner. Chopping the vegetables that she bought at the grocery, her thoughts returned to Mr. Travis. She wondered once again if it was just the cold that made him cover his new hat and scarf with his old battered ones. Her thoughts were interrupted by the sound of Sam's key in the lock and she went to greet him at the door.

Sam kissed Molly on her cheek. "You're so warm," he said.

"And you're so cold," Molly replied with a smile. "Come sit down and rest," she said. "I'll bring you something warm." Sam sat down at the table and immediately noticed the oranges sitting in the center of the table.

"Oranges!" he said, his voice rising with anger. "We can't afford oranges! You must take them back. How could you buy oranges, when I break my back every day for a few pennies!" Sam slammed the table-top with his open palm and the oranges spilled from the bowl and fell to the floor. Molly didn't answer. She walked to the table and bent down to retrieve the oranges and placed them back in the bowl in the center of the table. Molly was not at all surprised by Sam's reaction. She had antici-pated that he would react badly since they could ill afford such an extrav-agant purchase.

"You're right," she said softly, "I would never spend money on oranges, but they were a gift and I could not say no."

"What!" said Sam, his voice rising louder. "Who would give you such a gift and why?"

"It was Mr. Travis, the grocer," answered Molly, trying to stifle a smile.

"Mr. Travis, the grocer!?" raged Sam.

"Yes," said Molly, "the grocer. You see he is such an angry man, he would never say a word to me whenever I stopped in, and his hat and scarf were so old and tattered. When I got the yarn, I thought I would just make him something new. He was so pleased when I brought them to him that he gave me the oranges. I tried to say no, but he insisted. I felt a little guilty, especially when he told me that they were from Mr. Pimms's private stock."

"*What?!*" exclaimed Sam, "did you say Pimms's private stock?"

Molly was alarmed at Sam's outburst. She nodded slowly, *yes.*

Sam burst out laughing, "Mr. Pimms's private stock!" he repeated. "Can you believe it? Thank you Mr. Travis, I don't know how he will explain the missing oranges, but they will taste all the sweeter just knowing whose they were." Sam roared with laughter and picked up an orange and held it in his open palm for a long moment. Then he began to peel it, slowly savoring every second as the sweet citrus spray filled the air and the juice ran down his fingers. Molly watched the delight in her husband's face.

"Sam," she said with a giggle, "I guess you're not mad anymore?" Sam did not answer as he popped a juicy sweet section of the orange into his mouth and grinned.

CHAPTER 36

A Long-Awaited Letter

On a cold and blustery Tuesday morning in mid-February, Sam joined the long line of workers as they entered the factory doors. At the stroke of six, the main bell rang loudly and immediately the cacophony of hundreds of sewing machines operating all at once filled the air with lint and a sound like thunder. Sam worked quickly and accurately, intent on keeping his basket filled and his quota for the day met. He was so busy sewing that he did not notice when the factory supervisor, Mr. Sykes, stopped in front of his station. Mr. Sykes was someone to avoid if at all possible. He was a nasty little man and in order to get Sam's attention, Sykes tapped him repeatedly on the shoulder with his long bony finger. Sam was startled and he looked up angrily, and when he saw that it was Mr. Sykes standing in front of him, he stood up immediately.

"Yes, sir, Mr. Sykes, what can I do for you?" Sam asked, trying to keep the anger from his voice. Mr. Sykes handed Sam a crumpled letter.

The envelope was stained and tattered. From a quick glance Sam could see that the stamps were from far away, and his heart skipped a beat.

"*Gold*," demanded Mr. Sykes and there was true rage in his voice. "It is not company policy for employees to receive mail at work. See that it doesn't happen again!" and he thrust the letter out to Sam, crumpling the corner with his furious grip. Sam took the letter that Mr. Sykes held out for him. He stood there silently for a moment and watched Mr. Sykes turn defiantly from him and march away. Sam glanced at the letter quickly and placed it in his breast pocket. It was too dangerous to try and read it now with Mr. Sykes so obviously keeping an eye on him. He would have to wait until he was home with Molly.

But the wait to read it was agonizing, and his thoughts and concerns about the contents of the letter flooded his mind and flew as fast as the stitches he sewed. When the bell came at the end of the day, Sam moved as quickly as he could through the crowds in the coatroom and out the factory door. He didn't stop to wait for his usual group of friends who walked home together in the evenings. He just gave a fast wave as he passed. Sam had wondered all day if he should read the letter himself before he gave it to Molly in case the news it contained was disturbing. He had thought to protect her, to soften the blow if indeed there was one. In the end, Sam had decided to wait and now the anticipation and anxiety that had plagued him all day made him jog quickly through the snowy streets and home to Molly.

Molly was at the stove preparing dinner when the door to the apartment opened with a rush, the blast of cold air from the hallway making her shiver. She went to close the door behind Sam and to help him with his coat. "Dinner is ready," Molly said as she kissed him, "come sit down and eat."

Sam went to the table and sat down. He took the letter from his pocket and laid it down on the tabletop in front of him. When Molly saw the letter her eyes grew wide and bright. They had waited so long, sent so many postcards with never any reply, and now she hesitated, her hands shook. "Open it, Sam," Molly said softly. "Please let it be good news."

"It's from Mrs. Kinder," Sam said excitedly as he read the return address at the top of the envelope. Sam slit open the seal and removed the letter. Molly went to stand behind him and placed her hands on his shoulders. Sam slowly unfolded the brittle pages and began to read:

My Dearest Molly and Sam,

I hope this letter finds you both well and safe. There have been many changes here since last you were home. I am sure you read the newspapers and are aware of all the troubles and street fighting between the Red and Blue armies that have come to Pushkin. I heard from Moriah and Ari recently. Ari thought it would be smart to visit your mother's family for a while after you left, and we all agreed that that was a wise decision, and they left shortly after you did. With the mail here so erratic due to all the fighting around Pushkin, I have not heard from them again but I do keep trying.

Stella and Harold were kind enough to stay with me for a short while. Your father rescued his sewing machine from the shop and used his skills to alter a Red Army uniform that I had saved in the closet. He looked so handsome as they drove away. I believe they are with the Chernovs. I am so glad that old uniform came in so handy. War and hatred are ugly things, no one really wins and so many innocents are hurt and displaced. It is never easy to be a new person in a new place, but it is just as hard to be the one left behind. I think of you often and send you my love and best wishes,

Mildred Kinder

The tears that had filled Molly's eyes when she had first seen the letter now flowed freely down her cheeks as she slumped into a chair beside Sam. For a moment the room was filled with silence. The letter lay between them on the table. Molly slowly reached out for it and fingered the edges of the paper. "It has taken such a long time to arrive, do you think they are ...." Molly could say no more and she looked over at Sam.

He reached for her hand and answered her as honestly as he could. "We can only hope that they are all still safe, Molly. I believe that it was certainly wise for your parents to leave their home when they did. They really had no choice. If the Red Army was looking for you and I believe they were, then they would surely try to find your family for questioning. My parents too were in grave danger, since it was known that my father had fought with the Blues before this new war broke out. Mrs. Kinder is trying to tell us that my father wore her husband's uniform as a disguise in order to blend in with the Red soldiers in the area and escape from Pushkin. We can try writing to the Chernovs and to your Aunt Lena, but as you can see with a war on the communication will be very difficult."

"But there is still hope, isn't there?" Molly asked anxiously.

"... There is always hope, Molly, until we know differently. There is always hope."

CHAPTER 37

The Ladies

The winter storms blew more frigid than ever and the snow piled so high that the road to town was impassable. Molly was forced to stay inside. She paced endlessly around and around her tiny space and once in a while she would open the front door and look out in hopes that there would be another bag waiting there for her. She tried to stop herself, tried to think of something else when time after time there was nothing there, but she was unable to control the impulse and continued to check.

Then one early morning as Molly slowly sipped her tea, enjoying the warmth of the cup in her hands, she was startled by a loud knock at her door. Molly went to open it.

There in the doorway stood Mrs. Begley, her mother Mrs. Scott, and another woman Molly did not know. Each one of the women held a very large brown paper bag. Mrs. Begley pushed her way through the door and placed her bag on the table. Molly stood back and the other women followed Mrs. Begley, placing their bags down next to hers. When Molly saw the paper bags on her table she was stunned. *Could it be Mrs. Begley?* she wondered.

"Good mornin', Mrs. Gold," said Mrs. Begley. "I'm afraid there has been a wee mistake."

"A mistake?" repeated Molly, "what mistake could I have made?" Molly didn't know what to think.

"Not you, Mrs., … me," said Mrs. Begley. "You see, when my children showed me their new socks and mittens, I thought they said 'twas Mrs. Mullins who had made them." She pointed to the woman whom Molly did not know. Mrs. Mullins smiled warmly at Molly.

"So, this morning," Mrs. Begley continued, "when I chanced to catch Mrs. Mullins in the hall, I thanked her for the wonderful gift."

"I didn't know what she was talkin' about!" said Mrs. Mullins.

"Well, we couldn't figure out who 'twas. Then I thought, maybe they said Molly," continued Mrs. Begley.

"They do sound quite a bit similar," said Mrs. Mullins, interrupting again.

"Yes," said Mrs. Begley. "Anyway, I thought I'd give a knock on your door and see if 'twas you, and when we got here we found these paper bags in front of your apartment."

"Oh, Mrs. Begley," said Molly excitedly, "Did you see anyone in the hall while you were talking to Mrs. Mullins?"

"No, can't say that we did. Why?" Mrs. Begley asked curiously. Molly took the paper bags and placed them on her bed, then one by one she opened them and spilled out their contents.

"Ooohhh," sighed the women all at once and together.

"I haven't seen such color in a very long time," said the elderly Mrs. Scott in a whispery voice. She reached down to touch the rainbow of color on Molly's bed. "Such lovely wool too."

"Where did it come from?" asked Mrs. Begley incredulously.

"That's the mystery," said Molly, "I don't know where it's coming from, I only know that I feel that I should share it somehow."

"Really?" said Mrs. Scott excitedly. "I was a fair hand at knitting in my day, would you mind sharing some with me? My son Timmy could use a scarf under his old coat, and I wouldn't mind a warmer shawl if the truth be known." Mrs. Scott had the most beautiful silver hair that she wore in a tight knot on the top of her head.

Molly chose a deep lavender wool and held it out to Mrs. Scott. "This would be lovely with your hair," she said.

"Exactly what I would have picked. Thank you, Mrs." It was indeed the most perfect color for Mrs. Scott. It made her eyes sparkle and her cheeks pink.

"Please, call me Molly, and you are so welcome." Then Molly handed Mrs. Scott a pair of knitting needles.

The old woman grinned broadly. "I'm Alice," she said, looking down at the shiny knitting needles she held in her hand. "Now, let's see if these old hands have better memory than my head!" And she gave a delighted laugh.

"I'm Margaret," said Mrs. Mullins and she smiled again at Molly. "My ma taught me how to crochet when I was a girl, but 'tis a long time now," she said wistfully. "I'm a willing to try though, it's been that long since my Joe has had a warm coat or my kids socks or mittens."

"Aye," said Mrs. Begley, "and I am that grateful for the gift you gave my children." And she gave Molly a fierce hug. "I've been too busy workin' to do the finer things, but I am willing to learn, and help where I can," she said and patted Molly's shoulder.

"Well then," said Molly, "shall we get started?" She looked at Margaret, Mary, and Alice.

"No time like the present," said Alice excitedly and she pulled up a chair to the table.

"Exactly," Molly replied smiling with her heart. "The present."

CHAPTER 38

Mr. Pimms

The women sat together whenever they could, knitting and crocheting, chatting and laughing, and telling stories. Molly told the story of the day when the women of her village had sat together to make her wedding gown, of Mrs. Kinder and the soldier, and Mrs. Petrova and the soup. Alice had shared her memories of what Peabody had been like when the elder Mr. Pimms was in charge, and they all shared their memories of the homes and loved ones they had left behind. While they chatted, their hands were busy. Even Mary, who had never knitted before, was making good progress. At the end of each day, when the women had to leave for home, they took with them the things they had made. Alice gave an emerald green scarf to her son Timmy, and a watercolor aqua scarf to her son-in-law Fred.

After a little practice, Margaret had remembered well how to use a crochet hook and made sunshine yellow mittens for her children and a brilliant turquoise scarf for her husband Joe. Mary struggled at first and when she became exasperated, pulled out her stitches time after time. The women were patient with her slow progress and assured her over and over that they had experienced the same thing when they had been taught, and soon Mary's work began to even out. It was never quite like the others', but it would do. So she made scarves in simple stitches for her husband, Carl, and her uncle Frank.

Molly enjoyed the time she spent with these women, and while she listened, her hands were busy. It didn't matter what she worked on, and at the end of each day she would give away to the women whatever it was that she had made. It wasn't long before most of the men who worked in the factories were wearing the scarves that Molly and her friends had given them.

The men were happy to receive their gifts and the welcome warmth they provided was appreciated as they walked to and from the factories in the freezing winds. But they were worried that the colors of the scarves would be noticed by Mr. Sykes the Supervisor, so they hid the scarves as best they could when they hung their coats in the employee cloakroom. Or so they thought.

Mr. Avery Sykes was supervisor for factory A, the building where Sam worked, and he was also Mr. Pimms's right hand man. Mr. Sykes was not quite as tall as Mr. Pimms, but he was equally as mean. He was also a bit of a spy, which endeared him to Mr. Pimms even more. Each day, Mr. Sykes, dressed entirely in black, would hide in the shadows and listen to the talk of the employees as they entered the factory. He followed a strict factory code that stated: *All Pimms employees are required to wear only garments and shoes made by the Pimms Co. And therefore must dress in ONLY grey or black.* Then, because he was a stickler for neatness and detail, he would walk through the cloakroom as the morning bell would ring looking for stragglers. On this particular day as Mr. Sykes went about his routine in the cloakroom, he noticed out of the corner of his eye something very unusual. It was so unusual to Mr. Sykes that, for a moment, he wasn't sure if what he thought he saw was real. He went to investigate. Then he went to get Mr. Pimms.

Molly and Alice sat at Molly's table drinking tea and finishing up the last of the yarn. Molly was teaching Alice to crochet the beautiful roses she had made for her hat when there was a very loud and persistent pounding on the door.

"My!" said Alice. "Who could that be knockin' like that. You didn't fight with your husband did you?" asked Alice rising to her feet.

"Of course not!" Molly started to laugh and then the knock came again, louder this time. "My goodness!" Molly said, and she went to open the door. *Who could be knocking like that?* she wondered. "Mr. Pimms!" Molly exclaimed as the door swung quickly open. She was so startled to see this man standing in her doorway that for a moment she was frozen to the floor.

Mr. Pimms stood with his cane raised, just about to hit the door again when Molly opened it. The look of rage on his face was terrifying and he swept past her into the apartment as if she were not even there. He noticed at once the colorful balls of yarn and the knitting on the table and his anger knew no limit. "What do you mean by this!" he hissed and turned quickly to face Molly, waving a ball of yarn in the air. Molly was so terrified she could not speak.

Then Alice said in a calm voice, "You look just like your father."

Mr. Pimms was so angry, he had not noticed Alice who still stood by the table when he came in the door. "What did you say?" he asked, turning towards the sound.

"You look just like your father," Alice repeated in a calm and quiet voice.

"Do you think I care who I look like!" yelled Mr. Pimms. "I run this town and my businesses the way I like, and while you live here you will abide by my rules, and I will have no color in my factories *is that clear!*" he bellowed. Molly watched Mr. Pimms, who was red with rage and even angrier than when he first entered the apartment. His eyes bulged and he swung his cane threateningly as he vented his anger. Molly stepped back, her heart beating rapidly.

She took a deep breath. "Mr. Pimms?" she asked shyly. "What was it that took the warmth and color from your world?" Mr. Pimms was so startled by Molly's question that for a moment he could not answer and he dropped his arms to his sides, as the memories he always worked so hard to suppress came flooding back. Molly stood quietly waiting for his answer.

"I remember your father well," said Alice softly, trying to stay calm. "He was a good man and well respected." Alice was angry with what this man who stood before her had allowed to happen to the town and its people. She had tried hard to forgive him, but it was difficult.

"Come, Mr. Pimms," said Molly gently, "have we really done something so wrong? Please, sit down." She pulled a chair out for him at the table and offered him a seat. "Let me pour you some tea." Mr. Pimms reluctantly sat down. A bit of wind was gone from his sails after Molly's question. Mr. Pimms knew exactly when the color had left his world, but he could never speak of it and he held that memory close, a dark black memory.

Molly handed Mr. Pimms his teacup and his hands shook a little as he placed it on the table and watched it for a moment as the steam drifted off and it began to cool.

"Mr. Pimms," Alice asked boldly, a little of her anger rising to the surface once again, "why do you rattle around alone in that great dark house of yours, your father had high hopes for you, you know? He would not be happy to see how you live."

"What do you know about what my father wanted for me, " said Mr. Pimms, his irritation returning.

"'Tis what any father would want for such a son," said Alice wisely. Stewart Pimms looked intently at Alice. His shoulders sagged with the realization that he had failed his father and himself. He was no longer angry; his anger had popped like a balloon. This old woman was right. He had wasted so many years carrying his anger like a weight, not really living. His shoulders sagged with sadness and remorse.

"It's too late," he said, "I can't start again … I don't think I know how."

"Mr. Pimms," said Molly, "One thing I do know, there is always a chance for new beginnings and opportunities to make wonderful memories if only you will let it happen." Mr. Pimms looked at Molly and his eyes grew wide and he looked up at her and smiled for the first time in a very long while. He felt an enormous relief as the darkness that had plagued him for so long began to lift.

He took a little sip of the tea that Molly had poured for him. "Is there any sugar?" he asked.

"Of course," replied Molly with a laugh, "Of course there is."

Mr. Pimms smiled again and laughed a little too, as the realization of what Molly had really said rolled over him. *Maybe she is right*, he thought to himself. And he sat quietly for a time. Alice watched him closely as he sat there staring down at the floor. She could almost see the sea change happening in his soul. Then she picked up the pot and poured a little more into Mr. Pimms's teacup. She put down the pot and patted him on his shoulder and he smiled up at her.

"Forgive me," he said.

"I already have," Alice replied, and taking the sugar bowl from Molly, she added two rounded teaspoons to his cup.

Alice and Molly and Mr. Pimms sat for quite a while talking and drinking tea. Then Mr. Pimms glanced at his pocket watch. "I really must be going," he said, a little regretfully. As he stood to go, Molly handed him a white linen package tied with a rich purple string.

"Thank you," he said simply. "Thank you both," and he turned away and walked out the door. Alice and Molly looked at each other in surprise and happiness at what had just occurred. Then Molly rose quickly from the table and, going to her bedside cabinet, she removed the felt bag that held her great-grandmother's spectacles.

"I'll be right back," she said to Alice with a wide smile and hurriedly followed Mr. Pimms out the door. From the shadows, Molly watched as Mr. Pimms stopped at the entryway of the building and pulled the string off the package she had given him. The rich dark purple wool was patterned with interconnecting circles and the handiwork was beautiful. He held it gently in his hands for a moment enjoying its hue and detail. Then he slipped the scarf around his neck. *What a wonderful color*, he thought to himself as he walked lightly away. Molly stood on the front path and placed her spectacles on her nose. A soft warm rain had begun to fall and through the mist Molly watched Mr. Pimms as he moved down the path and crossed the street. The colors that surrounded him were changing rapidly, a spinning wheel of warm yellows and deep oranges that became ever stronger, sunnier, and brighter.

CHAPTER 39

The Colors of Music

M olly heard the gentle strains of violin music and, still wearing her spectacles, she looked a little further down the street. There she could see a tall man with a stubbly beard and a battered violin case set before him on the ground. The music he played was lovely and sweet, and as Molly watched the man through the glasses, she saw thin ropes and strands of magnificent and varied colors wrapping and unwrapping themselves over and over again all around him. The enchanting melodies which Mr. Garibaldi played seemed to pull her forward and she increased her pace a bit, delighting in the many rainbow colors that filled the sky. Her rapid steps made the spectacles she wore bounce lightly and they slid abruptly forward, coming to rest on the very tip of her nose, where Molly was able to look easily over their tops. Then, all at once, it happened. For the very first time since she had uncovered the spectacles in the garden, Molly found that she could see clearly all the brilliant colors that blew and twisted around Mr. Garibaldi, without having to look through their lenses. The colors she was able to see now without the glasses remained bright and strong.

She paused for a moment as the import of what she had just been able to do came to her. *Could it be? Do I not need them anymore? Can I really see without them?* she wondered in amazement. Slowly she slipped the spectacles off her nose and held them in her palm. They seemed to twinkle softly as they lay in her open hand, as if Great-Grandmother Ethel were winking at her once again, and delighted in what Molly had just discovered. *Just believe,* Molly thought to herself as she looked down at the spectacles. *Just believe!* The pride and excitement she felt in that moment made her stand a little taller, and closing her fingers lovingly around the spectacles, she placed them in the pocket of her apron. Then she looked directly at Mr. Garibaldi. The richness of the colors surrounding him seemed to increase and she watched in amazement as, without the glasses, she could see that each color was really a strand of fine wool yarn.

Molly knew then and all at once that it was Mr. Garibaldi who had given her the packages of needles and yarn. The fantastic colors that twisted and turned in time to the entrancing music told her so. *But why had he done such a marvelous thing for her when they were really strangers to one another?* she wondered. Molly's heart was filled by the overflowing kindness and generosity shown to her by this man who had nothing for himself. Her eyes stung with happy tears that rolled gently down her cheeks, and she reached up to hurriedly brush them away. As she did, the colors separated and vanished. Molly looked up and into Mr. Garibaldi's eyes.

"Ah," he said softly, "you have discovered my secret."

Molly's heart was so full it was difficult for her to speak. "Why?" was all she could say.

"You filled my belly, and that hadn't happened for a very long time. The music I played that night on the ship was full and satisfying, and I felt that I only wanted to give back to whomever it was who gave me that gift. When Mrs. Petrova gave you the first bowl of soup, I watched you as your heart swelled with happiness. When it was time to leave the ship, I watched you as you walked away. You seemed so uncertain and afraid. I wanted to make you happy like you had made me, and I wanted to give you what you needed for yourself. When we met on the street that day, and you told me how much you missed color in your world, I thought about you and let my spirit run free, open and clear, and in my heart I saw thread and yarn in all the colors of the rainbow and I knew what I wanted to do for you, who had given so much to me."

Molly's eyes grew wide with understanding. She felt a rush of love and gratitude for this sweet and tender man. She reached up and put her arms around Mr. Garibaldi's neck and hugged him tightly. "You gave me more than I can say, your kindness and generosity and the joy you have given me, I will never forget." A brilliant smile lit her face. When Molly hugged Mr. Garibaldi, she could feel the thin boniness of his tall frame and so she said, still smiling up at him, "I have some soup on the stove, would you like a bowl?"

"That would be delicious," Mr. Garibaldi replied. He placed his violin in its battered case and clicked the locks. Then he offered his arm to Molly. The warm rain that had fallen all morning stopped and as Molly and Mr. Garibaldi walked back arm-in-arm towards the apartment building, a brilliant sun began to shine.

EPILOGUE

Two Years Later

Jack the builder came quickly down the ladder. He had been up on the high peaked roof finishing the last of the repairs to the shingles. "That's it for this one," Jack called to his assistant. Jack had been painting houses and fixing things by order of the younger Mr. Pimms for the last two years. The town of Peabody was changing. But really it was Mr. Stewart Pimms who had changed the most.

Since the day he had sat with Molly and Alice, Mr. Pimms had begun to take an interest in the town once again and improvements of every kind were a frequent occurrence. The factory still made only garments and shoes in black and grey, but people were happier, and it seemed that the days were sunnier and warmer and that the icy chill that had lingered for so long was melting rapidly away.

Molly and Sam stood on the front porch of the apartment building where they had lived for the last two years. Around their feet were the trunk and suitcase that they had brought with them from Pushkin. And in Molly's arms, wrapped in a crocheted blanket of pearly pink, was a new baby girl named Aurora Rose Malkah Hannah Laurie Judith Phyllis Elaine Beth Bella Esther Chaya Dobrisha Elishah Alicia Marsha Pearl Sally Edie Sylvia Maria Raina Sophie Sarah Lily Francis Miriam Bette Rachel Evelyn Agnes Lucy Sadie Mary Ethel Goldah Ann. But everyone just called her Rosie.

The war in Pushkin had been over for several months and soon after peace was announced, Molly and Sam received a telegram. It read:

WE ARE ALL SAFE.
ARRIVE MAY 22.
CAN'T WAIT TO SEE YOU AND THE LIBERTY STATUE.
MORIAH, ARI, STELLA, HAROLD, MILDRED.

Molly and Sam had been overwhelmed with joy to know that everyone was safe and that they would all be together soon. Now the hopes and plans that they had made for the future were coming true. It was the right time to move away from Peabody and start a new life in the nearby town of Salem, where Sam had been offered a job managing a sewing factory. There were jobs for Ari and Harold too, and the new apartment they had rented was large and airy and bright with room enough for everyone.

It was really time to leave, but Molly and Sam hesitated. They had said their goodbyes at a little party the night before, but now that the reality of their decision had come it was difficult leaving the life they knew to start all over again in a new and different place. Then the front door to the apartment house swung open and Mrs. Begley stepped out of the door. She was quickly followed by her brood of children, her mother Alice, and Margaret Mullins. The little porch was crowded and, once again, hugs and well wishes were exchanged. Sam picked up the trunk and suitcase and placed them in the old wheelbarrow they had used when they first arrived. Molly carried the wicker basket her mother had given her on her arm and, holding her baby girl close, joined Sam as he began to walk down the path.

"Good luck!" called Mrs. Begley as she watched them walk away. "We will never forget you." And Mrs. Begley, who absolutely never cried, wiped away large tears as she repeated in a whisper, "We will never forget you."

Dedicated to my Grandmother Molly, and to yours, dear reader.

From tiny seeds miracles grow.

ACKNOWLEDGEMENTS

When a writer begins the long process of telling her story, it can for a time be a rather lonely experience and somewhat isolating. But that only lasts a very short time, because the most important thing to a writer is that people read and respond (whether positively or not!) to the stories that the writer creates. A writer needs readers.

As I began to create Molly's world in *The Girl With 35 Names*, I was fortunate to have input and direction from a variety of readers of all ages and experiences. Without their ideas, knowledge, and encouragement, I think this project would have had a very different outcome.

I wish to thank Carole Patmore and her granddaughter Violet Gibbs for being my earliest readers, as well as Dr. Sandy Wagenberg and his wife Betsy.

Special thanks to Sandy's son Justin Wagenberg for helping me shape the chapter "Along the way."

Thank you to Fay Zak and Herman Moonvess who believed in me and this book from the start.

Thank you to our dear friend James Mahoney who has followed Molly's journey from the beginning and has always been a wise and forthright mentor.

Thank you to UCLA and the English Department that enabled me to find my editor Maureen Shay, Ph.D. It was an added bonus that Maureen's dissertation concerned immigrants and migration. Maureen has helped to challenge me while asking the right questions and fixing my errors. I am so lucky to have found her.

Thank you to Andrew Bradigan, "My Biggest Fan."

Thank you to JJ Harrington, screenwriter for this novel. She has captured Molly's world of color and feeling in a most beautiful and magical way.

Thank you to my son Andrew Colbert for his understanding and guidance, his insightful advice, constant support, and sage wisdom.

And to my daughter Lauren Colbert Seaver who began this journey with me twenty years ago, when for a sixth grade school project she wrote a short story entitled "My Great Grandmother's Journey," which inspired me so much and started me on my way.

To my brilliant husband Jeff, who has been Molly's greatest champion and promoter from the first, and who always loves to hear me read aloud what I have written. I am deeply grateful and awed by all that you do for me. Without a magic man like you, there would be no rainbows.

As you turn the final page, know that this is not the end of the story but the beginning of a much larger journey! We invite you to discover what happens from here …

Join us at www.Girlwith35Names.com for an immersive and interactive experience. Upon visiting you will be able to learn about the inspiration behind our story and the author who wrote it. You will also be invited to "Join the Journey," gain exclusive access to sequel chapters, and much more.

The Girl With 35 Names is available on eBook, Audiobook, Apple & Google App Stores, Print, & Podcast.

To request access or discuss opportunities related to the recently completed screenplay by award-winning screenwriter/director JJ Harrington, please email us at: outreach@Girlwith35Names.com.

Follow us on Twitter, Facebook, Instagram, LinkedIn, & YouTube@ Girlwith35Names.